PENGUIN BOOKS

The Last Laugh Club

Steve Jones's first job was in a petrol station. It was also the first job he was fired from for putting diesel in Dai-the-Milk's petrol truck. From there he gained employment in a printing factory before setting off for distant shores to 'find himself'. He subsequently found a mediocre career in modelling which thankfully segued into a fairly successful twenty-year (to date) career in TV presenting. His cherished accomplishments: he was crowned Welsh Rear of the Year in 2002; his suitcase has come out first at the airport on no less than two occasions; and now, he has written *Call Time* and *Terminally Kill*, which he very much hopes you will enjoy.

By the same author

Call Time

The Last Laugh Club

STEVE JONES

PENGUIN BOOKS

PENGUIN BOOKS

UK | USA | Canada | Ireland | Australia
India | New Zealand | South Africa

Penguin Books is part of the Penguin Random House group of companies
whose addresses can be found at global.penguinrandomhouse.com

Penguin Random House UK,
One Embassy Gardens, 8 Viaduct Gardens, London SW11 7BW

penguin.co.uk

Penguin
Random House
UK

First published as *Terminally Kill* by Penguin Michael Joseph 2024
Published in Penguin Books 2025

001

Copyright © Steve Jones, 2024

The moral right of the author has been asserted

Typeset by Jouve (UK), Milton Keynes
Printed and bound in Great Britain by Clays Ltd, Elcograf S.p.A.

The authorized representative in the EEA is Penguin Random House Ireland,
Morrison Chambers, 32 Nassau Street, Dublin D02 YH68

A CIP catalogue record for this book is available from the British Library

ISBN: 978-1-405-95872-1

Penguin Random House is committed to a sustainable future
for our business, our readers and our planet. This book is made from
Forest Stewardship Council® certified paper.

For our Ray. We knew you'd beat it.

Prologue

Mac and Fish dragged the injured insurgent to cover. Dowe provided fire support as the four of them entered a nearby blown-out compound.

'Thought you'd try a sneak attack, did you?' growled Mac at the thrashing Taliban fighter. He wailed something in Pashto as they slung his body onto a pile of rocks in the corner. Landing with a grunt, a grenade fell out of his jacket. It came to rest with a precarious spin amongst the rubble on the floor.

They froze for a millisecond until the sight of the pin still engaged brought sighs of relief.

'Get that, Fish, before he does himself a mischief,' said Mac.

The wounded man, his face twisted in agony, looked down at the grenade and made a weak grab for it with bloodied fingers. But Fish quickly batted away his hand and scooped it up.

Dowe stood watch at the blasted hole that formed the room's makeshift entrance, his rifle primed in the direction of the sound of gunfire.

'You don't look too good, pal,' said Mac to the squirming man who grasped at the gunshot wound at the top of his inner thigh. 'Sorry about that,' he added with a smile and a nod at the bloody mess, before he put his boot on it.

The man screamed.

'Corporal . . .' said Fish, placing a firm hand on Mac's shoulder.

Mac ignored him. 'It's an early shower for you. Go on. Fade to black, you wee fucker.'

'*Mac!*'

'What?'

'We should patch him up.'

Mac removed his boot and turned to Fish. 'We look like the fucking St John Ambulance to you? This isn't some honourable adversary. He's Taliban shite. This is a man who'll use kids as shields. Who'd hang our blown-off limbs from trees.' Blood was now pumping from the Taliban soldier's leg. 'You wanna fucking kiss it better, Fish?!'

'You cannot let him –'

'Can't we? This is what winning looks like – one less of them.'

'Stripey inbound!' announced Dowe, giving Mac and Fish the heads up.

A man entered the scene and paused to observe the dimly lit stand-off between Mac and Fish. 'What's going on here?' he asked.

'Injured insurgent, Sergeant,' said Fish.

Their commander pushed past the two and looked down at the now silent man. The blood flow from his leg had slowed significantly and the agony that had creased his bearded face was gone, replaced by a near-death calm.

'Help him. *Now.*'

Fish removed his field dressing kit and went to work as the Multiple Commander, Mac and Dowe looked on. After a while, Fish stopped. 'I'm afraid he's gone,' he said, dragging a hand over his face in frustration.

Their commander followed the blood trail from the wounded soldier's leg to the blood-spattered boot of Lance Corporal Neil 'Mac' McCrindle. 'You know what you've done here?' he asked, meeting the much bigger man's defiant gaze. 'You've broken the Geneva Convention. You let that man die.'

I

'Do you mind me asking where you got the scar?' the pale man opposite asked.

'Do you mind me not telling you?' replied Ray, holding the younger man's gaze until he decided his lap was a better direction to look in.

Ray immediately felt bad. He knew the man didn't mean anything by it. He was just trying, albeit clumsily, to make conversation and alleviate the awkwardness of their dire situation. There were four of them sitting in oversized white leather armchairs in a small room. The chairs were set up in two pairs, so that the members of the unfortunate group faced one another like the host and contestant of the last game show on earth anyone would want to be part of.

All things considered, Ray wasn't in a talkative mood. Frankly, he was feeling sorry for himself. Lamenting his luck. He mused that there are only two kinds of luck in the world – good and bad. A slight limp and a deep, jagged scar that cut a vivid crescent from the corner of his left eye to his jawline, reminded Ray every day what good luck looked like. Right now he needed that, because all he had known recently was luck of the bad variety. He wasn't about to share his sad story with a man he had met only moments earlier just because cruel fate had decided to place them opposite one another.

Ray glanced across at the pale man who now stared forlornly down, and relented. 'I cut myself shaving. Just a nick. So I popped a square of tissue on it and as you can see – good as new.'

The man looked up to meet Ray's lopsided grin. 'Really?' he replied with a laugh. 'Maybe we're wasting our time here. Maybe we should all go home and wrap ourselves in toilet paper?'

'All that whining,' said the painfully frail elderly lady sitting in the chair to Ray's right. 'You're a proper pair of *mummy's* boys.'

'Oh, very good, Rose! Such wit. A pier somewhere is missing its comedian.' The pale man rolled his eyes, before bringing his attention back to Ray. 'I'm Luke Kellner. You've just met Rose and the big man here is Gog.' He tapped the shoulder of a huge man to his left who managed to fill his oversized white leather chair with awkward ease. He gave Ray a glance and a nod of his shaved bowling-ball head before looking back down at a spot on the carpet that had held his attention until now.

'Gog? That's an unusual name,' said Ray.

'It's a nickname,' the big man replied in a gentle Welsh brogue. 'It's short for Gogmagog – the last of the Welsh giants. My real name is Paul.'

'Do you prefer Paul or Gog?' Ray asked.

He broke into a wide smile revealing a missing incisor. 'I like Gog.'

'Then Gog it is,' said Ray, returning the smile.

'So that's us, Earth, Wind and Fire. How about you?' asked Luke.

'Ray Leonard,' he said, extending his hand before

6

coming to an abrupt stop as he realized the tether wouldn't permit the distance required for a handshake. An embarrassed wave to all would have to suffice.

'Oh wow! That's funny. Just like the boxer,' said Luke, lighting up at the notion.

'Yes. Like the boxer,' said Ray, with the air of a man who had said that a lot over the years since 1979, when Sugar Ray Leonard had come to prominence after fighting and beating Wilfred Benitez for the WBC Welterweight title.

'I bet you get called Sugar quite a bit?'

'Sometimes.'

'May I?'

'As we are in this getting-to-know-you period . . . I'd prefer Ray.'

'Roger that,' said Luke, with a no-hard-feelings shrug. 'What a boxer, though. Speed. Footwork. Punching power. And an absolute master of ring strategy.'

'I'm surprised you know him. How old are you?'

'Thirty-four,' Luke replied, rubbing at his designer stubble. 'I like the fights. I've taken a lot of clients over the years.' Ray nodded and thought – *investment banker?* 'Pound for pound one of the greats, old Sugar Ray.'

'If you say so.'

'You don't like boxing?'

'I don't mind it. I just wouldn't put it on TV.'

'Where would you put it?' asked Luke with an incredulous chuckle.

'In a barn? A clearing in the woods?' said Ray after a moment's thought, in his practical way.

'A clearing in the . . . *Why?*'

'If a couple of men want to hit seven bells out of each

7

other then be my guest. But do it away from prying eyes. Let's not call it entertainment. There's enough pain and suffering in the world.'

'The world!?' laughed Luke. 'There's enough pain and suffering in this room.'

A solemn hush came over the group as they considered the truth of his words. For several long moments the only sound that could be heard was the ceaseless din of the twenty-four-hour news cycle coming from a small, wall-mounted television in the corner of the airless room.

Ending the group's reverie, Luke said, 'What are you in for, Ray?'

'You make it sound like we're in prison.'

'We are in a way, don't you think? We've all been given life sentences. For some reason or another we've pissed off the guy upstairs. What's the verdict from the bearded sadist?' At this, Gog shook his head and gave an irked grunt but Luke didn't seem to notice, and continued. 'Hanging? Lethal injection? Firing squad?' Ray gave Luke a long un-appreciative look. 'No dice?' said Luke. 'Surely this is the one room we can all cut through the bullshit? No need for tippy toes in here. Life's too short – pun intended.'

In the soft dim of the spotlights above (dimmed, Ray supposed, in an attempt to create a soothing environment for those going through a challenging time) Ray looked down at the tape under which an unseen needle pierced his skin and entered his vein. His eyes followed the line of the rubber tube connecting the needle to a liquid sack, full of a combination of drugs designed to extend his life, which hung from a stand beside his chair. It was a set-up mirrored for the room's other three occupants. Ray mused upon the irony that the slow drip of the IV brought a sereneness to the clinical space, which was otherwise stark but for a low table full of magazines and a small window without a view.

'All right, I'll go first,' said Luke. 'GBM. Glioblastoma. I'm told it's the most dangerous and aggressive form of brain cancer. I don't do things by halves.' He tapped his temple. 'It's way in the centre of my noggin so they can't operate. Hence my second chemo cycle and laser beams blasted into my skull to try and shrink the little beastie. The rest of me –' he held his arms aloft and struck a Her-culean pose, showcasing what Ray suspected would once have been an impressive physique but was now thin ver-ging on gaunt – 'pure beefcake.'

'Eurgh,' said Rose.

'What?'

'A cake made of beef? Sounds disgusting,' she said through a grimace.

'You're in a jolly mood today, aren't you, Rose? Did you see a child drop their ice cream on the way in?'

'Luke,' said Ray, recapturing his attention. 'You seem . . . unperturbed.'

'"Perturbed", *me*? Why would I be? What have I got to live for? It's not like I'm young, good-looking, rich and successful,' he said with bitter sarcasm. 'I eat right. I exer-cise constantly. I look after myself. What was the point? Fucking brain cancer. *Brain cancer!*'

'Maybe you should have exercised your brain more?' Rose said with a cackle.

After a long sigh, Luke asked, 'Why don't you tell us what will rob the world of your wonderful presence?'

'None of your bloody business,' she fired back, running a hand through the few wisps of hair that remained on her head.

'Charming,' said Luke. 'Gog?'

'Pancreas,' he replied, rubbing his stomach. 'It's my first cycle. The doctors said chemo might be the best bet. If it doesn't work the hope is that my cancer shrinks so it's easier to do surgery on. They're nice people, the doctors, I do trust them.'

'Oh, yeah. They're good here. They could do that surgery blindfolded . . . if it's even needed after this, buddy.'

Gog made an appreciative smile.

The eyes of the group turned to Ray. He took a moment to consider whether to deploy the Rose-defence but thought better of it.

'Prostate,' he said quickly.

'Excellent mortality rate,' said Luke.

'Stage three.'

'OK.' Luke's voice took on a serious edge. 'First time in chemo?'

'Yeah. I had surgery . . . but, ahhh, here I am.'

'That's shitty. How long is your cycle?'

'First stint is six weeks.'

'Tough. But stage three is still beatable.'

'That's why I'm here,' said Ray with a shrug.

'That's why we're all here. Trying to beat the clock,' Rose said, squinting distractedly at the TV.

'What do you do for work, Ray?' Luke asked.

'I'm retired. You?'

'Private equity investor.'

Close enough, thought Ray. 'How about you, Gog?'

10

'I work in security. I like to make people feel safe.'

'Good of you.' *Yup, bouncer if I ever saw one*, thought Ray. 'Rose?'

'Retired,' was all she offered, still staring at the TV.

'Well, look at you two in the same business,' Luke said with a grin. 'You've got people to help you through this, Ray?'

'Yeah,' he replied.

'That's good. No one should go through it alone.'

'You?'

'Yeah. Got a good family. It's everything, isn't it . . . family.' Luke considered his words. 'But if I'm completely honest, when I'm with them, most of my time is spent trying to comfort them because they're all so upset I might die . . . and that's bloody exhausting,' he said, to unanimous grumbles of agreement from the rest of the group. 'Even my nephew understands Uncle Luke needs his brain if he wants him to help build Lego for a few years yet.'

'Don't do yourself a disservice, Luke. You've got this far without one.'

'You know what, Rose, I actually feel sorry for whatever your cancer is,' snarled Luke. 'I can't imagine what it's like having to live inside your bitter, rotting, lizard-witch carcass.'

Rose slowly turned from the TV and looked to the young man with unbridled venom.

'All right, why don't we all calm –' began Ray, only to be silenced by the eruption of laughter between Rose and Luke.

'That's a good one,' said Rose, cackling.

'I've been sitting on that one for a while,' Luke replied, with a wink.

'So you're a double-act. That's . . . great,' said Ray, stone-faced. 'I had no idea chemo would be this fun.'

2

'So how was day one?'

'It was fine.'

'How do you feel?'

'Fine.'

'You want to give me a bit more, Ray?' Chaynnie asked, not taking her eyes off the road as she navigated the busy city streets in the old Vauxhall Corsa Ray had bought her for her eighteenth birthday.

'I don't feel as bad as I was expecting. Little drained. But not bad.'

'And the people in there? Were they nice to you?'

'I'm a little uncomfortable with this reverse parent–child dynamic, Chay,' said Ray, in jest.

'Sure,' she said, rolling her eyes. 'There's a *child* driving this car.'

Ray wasn't related to Chaynnie by biology but where his heart was concerned she was his daughter. When he had met Odette, her mother, eleven years earlier, she was a divorcee with a harrowing past. Ray was initially reticent to get involved with a divorcee (he had always tried to keep a healthy distance between himself and drama of that variety), and then even more so when he discovered that there was a ten-year-old girl in play.

That trepidation, on some level, had been justified. Bringing Odette and Chaynnie into his life had brought him gut-wrenching pain. Moments that haunted him and would continue to haunt him for the rest of what could be his rather short life.

But they had also given him happiness and meaning beyond anything he had ever hoped for. There was no contest – to have Odette and Chay in his life he would do it all again without hesitation.

'Well? Good people in there?'

'Yeah.' He nodded. 'They seemed like good people.'

From the corner of his eye he watched Chaynnie's intense scowl in profile. Odette had worn that exact same look when she drove. Chaynnie's mixed heritage meant she didn't have her mother's sable skin but nevertheless Ray couldn't help but see his dead wife, living and breathing in her daughter's youthful face, every time their eyes met. That tore his heart from his chest, not just because it reminded him of what he had lost too soon, but because Chaynnie would have to see her mother too every time she looked in the mirror.

Sadly, Chaynnie had experienced more heartache than most. A childhood trauma that he feared would dictate the rest of her life was at the route of her underlying issues. And then, compounding that, two years ago she had lost her mother. Inevitably, she had been robbed of the carefree demeanour that she should have been entitled to as a now twenty-one-year-old student in the prime of her life.

'How's school?'

'University,' she corrected.

'Sorry. How's university?'

'Good.'

Ray watched her expectantly as the silence stretched out between them.

'What?' she said, eventually.

'Would you like to give me a bit more, Chay?' he asked, smiling.

'You always do this, Ray.'

'What do I do?'

'You're deflecting. You've just had day one of what is arguably the most important period of your life, and you're asking me about university? Who gives a shit about university!?'

She kept her eyes on the road. But Ray could tell by her voice that there were tears there. He looked out of the passenger window and watched the high street go by, full of people living their unworried lives.

'The room is approximately twelve feet by eight feet,' he began, 'with one small window looking out onto other windows. The buildings are clustered around a shaded courtyard below. The decor is plain white walls and a brownish carpet that hides stains well. There is a small wall-mounted television poorly positioned at the room's exit/entrance. Every time the door opens it blocks the TV.' He turned to Chay and was instantly gratified to see a smile on her face.

'OK. Got it,' she said, nodding to continue.

'There are four chemo stations within the open-plan space. Each of the stations consists of a large white leather chair with meds hanging next to them, ready to be administered intravenously by a very pleasant nurse called Donna, who is approximately fifty years old. One of these stations is mine, the other three are occupied by the following. Luke Kellner: a thirty-four-year-old private equity investor with brain cancer who looks a bit like a young Pierce Brosnan.'

'That's quite a look,' said Chay, blowing out her cheeks.

'Rose – surname unknown, cancer unknown – is a very old woman with a sharp tongue who looks like a Disney witch. And Paul – surname unknown – is a Welshman with pancreatic cancer who I estimate to be in his mid to late-forties. Paul prefers to go by the nickname Gog.'

'Gog?' she repeated.

'Yup, Gog. It's a contraction of Gogmagog.'

'Gogmagog!' Chay laughed. 'You're making that up.'

'I'm not. Apparently, he was a Welsh giant. Which makes perfect sense because Gog is the size of the QE2 and looks like every bouncer I've ever seen outside of a night-club. Which, again, makes a lot of sense, because he is a bouncer. How's that?'

'It's like I'm in the room with you,' she replied, smiling but sad at the same time.

'It's a strange room, Chay.' He saw it recreated in his mind's eye. He wasn't sure if it was the dread the space represented or the drugs coursing through his body that triggered a sudden sickly feeling in his stomach.

'I'm so sorry you have to go through this, Ray.'

'We'll get through it.'

'I wish Mum was here.'

'Me too, kiddo.'

3

A week later and Ray had started to settle into the draining, nauseating, repetition of chemotherapy. The experience would have been much more bearable if he were allowed to quietly sit and pretend to read one of the room's stack of trashy magazines. But, like a bored taxi driver, Luke Kellner seemed to be wholly unaware or uninterested in other people's boundaries.

'It's a minefield out there, Ray,' he said. 'Since the Me Too movement women are just floating heads to me. I don't look below the neckline.'

'Well, that's progress,' said Donna, with a roll of her eyes, as she inserted Ray's IV.

Ray felt the 'scratch' of the needle entering his vein. Why did they call it a scratch? It felt nothing like a scratch: unpleasant, yes, but not a scratch. Maybe 'pinch' would be a better description?

'You know what I mean, D. I'm merely attempting to illustrate that I am not a creep like those countless shitbags before me.'

'Women like to be looked at, Luke. We like dressing up and looking good. It's nice to be noticed. You wouldn't make a film, put it in the cinema, and then complain when people go to see it, would you? But there's a country mile between getting leered at and catching someone's eye with a smile.' The nurse's point registered on Luke's face in a smiling epiphany. 'That OK?' she asked Ray.

'I didn't even know you'd put it in,' he replied.

'That's what she said,' said Luke, beaming.

'Inappropriate,' said Donna, but her chuckle suggested otherwise. 'Okey-cokey, campers. You know where I'll be. Just buzz me if you need me.'

'Who do I buzz for mercy killing?' asked Rose.

'Very funny. Don't forget to stay hydrated,' she said, closing the door behind her.

'What did I say that was so funny?' asked Rose, fidgeting with the placement of the purple bandana she had decided to wear that day.

'I'd be up for the job. I can't guarantee any mercy, though,' Luke said with a grin.

'What are you going to do? Bore me to death?' Rose replied, to a snort of laughter from Gog.

'What's the deal, big man?' said Luke with faux hurt. 'I thought you were on my side?'

'It was funny,' said Gog, smiling apologetically. 'I'm on the side of funny.' He turned to Rose. 'I like your bandana.'

'It's a head scarf,' she snapped, before mellowing somewhat. 'But thank you. It's made in Bangladesh.'

'Lovely,' said Gog, impressed.

'Yeah, lucky me. Of course the woman loses her hair. Typical.'

'God, I wish I was at the races now,' Luke said longingly, pointing a finger at an advert for an up-and-coming horse racing meeting on the room's small TV. 'There's nothing more exciting than a day at the races. The baying crowd.

Everybody wearing their finest. The smell of grass and money in the air. Nothing like it,' he concluded, looking down at the needle in his vein. 'But here I am.'

'What's so special about horse racing? Horses are just thin, fast cows,' said Rose. 'The Swedes have got it right. They're dumb, and we should be eating them.'

'Who? The Swedes?' asked Gog.

'No! Bloody horses!' she barked back at him.

'Are you hearing this, Ray? We're doing chemo with the anti-Christ. Now she wants to eat horses.'

'I'm hearing it, Luke,' Ray replied flatly.

'You OK? How are you feeling? Nausea? Metallic taste in your mouth? Any strange food cravings? I remember my first time I couldn't stop eating cheese.'

'Nausea,' he nodded.

'Yup. It's a constant battle. Fatigue? Irritability?'

'Now you mention it,' said Ray, glancing from Rose to Gog to Luke, 'I do feel a bit irritable.'

'Yeah. That's probably the human hemorrhoid here,' said Luke, with a thumb in Rose's direction. That got a big laugh from Rose and Gog. Even Ray cracked a smile. 'In all seriousness, though, Ray. There are some great forums on Facebook that can give you some support specific to you. It's sad but with cancer there's always some poor bastard out there going through the same thing. That person could give you some invaluable advice.'

'I don't think so, Luke. I've got this far without Facebook.'

'I know. Facebook in general is the devil's notice board. But it can be a useful tool.'

'Oh, I have no doubt. Question is – for who?'

'You've lost me,' said Luke, his forehead lined in confusion.

'The Government employ agencies to gather information on people. But now there's hardly a need to because we do it for them. If you'd like to know where I am? What I do? Who I know? Which god I pray to? What my ideological beliefs are? Just take a look at my Facebook page, because I've handily gathered all that information for you.'

'Hmmm . . . never thought of it like that. Yeah, you're spot on,' Luke replied, rubbing the underside of his stubbled chin. 'What did you say you do for a living again?'

'I'm retired.'

'Oh yeah. A man of leisure.' Luke smiled, before his forehead creased in thought again. 'But saying that, if you've got nothing to hide, what's the big whoop if someone does look at your Facebook?'

'Does your home have walls and doors?'

'Well, yeah . . . of course.'

'It's nice to have privacy, isn't it?'

'Touché,' he said, returning Ray's lopsided grin. 'Well played.'

'There's only one God!' said Gog, with unusual force.

'Come again, big man?' Luke asked, turning to the seemingly irritated Welsh giant.

'Ray said Facebook knows which god I pray to. There's only one God – our Lord and Saviour Jesus Christ.'

After a moment's scrutiny, Luke said, 'I can't tell if you're joking or not?'

'Oh Christ! He's not. He's one of them,' said Rose, putting her face in her hand.

'You shouldn't take his name in vain, Rose,' Gog said.

'Why? What's he going to do – give me some kind of horrific form of cancer? I think at this point I can say and do anything I fucking well please.'

4

Ray stood in the sunlight outside the clinic and breathed in the familiar smog-infused air of his city. It was a vast improvement on the chilling sanitized odour of the clinic. Chay had messaged him to say she was running late. Checking his watch, he saw that she would arrive in fifteen minutes. Yes, he could have driven himself, but the opportunity to see Chay was a welcome boost to his day he was not willing to pass up. A coffee shop a few minutes away that he had started to frequent would bridge the gap before her arrival. He started to walk, favouring his right leg as he had every day for the last twenty years.

Around halfway to his destination the sensation to urinate hit Ray like a tsunami in his bladder. It was a horrible side effect of his condition and something he was getting used to. He had managed it well . . . until now. It was too far back to the clinic's facilities, and the same distance again to the coffee shop.

He realized with horror that at fifty-seven years of age, on the high street in broad daylight, he had arrived at the point in his life where he would wet himself in public (and his grey jeans would highlight his shame with devastating effect). Just as all hope seemed to be lost, Ray's peripheral vision spotted a lifeline on the other side of the road. Barely checking for cars he darted across the street and into the shady alleyway.

Unzipping his flies, he desperately relieved himself between two industrial-sized recycling bins, noticing with disdain the bright orange colour of his urine; an unfortunate side effect of the chemo. Finishing, with as much dignity as he could muster, Ray began to zip himself back up.

'Gimme your phone and wallet,' demanded a voice from behind him. Ray turned. A tall thin man stood around six feet from him, holding a knife with a blade Ray estimated to be six inches in length. 'What the fuck are you waiting for? Give 'em to me!'

'Take it easy,' said Ray, holding one hand up in a placating manner. He unzipped his jacket and reached into his inside pocket for his phone and wallet. 'Here,' he said, offering them. 'My name's Ray. What's yours?'

'Dick Turpin.'

Unless this guy is three hundred years old, that's a fake name, thought Ray.

'Dick' snatched the items and caught the hint of a gleam from beneath Ray's jacket cuff.

'And the watch.'

'Can't do that.'

'What did you say?'

'I can't give you my watch.'

'Do you see this knife I'm holding? Do you want a scar to match on the other side of your face? Give me the watch or I'll cut you, old man.'

'You've got my wallet. I bet you could buy yourself a nice watch with the money that's in there. Why don't you walk away?'

'You think this is a fucking negotiation? *Give it to me!*' he spat, grey teeth revealed behind an ugly sneer. Not that Ray noticed – his unblinking eyes hadn't left the blade clutched in the man's hand since the moment he first saw it. The steadfast way he held the knife loosely against his hip suggested this was not his first time holding one.

A bus idled on the high street at the end of the alley and its red bulk cast further shadow onto Ray and Dick's impasse. When the bus moved off, meagre light returned to the alley, illuminating Dick's dirty thin face. With a quick glance up from the knife, Ray caught the desperation and uncertainty that lived there.

'OK. You can have it,' said Ray.

Ray knew that the safest practice in a mugging was to immediately hand over any items on your person. A wallet, or a phone, was not worth dying for. The problem he currently had was that he was willing to defend the watch that his dead wife had given him with his life.

To Dick's eyes, Ray would have been perceived as some old geezer (average height, not much meat on him, nice jacket, good jeans) hurriedly hobbling his way into a dead-end alley. He was an opportunity not to be sniffed at. A rube. A crippled gift now trapped between two bins.

Expected to cow to Dick's will and hand over the watch, Ray realized that doing the opposite would be to his advantage.

He pulled up his sleeve and brought his fingers to the clasp of the watch . . . and then surged with astonishing speed towards the knife, closing the gap between them in the blink of an eye.

Taken by surprise, Ray expected Dick to instinctually use the knife to defend himself. And that is exactly what happened. He swung the knife as hard and as fast as he could in Ray's direction. At least that was his intention. What actually happened was – nothing.

Ray's hand gripped Dick's clenched fist that held the knife. Pinning it to his hip with a strength that no 'old geezer' should have had any right to.

Ray saw the look of confusion in Dick's eyes, which he turned to his advantage by quickly bringing the top of his head into the underside of his mugger's jaw. Grey teeth came together with a sickeningly sharp crack.

Before Dick could even register the damage to his mouth, Ray rammed the point of his elbow, with brutal force, into the centre of Dick's chest plate.

An explosion of pain drove him staggering with a high-pitched scream into the brick wall behind him, adding insult to more injury.

Bent double against the wall, clutching his chest and jaw, Dick looked up to see the old man, who wasn't even out of breath, standing over him.

'*Fucker . . .*' he gasped.

'Now that didn't go the way you were expecting,' said Ray, matter-of-factly.

'You broke my teeth,' said Dick. His diagnosis was confirmed when he spat a mouth full of blood and teeth to the ground.

'I did. But they really shouldn't come out that easily.'

'*Bastard*,' he wheezed.

'In my defence, you were trying to stab me. Get them fixed with the money in the wallet and let's call it quits.'

'*You broke my fucking teeth*,' Dick hissed, gradually

bringing himself back to his full height, blocking Ray's exit once again, the knife still clenched in his hand.

'Careful now. You've taken a couple of big hits there. Your body is trying to compensate by flooding itself with adrenaline. In your case that adrenaline is for flight not fight. You might think you're in a better position to have a go. But you're not,' said Ray, his words apparently hitting the mark as Dick's eye-line was pulled towards the end of the alleyway, to the spot where the bus had idled before. 'That's the right choice. Let's both walk out of here.'

'I'll walk out of here . . . with that watch,' Dick said, turning to Ray with that sneer back on his face, bloody red teeth clenched within.

'All right. No more talk,' Ray said, as Dick raised the knife out before him, denying Ray the opportunity to pin it against his body this time – *he's a quick learner*, he thought.

Dick began to slowly stalk his way towards him, waving the knife from left to right in what seemed to Ray like an approximation of what he must have seen in a knife fight in an action movie. Turning his body to offer the smallest target, Ray took a few steps backwards in the hope that Dick would telegraph his intentions. Two details immediately worried him: the edge of the knife faced upward and his attacker's thumb was resting on top of the knife's handle. Both were incorrect practices for a knife fight. Dick's evident lack of experience wielding a knife was ultimately more challenging for Ray: he couldn't telegraph his intentions if he had no idea what they were. Relying on reflex and adapting to whatever came next was now Ray's best chance of survival.

Dick edged closer. He continued to wave the knife

erratically, his eyes wide and wild behind its glint in the gloom. Ray watched with forced calm, shuffling further and further back into the dead-end, his hands open, waiting for an advantageous opportunity.

Suddenly a loud clang rang out behind him, and Ray turned. Before his eyes even came to rest upon the discarded glass bottle he had kicked, he knew he had made a mistake. Snapping his head back front and centre, Dick was already cutting the knife through the air with deadly intent. But Ray was equal to it. His left hand snapped into a solid block but was unable to stop the knife from cutting through the material of his jacket. Thankfully the blade didn't seem to make contact with his body. Not that it would have mattered to Ray. You expected to get stabbed to some degree in a knife fight. Any other childish notion to the contrary would only serve to break concentration.

Dick would have to retract the blade and try another attack. Unfortunately for him the process was interrupted by Ray's foot kicking his balls into his stomach. Dick gasped in shock, his hands instinctively heading to the point of impact. Ray pressed his advantage, all business now, nothing personal.

'*Wait!*' Dick grunted, feeling the point of the knife's path. Unlike the movies he had watched, it was over quickly. Ray's hand encircled Dick's, which held the knife's handle. The rest of it, six inches of steel, was buried to the hilt in Dick's chest. Ray let go, the blood on his fingers warm and thick, and Dick collapsed to his knees before slumping onto his side.

Ray exhaled a long shaky rush of air. Adrenaline registered on his skin in a wave of goose flesh.

He bent down alongside Dick's body, '*Hey,*' he said, even though in the dim alley it was clear to see the light of life had left his attacker's eyes, now two dull, unseeing marbles. He reached out to close them, then stopped short. Instead he roughly rubbed his own eyes in disbelief, half expecting the man he had just killed to be gone when he opened them. But he was not; he was still there, motionless apart from the blood pooling beneath his chest and slowly making its way towards Ray's shoes.

He was suddenly aware of his heart pounding, each beat screaming leave – *flight!*

Ray looked quickly in the direction of the alley's exit, obscured somewhat at his current eye-level by the industrial recycling bins. He had some partial cover, that was good. With his clean left hand he reached into Dick's pocket and recovered his wallet and phone. He lingered on the phone. Should he call 999? The question was answered when he put the phone away. He then glanced at the tear in his jacket (careful not to touch it with his bloodied right hand) and knew he hadn't been cut. Good.

Looking at the knife protruding from the man's chest, still held in his hand, Ray was positive that he hadn't touched it at any point. This was also good. The bad was that his right hand was covered in Dick's blood. His own T-shirt was the safest place to hide the blood for now. Wiping off as much as he could he then zipped up his jacket (it turned out maroon was a fortuitous choice that day) which hid the incriminating gory evidence. Next he surveyed the alley and its entrance for security cameras. With a sigh of relief, he found none. The high street would be a different story. There were bound to be cameras there that covered the entrance to the alley. But that couldn't be helped; he would have to take his chances. He looked at his watch, the catalyst of Dick's demise. Chay would be arriving in seven minutes. The whole altercation between himself and Dick had taken around five, possibly six minutes. It had felt a lot longer.

He stood up and stared down at Dick's dead body lying on the ground amongst the piss and filth you'd find in any alley in any city. This was not the way Ray had imagined his day unfolding. But, he reasoned, if you chose the life of a criminal, petty or grand, there was a good chance this would be your end. Ray knew that better than most, as he had spent a considerable amount of his life around grisly scenes like this one. The only difference was that up until now his role had been to find the people responsible, arrest them, and put them in prison.

5

'You're quiet,' said Chay, glancing at Ray quickly before returning her eyes to the road. 'I mean, more quiet than usual.'

'I'm fine,' Ray replied, falling short of selling the sentiment.

'You sure?'

'Chay, I'm fine,' he repeated.

'OK. How was it in there today?'

'Much the same as last time.'

'Well, let's do something different today. If you're feeling up to it I thought we could go to the pub.'

'I don't know. I'm a bit tired.'

'You just said you were fine. *Twice*,' she said with an arched brow. 'It'll do you good to get out, Ray.'

He took a moment to consider the idea. Would a man who just murdered another man casually go to the pub for a pint immediately after? No, he would not. He would go home, draw the curtains, and climb the walls.

'Yeah, why not –' he began then suddenly stopped, noticing the tell-tale red beneath and around the finger-nails of his right hand. He quickly placed his hands in his pockets. 'I could use a drink.'

'Great.'

'I'll just change into something else first,' he said, horribly aware of the bloody T-shirt stuck to his stomach.

'Change? Who are you, J-Lo?' she said with a laugh. 'It's just the Green Oak.'

'I know. I can smell the clinic on me.'

'Oh. Of course. Sorry.'

'It's OK. I'll quickly pop into the house and you go ahead and get us a table. Sound good?'

They lapsed into silence and eventually arrived at Gilmour Avenue, the leafy suburban street where Ray lived.

Ray lived.

Not Ray, Odette and Chay. Odette was gone and Chay had moved out to be closer to the university campus. She had wanted to move back in after learning of Ray's diagnosis. He had politely, and with great effort, refused. It was important she be with people her own age. He didn't want his condition stalling her life.

'Dream space,' said Chay, reversing her car into the tiny gap almost exactly outside Ray's house.

'Beautiful control,' said Ray, opening the passenger door and stepping onto the pavement. He glanced down at the seat. No traces of blood. He slammed the door.

'I learned from the best,' she replied, closing her door before beeping the car locked.

Ray gave a broad smile from over the car's roof. 'Your mother.'

'Exactly,' she said.

'Go on, head to the pub. You know my tipple. I'll be with you shortly,' he said, heading to his front door, key ready in hand. He wanted to get in the house as soon as possible. He believed the blood to be safely hidden against the maroon of his jacket, but the rip in its shoulder (unnoticed up until now by the fact it was on his left-hand side and he had sat in the passenger seat) might prompt a question and the need for an excuse. Ideally both would be best avoided.

'Are you sure you're OK?'

'Chay, please stop asking me. I'm fine, honestly.'

'You just seem a little off?'

'A little off? I've got *cancer*,' he snapped, and immediately regretted it. 'Sorry, Chaynnie. That was uncalled for.'

'It's OK,' she replied, showing no signs of being hurt. 'It's OK to be angry. You're allowed to be pissed off. You're allowed to be anything you want, Ray. Just don't be a stranger. Speak to me. You know you can do that right?'

'More of this reverse-parent thing,' he said with a grin.

'Ray!'

'Sorry.' He really wanted to hug her in that moment, but that wasn't going to happen and not just because he was covered in blood. Only one person had been able to hold Chay, and, tragically, she was gone. 'I know. You're right.' He turned the key in the lock. 'Won't be long. A pint of the usual, if you please.'

'Of course the student is paying. Outrageous.' She grinned, walking off towards the pub.

Pink water swirled its way into the plug hole at his feet. Sadly for Ray, his prostate cancer meant that he had stood in this shower, pain resonating in his lower back and pelvis, washing blood from his body on a number of occasions.

As the piping hot water gushed over him, he couldn't believe that he was currently in a worse situation: washing the blood of another man off his skin. The blood was soon gone but Dick's lifeless eyes persisted in Ray's mind. What had he done? The fact that he had killed a man forty-five minutes ago was difficult to accept but his actions immediately after the event troubled him even more so. Instead of what he knew to be right (call the police immediately), he had put his phone away and then sought to remove any evidence of his presence in that alleyway.

Even now, in his own home, he continued the quest to erase any evidence that might connect Dick's murder to himself. His bloodied clothes were sealed in a plastic bag and ready to be incinerated in his log-burner. He had been attacked, his life had been threatened, he had acted in self-defence. So why was he acting like a criminal – like a murderer?

He turned the lever, stopping the flow of water, and the answer came to him in the sudden silence of the shower cubicle.

Time.

He didn't want any more time taken from him. His time with Odette had been taken from him. Cancer was now taking time away from him, and Dick would have taken his life there and then in that terrible alley. It was him or Ray. And Ray wasn't about to live his final moments on his back amid the refuse watching a sliver of sky fade from his sight.

He knew all too well exactly how much time would be wasted attempting to explain to the authorities what had happened. The outcome of those conversations was unclear. Prison could be one of them. The thought twisted his stomach in a cold knot. As an ex-cop, it did not bear thinking about. Fighting cancer whilst looking over his shoulder sounded like hell on earth.

No. There was only one place he wanted to be right now – sitting in a pub with Chay. And there was nothing that was going to stop that from happening.

Not the police.

Not Dick.

Not cancer.

Ray nodded in silent agreement with the stoic outcome of his wet deliberations. But there was another thought in his head, voiced by the darkest part of him. A vengeful place that whispered a command he knew he could not ignore: *You need time to find your wife's murderer.*

6

He noticed Chay check her watch for the third time in the last five minutes.

'Everything all right?'

'Yeah. Why?'

'You keep checking your watch.'

'Do I? I didn't notice,' she said, finishing the last of her gin and tonic. She had barely placed the empty glass upon her beer mat when an eager voice asked, 'Can I get you another one?'

Chay looked up into the handsome smile of the young barman. Ray noted the tea towel draped over his arm in a pleasingly professional manner. 'Why not,' she said, with a tight polite nod.

Quickly scooping up the glass, the barman said, 'Hi, Mr Leonard.'

Having not long arrived in the Green Oak, this was Ray's first look at the handsome young man. He now recognized him.

'Oh! Hi, Miles,' he said to Chay's old school friend and the son of the landlord. 'You work here now?'

'Just helping Dad out,' he said, unable to stop the shift in his eyes to the jagged crescent of Ray's facial scar.

'Table service,' said Ray. 'I could get used to this.'

Miles laughed nervously, flashing a line of perfect white teeth. 'Can I get you another lager?'

'Let me see.' In one fluid action Ray poured the remaining half-pint down his throat. 'Yes, you can,' he said, wiping his mouth with the back of his hand.

Miles took Ray's pint glass and turned his attention back to Chay. 'How's uni going?' he asked.

'No complaints,' she said, his puppy-dog gaze ricocheting off her stern, beautiful features.

'Great ... that's great,' he said, nodding a head of shaggy blond hair as he brushed some non-existent crumbs from the table. 'Things are going pretty well up in Leeds. It's a fun city. But it's a long way to go. I feel a bit detached from everyone down here. It's a long way . . . up there. You know. Leeds, I mean.' He glanced at Ray. Ray gave him a pitying smile. 'OK, I'll go grab those drinks. Catch you later . . . well, when I bring them back.'

Ray watched him walk to the bar and even though he couldn't see his face he still managed to register that shake of the head that said – *Miles, you bloody idiot.*

'Always was a nice kid, Miles,' he said out loud.

'Yeah. He's a good guy,' agreed Chay, correcting the angle of her beer mat.

'He seems to like you.'

'I hadn't noticed.'

'Really? I'm pretty sure the stuffed stag above the bar noticed,' said Ray, nodding towards the taxidermy.

'Don't start, Ray.' She sighed.

'What am I starting?'

'Playing Cupid.'

'Cupid?'

'Yeah. It's really annoying.'

Ray knew that Chay had never been in love. It was not

her fault. Ray knew whose fault it was. Chay knew whose fault it was. But they danced around that subject, as people do when the subject is the stuff of nightmares.

'I was just pointing out that he clearly likes you. I'm sure he would love to take you out some time,' Ray said, trying as hard as possible to sound breezy. The truth was that knowing that Chay was unable to give herself to one of life's most meaningful experiences left him in a constant state of heartbreaking sadness and immense anger.

'It's no concern of mine what Miles wants,' she said, feigning disinterest by looking out of the window. Dappled light that made its way through the big oak tree outside flickered across her face.

'What about what I want?' asked Ray.

'What do you what?'

'I want you to be happy.'

'I am.'

'Your mother would want you to be happy.'

'I know she would.'

'She'd want you to be young.'

'I know.'

'To meet someone.'

'I know.'

'Make a few mistakes. She'd want –'

'You know what Mum would really want, Ray?' Chay said, an edge to her voice. 'She'd want to be alive. That would be at the top of her list. Not my fucking dating life.' She looked back out of the window, a quiver in her lip.

Ray looked at the empty seat to Chay's left and gave a long silent sigh. 'Chay . . .' he began, only to be interrupted by Miles.

'One gin and tonic —' placing the drink before Chay — 'and one pint of lager. Can I get you guys anything else?' he asked, with that eager smile.

'We're good, thank you, Miles,' said Ray, not taking his eyes off Chay.

'OK . . . I'll leave you to it.' He walked away, the spring in his step somewhat less evident.

'I guess it's my turn to apologize,' said Chay, meeting Ray's gaze.

'Then it's my turn to say it's OK.'

'No. That was a pretty shitty thing to say. To you and Mum,' she added, rubbing at her temples.

'I'm not so sure. I seem to remember your mother saying she'd swim with sharks if it meant you'd meet a nice boy.'

She smiled. 'Did she? She was terrified of sharks.'

'Absolutely petrified. She told me after the first time she saw *Jaws* she couldn't put her hands in the sink to wash dishes for a good month, let alone take a bath.'

They both laughed. Easy and light. Rare.

Chay picked up her drink. Steeling himself, Ray decided to push the point. 'Look, Chay, I get it, I really do. It kills me . . . the thought of what you went through. But at some point —' He stopped. He could tell by following her line of sight that she wasn't listening to him. She was looking at someone behind him.

He felt a heavy hand come to rest on his shoulder.

'Mr Ray Leonard, I'm placing you under arrest.'

7

Ray's blood froze in his veins.

'You do not have to say anything –'

They had found Dick's dead body slumped in that alley-way, murdered. And now they had found the man who had plunged the knife into his chest, sitting in a pub without a care in the world, having a drink with his stepdaughter.

'– but it may harm your defence if you don't mention –'

Jesus Christ. What would Chay think of him? Ray opened his suddenly parched mouth to say something to her but no words were forthcoming.

'– that you're the worst brother-in-law in the world.'

Hold on.

What?

At first Ray didn't understand the words that had been spoken. Only when he saw Chay's face light up did the dark thoughts that had been racing through his mind come to a complete halt.

'Surprise!' she exclaimed.

Ray cautiously turned and looked up into a familiar face. 'John,' he said, blinking in relief.

'Hi, Ray,' said Detective Inspector John Facey.

How one might address John Facey depended on your relationship to him. He was DI Facey to his colleagues, Facey to acquaintances. His impossibly chiselled good looks had earned him his nickname Handsome John to his friends and family, a moniker he retained with ease into his mid-forties. Ray had been able to call him all of these names as he was all of the above to him at one time or another.

Ray and John had first met as a pair of uniformed officers. John (the younger by some ten years) had quickly latched on to Ray as a father figure of sorts. John's own father had abandoned him before he had even had a chance to memorize his face (at a guess it was extremely handsome; a bastard's face, but handsome all the same). Their friendship continued to grow as they both rapidly ascended the ranks from uniform, to CID, to Divisional Headquarters: Major Crimes Unit.

Ray's age, coupled with a keen attention to detail and a cool head, meant that he achieved the rank of Detective Inspector first. John had been extremely happy for him. And then extremely sad for him when, one day, almost eighteen months ago, Ray beckoned him into his office. He entered as a Detective Sergeant and left as Detective Inspector. Having chosen his replacement Ray took early retirement, stating ill health and the need to spend more time with his stepdaughter as reasons.

John was there now at the Green Oak because their relationship extended beyond serving together as police officers. They were family. John had introduced his sister, Odette, to Ray eleven years earlier.

'I thought it might do you some good to see Uncle John,' said Chay, as his friend sat down in the empty seat next to her.

'Being a man who detects for a living I'm embarrassed to say I had to rely on Chaynnie to pin down your whereabouts,' John said, leaning his long, well-maintained frame back into the chair, instantly at ease with his surroundings. 'I know you're more of a quill and parchment kind of guy, but you need to check your phone from time to time, Boss.'

'You're right. I'm sorry I haven't been in touch,' said Ray, the warm regard on John's face thawing the blood in his veins. 'I'll make more of an effort . . . if you'll stop calling me "Boss".'

'Old habits,' said John, returning Ray's grin.

'When can I see the girls next?' Chay asked her uncle.

'I've got them at the flat this weekend.'

'Fab. I'll come by.'

'They'd love that. How about you, Ray?'

'I'm not good company at the moment.'

John's easy smile turned grave. 'How are you doing?'

'I'm doing OK. Taking each day as it comes. Some days are more . . . challenging than others.'

'Wow, Uncle John,' said Chay. 'You've already got more out of him than I've managed.'

'That's why they call me the Ray-whisperer.' He grinned and Chay giggled.

Ray shook his head and asked, 'How are the girls?'

'A pair of terrors.'

'And Angie?'

John's smile wavered. 'She's moving on.'

'She met someone?'

'Yeah. Seems like a good guy.'

'All right . . .' Ray said, tentatively.

'Hey. I'm over the moon for her,' John said, seeing their pitying looks. 'The sooner she gets married the sooner I can have my entire pay packet. Ex-wives are far more expensive than wives.'

'You're OK, though?' asked Chay.

'Broke . . . but rich in spirit,' he replied with a wink.

'How's work?' asked Ray. 'Caught any bad guys lately?'

'And so ends the family heart-to-heart,' said Chay, with a raised finger catching Miles's eye (an easy thing for her to do). 'Another pint of lager, please.'

'I can't, Chay. I'm still on the clock,' said John, halting Miles's journey to the tap. 'Sparkling water for me, son.'

'So?' Ray nudged. 'Any interesting cases recently?'

Chay rolled her eyes.

'Once a cop,' said John, in amusement. 'All right, I've got an interesting one for you. A guy tries strangling his wife to death . . . over chewing gum.'

'Gum?' said Chay, confused.

'Yup. Gum,' confirmed John. 'Any theories?'

Ray sat for a while in thought.

'The husband found some chewing gum in their home, possibly in the bedroom. The wife does not chew gum,' he eventually said.

John slowly started to clap his big hands together. A few heads turned towards them at the racket.

'Wow, Ray,' said Chay, impressed.

Ray gave her a semi-embarrassed shrug.

'Ray Leonard, ladies and gentlemen. The best to ever police . . . apart from Nick Sutter.'

'Funny,' Ray replied, rolling his eyes.

John threw his head back in laughter.

'Who's Nick Sutter?'

'Sorry, Chay. In-joke,' said John. 'He's the meanest, most horrible Manc detective you'll ever meet.'

'Can we get back to the case at hand, please?' asked Ray.

'Yes, Boss . . . I mean, Ray.' John grinned. 'OK. So, you were spot on. Except it wasn't the bedroom, it was the bathroom. And it gets better. Believe it or not, chewing gum in a toilet bowl triggered this maniac. You should have seen this guy, Ray,' he said, giving their surrounding area a quick scan and lowering his voice. 'Myself and DS Greylag joined William – the suspect – in the interview room. William is a real uptight type, and I mean *really* uptight. Like, spandex-on-an-elephant tight.' Ray and Chay chuckled. 'He's wearing those creepy little round specs. He kind of reminded me of one of Vader's henchmen at the controls of the *Death Star*, all pasty and gaunt. Anyway, he's sitting in the interview room in a buttoned-up cardigan and shirt and tie. It's hot as hell in there and he hasn't loosened a single button. But either way, it's a hell of a get-up for attempted murder.

'The old black box tape machine is barely up and running before William starts giving his version of events. His solicitor, fresh out of school by the way, has zero control over him. Which is great,' said John, accepting his sparkling water from Miles, with a smile and a wink. 'So, I say to him, just slow down, take it easy, and tell us what happened. You ready for William's version of events, Ray?'

'One moment.' Ray took a big gulp of beer. 'Ready,' he said, returning the glass to its mat.

'OK. A long time ago . . . in a galaxy far, far away . . .' Chay laughed, but Ray looked confused. '. . . William returned home early from a work meeting that had been cut short in the city. He found a piece of chewing gum stuck to the inside of the toilet bowl in the en-suite. As you correctly deduced, Ray, William confirmed Sarah, the wife, has never chewed gum. Apparently, William does chew gum and his wife once told him chewing was for ruminants. But he knows it's definitely not his in the bowl because he wraps his gum in tissue and disposes of it in the bin.' John rolled his eyes. 'So, he confronts Sarah, who's chopping some veg in the kitchen.'

'Copy that,' said Ray, his fingers steepled beneath his chin.

'William asks her where has the gum come from? She says it was hers and that she'd recently taken up the habit. William does not believe her . . . so –' John wound a finger at his temple – 'this nutter gets a pack of chewing gum from his work bag and asks Sarah to chew. He wants to see this "miracle of self-development". Sarah eventually obliges and that's when William put his hands around her throat.'

Chay gave a small gasp.

John raised a calming hand. 'She's in the infirmary but she's going to be fine.' He continued. 'William denies he did it. He said he blacked out. But it couldn't possibly be him. She must have done it herself somehow because it's not something he would ever do. But we know he did . . .' He met Ray and Chay's eager stares, eking out the suspense. '. . . because we have an eyewitness.'

'Oh, snap!' said Chay.

'Indeed. So I ask you –' John swirled the half-drunk sparkling water in his glass – 'who is the eyewitness?'

Chay was first to guess.

'A neighbour saw in through the kitchen window?'

'Incorrect. Would you like to phone a friend?'

'No need,' she said with a look of triumph. 'I've got it . . . security cameras!'

'That's not the answer we're looking for. You're out of the game. So sorry. Thanks for playing, gorgeous. Which means Ray Leonard has a chance for the win. How are you feeling? Nervous?'

'A little,' said Ray, puffing his cheeks.

'Don't be. You got this. To win the lot – that's the caravan, the dishwasher, and the romantic getaway to Bognor. Ray, who is the eyewitness?'

Ray let both sets of eyes linger on him expectantly. 'Gonna have to rush you, I'm afraid,' said John, as he started to hum the theme tune from *Countdown*.

In the last frantic notes, Ray said, 'The man Sarah is having an affair with. He was still in the house.'

'Bing! Bing! Bing! Winner!'

'That's amazing,' said Chay, stunned.

'Your old man's a genius, Chay,' said John, beaming. 'I could use some of that magic on this other case I've got brewing.' His smile faded.

'What is it?'

'Missing teacher. We don't have anything to go on just yet.' John shook his head, grimly. 'It's only been a few days, but it's one of those you know isn't going to end well. I just –'

John's phone rang. Looking down at the number on the screen his face hardened further. 'Sorry, guys, got to take this.' He quickly rose from his chair and stepped out of the pub.

'How did you know the guy was still in the house?' asked Chay.

'Lucky guess. Don't tell your uncle,' Ray told her with a coy grin.

John returned, still speaking into his phone. 'Yeah . . . I'm on my way,' he said before ending the call. 'I got to go, lovely people,' he said, his face still serious.

'Everything OK?' Chay asked.

Ray sat silent. He already knew.

'I have to head over to Harringdon.'

'We were just there,' said Chay.

'Really?'

'Yes, that's where Ray's clinic is.'

'Small world,' John said, looking at Ray.

'What happened?' Ray asked with forced calm.

'The usual. Someone was alive, now they're not.'

8

'DI John Facey. Major Crimes Unit.' He raised his ID to the two uniformed officers on point duty, responsible for keeping prying eyes away from the sight of the terrible things that can happen to other people.

'Inspector,' they both said in unison. One of them hurriedly scribbled John's details in the major incident log, the other let him through, lifting the blue-and-white taped police cordon that mushroomed out into the high street. Within, a squad car, ambulance and a crime scene van obscured the entrance to the alleyway. DS Greylag met John at the van.

'Boss,' he said, pulling his blue face mask down and letting it snap snugly around the portly fold of his second chin.

'Ben. What have we got?' asked John, as he started to open the sterile packaging and pull on the white forensic suit he had just taken from the van.

'Male, early thirties, with a very big knife buried in his chest,' the DS began, consulting his notebook, 'found by the kitchen hand, a Mr Arjun Doshi, of the Chutney Ranj restaurant, who was on a smoke break.'

'Is he OK?'

'No. He's definitely dead,' said DS Greylag, with a wicked grin.

'I meant the kitchen hand,' said John, rubbing at his

forehead in an exasperated manner. 'I know we all develop coping mechanisms for the horrors we see day in, day out. But your dark, *dark*, comedic bent is truly worrying, DS Greylag. Can't you just drink too much like the rest of us?'

'I'll work on it, Boss,' he said earnestly, though his grin remained. 'Mr Doshi was quite shaken up. He actually had a bit of a trip and fell in the blood.'

'So he's covered in the victim's blood?' said John, arching an accusatory brow.

'Yeah. But he's not our man.'

'Why not?'

'He's eighty-three years old and he looks like he couldn't push his finger through wet paper.'

'That's a pretty good alibi.'

'Rock solid. Either way, the paramedics have looked him over and he's going to be fine thanks to some bin bags breaking his fall, so we can start getting more details off him.'

'Do we have an ID on the deceased?' John grunted, reaching down to wrap his shoes in the sterile booties.

'He didn't have any on him but one of the uniforms up front recognized him, which is a nice break,' DS Greylag said, turning a page of his notebook. 'A James Pentecost.'

After a moment's thought, John said, 'I'm drawing a blank. What do we know about him?'

'Not much. As I said, PC Wickham has had a couple of brushes with him. Judging from what he told me he's a run-of-the-mill local ne'er-do-well. Small-time drug offences, bit of pickpocketing, shoplifting, stuff like that. Edie is digging deeper back at the office as we speak – family, friends, associates, taking a look at his PNC record.'

'Good, good. If there's anything worth knowing she'll find it,' said John, looking beyond DS Greylag to the alleyway, which was now heavily flood-lit despite the day still clinging to the last of its sunlight. 'CSI are already hard at it?'

'Yeah. Lanegan is with them too. The body is just beyond a group of large recycling bins towards the back of the alley. It's a bloody mess in there, Boss.'

'It always is,' said John, securing a mask over half his face. 'Let's head in.'

They negotiated the narrow corridor created between the van and squad car, the flashing lights turning their white booties, hooded suits and gloves intermittently blue and red. As soon as they entered the alleyway the floodlights brought their figures back to an uninterrupted pristine white.

'As you can see, we are entering through the one access point from the high street,' began DS Greylag, John's guide on the worst tour ever. 'The only other points of entry or exit are four doors either side – two east, two west. They belong to four businesses: two restaurants (one of which is the Chutney Ranj), a nail salon, and a charity shop. Employees are being vetted as and when, it's getting on so the salon and charity shop are shut. There are flats above that are accessed from the high street but they don't have windows overlooking the alley.'

With the stench of urine and piled-up refuse assaulting his nostrils despite his mask, John stopped to survey the crime scene. At the far end techs in white suits busied themselves collecting and tagging. A camera clicked and flashed around a woman who was crouched over James

Pentecost's body, which was lying in a pool of its own blood. The floodlights gave the entire scene an eerie, hyper-reality quality. Piss-soaked spaces such as this were rarely, if ever, afforded this level of clarity, he thought.

'CCTV?' asked John, craning his neck.

'None in the alley itself, unfortunately. We're hoping the high street will have something for us and we're approaching surrounding businesses for whatever footage they might have. It'll be a lot to sift through.' Greylag snapped his notebook shut. 'Now, if you'll follow me, I'll show you where the gift shop is located.' The face mask concealed his grin but John knew it was there anyway.

They arrived beside the crouched woman – Eloise Lanegan, the Home Office registered forensic pathologist.

'El,' said John, as she placed some signed and sealed swabs into her old battered medical bag.

'Hello, handsome. Fancy meeting you in a place like this,' she replied. Understandably, thirty years of proximity to all kinds of nightmarish scenarios had left Eloise Lanegan somewhat desensitized. Rumour had it that she was once seen performing an autopsy whilst eating a tin of cold baked beans.

'How are you two getting along?' John asked as he and DS Greylag crouched beside her at the edge of the dark red pool. A streak of blood jetted out of its congealed mass, thick at first before fading and then disappearing altogether under a pile of black bin bags.

'Mr Doshi,' said DS Greylag, pointing at the smear.

'Not particularly helpful. The surrounding area will be a tough scene to process, considering all the detritus,' said Lanegan, pushing her horn-rimmed glasses up her nose with the back of her hand. 'He died from either an incredibly precise knife wound to the chest, or an incredibly lucky knife wound to the chest. Or unlucky, depending on which side of the transaction you're on.'

'So, our offender may or may not know how to wield a knife,' said John.

'I know. Not particularly helpful. But there's no getting away from the fact that you're looking at the champagne of knife wounds to the heart. Lights out. No muss, no fuss. It's even more impressive – *or lucky* – when you factor in the victim is actually holding the knife.'

'Have we ruled out hara-kiri?' said DS Greylag.

John rolled his eyes.

Lanegan gave a short *Ha!* before continuing, 'It's very unlikely we'll find any prints around this bloody mess.' She pointed at Pentecost's hand still gripped around the knife.

John's gaze made its way from the knife to Pentecost's face. The victim's grubby features were ghostly under the crime scene lights. 'What about this?' he asked, gesturing to a dark purple patch around the underside of his small weak chin.

'Blunt trauma. Something hit him hard just there.'

'Kicked when he was down?' asked DS Greylag.

'Unlikely. If you look at the blood dried and gathered around the corners of his mouth, it's gathered in a way that suggests he was vertical at the time. Inside his mouth there are some broken teeth, which also suggests impact in an upward motion. We'll have to wait till I get him back to the lab to see if there is any other bruising or damage to his body. But my guess is there's more.'

'Time of death?'

'Hour and a half. Two hours tops.'

John did a three-sixty of the area. 'Either of you having difficulty giving this guy the label of innocent victim?'

'Hard to believe he was down here collecting for charity,' said Lanegan.

'Definitely has notes of criminal-on-criminal. A low-life summit gone wrong?' pondered DS Greylag. 'Maybe a drug deal gone askew? Some kind of argument ensued and the resulting scuffle ended with a one in a million shot to the heart.'

'Or, for reasons not yet apparent, he was executed by a professional,' said Lanegan.

'Hmm. There is another possibility,' said John, looking at Lanegan and then, in turn, the body. 'As you said, this wound is instant death. Which tells us that he was holding the knife when it went in . . . there was no time for him to grasp it post insertion. So, the knife probably belongs to him. Which means perhaps *he* was threatening someone. This could be a mugging gone horribly wrong for Mr Pentecost.'

'The hunter becomes the prey,' said Lanegan.

'Who was he trying to mug, Batman?' said DS Greylag.

Lanegan gave another snort of laughter. John did not.

'The CSIs will have to perform a fingertip search of all of these bags and bins. All of it will have to be examined, photographed, logged and seized. Christ, it's going to take forever.' John sighed.

'I'll hang back and coordinate the removal of St James here,' said Lanegan.

'Thank you, El. We'll meet you in the lab tomorrow in the AM. I'm going to walk the alley,' he said to no one in particular, as he stared down at Pentecost.

Something felt off.

He knew there was a critical detail here he was missing. And that made no sense. He didn't know this man. This was the first time he had seen him and the first time he had been in this alleyway. But the thought persisted that he was overlooking a key point. 'I'm going to walk the alley,' he repeated.

'OK, Boss,' said DS Greylag, knowing to give DI Facey space when he saw the look that was currently in his eye.

John slowly moved around the area (saying his hellos to the CSI team when prompted), taking in its squalor in broad brushstrokes, feeling it out, wondering what might jump out at him. But in the immediate vicinity of James Pentecost's corpse, nothing did. On the surface it was just as it seemed – a horrible, disgusting, stinking place to die. The stench of his workplace for the evening hit John with renewed vigour. It was time to get a breath of fresh air outside of the crime scene. John made his way back towards the high street, absently glancing here and there.

Stop!

A good twenty feet from the body, close to the entrance, was one of the few small pockets of shade still left in the alley. John stood frozen, peering into the dark void between two large industrial recycling bins.

'*Shit*,' he said quietly to himself.

9

'Did you hear about the stabbing in that alley across the street from here last night? I heard some guy was found with a machete sticking out of his head,' said Luke, with a mixture of excitement and dismay. 'It's like *Grand Theft Auto* out there.'

After the observation was met with silence he recalibrated his reference for an older crowd. 'It's getting like *Mad Max* out there.' That worked, setting off a flurry of nods of recognition, so he went with the metaphor. 'What are we . . . ten, twenty years off roaming the tundra for food? Human food, by the way. The future is no place for a veggie.'

'Ironically, vegetable-fed human will be quite the delicacy,' chimed in Rose with a flick of her old tongue and a cackle of laughter.

'I'm a vegetarian,' said Gog, his worried eyes darting between Luke and Rose.

'No way!' Luke exclaimed. 'How many carrots does it take to keep you running all day?'

'I hate carrots,' Gog said, sticking his wide tongue out in a 'yuck' gesture.

'Why did you stop eating meat? Was it hard?'

Gog mulled the question for a moment. 'No, not really. When we had our first drive-thru McDonald's in the Valleys, years back – we used to have to go to Cardiff before then — I got my Happy Meal from the little window and pulled up in the car park. I went to put the burger in my mouth and I looked up and there was a cow looking over the bush at me from the next door farmer's field. Our eyes met, and that was that, I stopped straight away. Pizza cake.'

'Pizza cake?' Luke said, confused.

'Yeah. Pizza cake.'

'What's a pizza cake?'

'You know. Easy. No problem.'

'The phrase you're looking for, you big lummox,' said Rose, with her forehead in her hand, 'is "piece of cake".'

'That's what I said?!' Gog protested. 'Pizza cake.'

'Oh my God. Let's move past it,' said Luke, shaking his head in bemusement. He turned his attention to Ray. 'You look like a man who would fare well in the end times? I can see you with a mohawk, and a shotgun strapped to your back.'

'If they're end times I don't think anyone is going to fare well . . . regardless of hairstyle.'

'Oh, I think some would. I'd do well in the apocalypse,' Luke said, cockily running a hand through his jet-black hair.

'You think so?'

'No diggity. If it came down to it. If anyone was dumb enough to cross me or the people I love . . . well, I'd do what was necessary in a heartbeat.' He snapped his fingers for emphasis.

'You think you could do that? Take someone's life?'

'I wouldn't want to . . . but don't fuck with me.'

'Noted,' said Ray, holding his hands up in surrender.

'I don't think we'd have a problem out on the tundra, Ray. You're one of the good ones. I can tell.'

'I'm flattered.'

'I'm good at sniffing out bullshit. That's what would give me the edge. I can read people. You have to be able to do that in the corporate raiding game.'

'The what game?' asked Gog.

'Activist Investor. Corporate Raider. That's what I do.'

'How do you do raiding?' Gog repeated, even more confused.

'Basically, I acquire a controlling stake in a company, say something in retail or tech, then gut the hell out of it. Sell off unprofitable divisions, change structures, streamline operations –'

'Sack people,' said Rose, disdainfully.

'If need be,' Luke replied with a shrug. 'The ultimate goal is to sell off the company for a higher price than what was paid to acquire it.'

'That doesn't sound very . . . nice,' said Gog, unsure of his own observation.

'That's because it's not. Trust me, I've mulled over what I do and how it might have influenced my current situation. Cosmic karma and all that.'

'You sound as bad as him with all his God nonsense,' Rose jabbed a finger at Gog. 'Do you really think that has anything to do with you being here? Silly boy.'

'I'm just saying, that's all. I've taken a few shits on the little guy. If someone is taking notes, I've got to offset some "not very nice" with some "very nice". And it looks like I've got limited time,' Luke concluded, with a flick of his IV bag.

'How do you read people?' Ray prompted, in the hope of lightening the mood.

'Oh yeah.' Luke repositioned himself in his chair. 'All right, so I look for quirks, patterns, gestures, even the way someone walks.' His gaze briefly dropped to Ray's legs, before he continued. 'When huge amounts of money are in play, you have to be able to pinpoint the most powerful voice in the room. Because it's not always the guy at the head of the table.'

'Well, we all know the loudest voice in this room,' said Rose, rolling her eyes.

'Don't confuse a loud voice with a strong one,' came Luke's quick reply, which was met by silence from Rose. With a smile he continued, 'But my secret weapon is my trusty internal lie-detector. It cannot be beaten,' he said, rubbing his hands in glee. 'It's flawless. You can't lie to me. It's all in the eyes. Like the Eagles sang, "*You can't hide your lyin' eyes*".'

'Can't hide them, you say?' said Ray.

'No, sir.'

'Have the Eagles never heard of sunglasses?' Ray deadpanned.

Gog and Rose guffawed. 'Superman's got Kryptonite. Luke's mortal enemy is the Sunglass Hut,' poked Rose, finding her voice once again.

'Laugh it up, Chuckles. I dare one of you to try and tell me a lie. Go on, Rose. Give it a go.'

She raised the remote and muted the TV, which had been humming away in the background.

'Challenge accepted,' she said, with a stern look in her eye. After a moment's thought, she said, 'I've swum the English Channel.'

'OK,' said Luke, as his eyes bored holes into Rose's soul. 'Got it.'

'I've had lunch with the Queen,' she said, the many lines on her face unwavering.

'But she's dead?' Gog pointed out.

'When she was alive, you twonk,' she hissed at Gog, but her eyes never left Luke's.

'She's good,' he said, nodding his head in appreciation. 'But not good enough. You've never swum the channel but you *have* had lunch with the Queen.'

Ray and Gog looked at Rose.

'Correct,' she said, through gritted teeth.

'You did have lunch with the Queen?' Gog asked in amazement.

'Why wouldn't I have had lunch with the Queen?' snapped Rose.

'Because you're bloody horrible,' said Luke, turning to Gog. 'What have you got for me, BFG?' Gog wilted under the spotlight. 'Come on. It's super easy. One thing about you that's true and one that's not.'

Gog's eyes slowly circled their sockets, searching for inspiration, then they suddenly stopped, his big round face lit up in excitement.

'All right. I can whistle. I . . . can't whistle.'

'God help us,' said Rose, putting her head into her skeletal hand once more.

'You can't whistle,' Luke said, minus any kind of deliberation.

'Urethra!' said Gog, throwing his arms up. 'Spot on!'

'I think you mean Eureka!, Gog,' said Ray.

'What did I say?'

Ray paused for consideration. 'Doesn't matter.'

'Yeah, can't whistle,' said Gog, proving himself by pursing his lips and blowing nothing but air and spittle out of his missing incisor. 'My nan reckoned it's because my tongue is too big in my head.'

'That's the only thing that's big in that head,' said Rose.

'Thank you, Rose,' said Gog, placing a big hand on his heart.

'What about you, Ray? Think you can beat my lie detector?' Luke goaded.

Ray waved a dismissive hand.

'Come on, Ray! For old times' sake,' said Gog, excitedly.

'We don't have any old times, Gog. We just met,' said Ray, chuckling. He looked to Luke, who fanned his fingers temptingly. 'All right. I'll give it a crack.'

'*Yes!*' said Luke, leaning forward in his chair as far as the intravenous drip would allow. He locked eyes with Ray. 'Bring it.'

Ray shuffled in his seat so that their faces were just inches apart. Luke's head bobbed excitedly as he bit down on his lip in concentration.

Unblinking, without a trace of emotion, Ray said, 'I killed the guy in the alley across the street.'

Luke started to smile but the intensity of Ray's gaze stalled the movement. Rose and Gog looked on in a similar state of *should we, or shouldn't we laugh?* Ray milked the moment for another beat before he offered, 'I'm a retired cop.'

'I knew it!' Luke shouted.

'DI Leonard, at your service.'

'I knew it. I said to Gog, I'm getting a whiff of the Old Bill or maybe ex-army. Didn't I say that, Gog?'

'He did, yeah. He said, I smell Frazzles –'

'Gog,' said Luke, suddenly panicked.

'– and I said, Frazzles? And then he said, crispy bacon flavour.'

'Thank you for that.'

'What did I say?' asked Gog, oblivious.

Luke turned to Ray. 'Bantz,' he said, his cheeks suddenly flushed. 'Sorry, Ray.'

'Never apologize for Frazzles, Luke,' he replied, with a no-hard-feelings grin.

'I knew you were a cop,' Luke said again, through narrowed eyes. 'You've got a hell of a poker face, too. For a moment I really did think you chopped up that bloke across the street.'

'Eh, Rose,' said Gog. 'How did you have lunch with the Queen, then?'

She considered the question for a time, before deciding to share something of herself.

'I worked at a dog shelter for a long time. Apparently that kind of thing sits well with the monarchy.'

'You like dogs?' Gog replied, in surprise. She shrugged. 'Was it nice at the Palace?'

'There were no locks on the bathroom doors. Very strange.'

'I'm still trying to process . . . *charity work*?' Luke guffawed. 'I did not see that coming.'

'Charity? It was a job. The shelter is just down the road from my flat. It was convenient. I still pop in from time to time,' Rose said nonchalantly.

'I'm not entirely surprised,' Ray chipped in. 'Especially considering Rose's love of dogs.'

'What? No. I don't love them. Filthy animals.'

'Oh, I think so,' he said, leaning closer to her. 'You reached for a hanky in your pocket recently. I saw the corner of a small plastic bag before you pushed it back in. And those coarse little hairs on your skirt suggest a Jack Russell or maybe a West Highland White enjoys the warmth of your lap?'

Rose brushed a hand over her skirt. 'Not even the lint roller can get it all,' she said, as a yellow-toothed grin spread across her face. 'Little Alfie. And yes, he's a Jack Russell. Not much gets by you, does it, Detective Inspector?'

Ray leaned back in his chair with the usual slight embarrassment sharing his insight brought him.

'DI Leonard,' said Luke, shaking his head in delight. 'It's like doing chemo with Columbo. And you,' he added, turning to Rose. 'I always assumed the lap dog of the

Princess of Darkness would be a three-headed snarling wolf beast not a cute little Jack Russell named Alfie.'

When Ray left the clinic John Facey was stood waiting for him on the pavement. In stark contrast to the 'scruffs' (jeans and a T-shirt) his brother-in-law had been wearing at the pub last night, he now wore the standard business attire of a cop at his level. But, of course, it being Handsome John, he elevated the look to something you might find browsing the pages of *GQ*.

'John?' he said, unable to hide his surprise.

'Hi, Ray. I hope it's OK but I asked Chaynnie if she wouldn't mind if I gave you a ride ... I was in the area anyway,' he said, pointing a thumb at the alleyway just down the street.

It was still, as Ray had noted heading into the clinic, the polar opposite of the dim maw he had rushed into so desperately the day before. The cordon was still being enforced, protecting the well-lit and probably well-preserved scene of Ray's crime.

'That's very nice of you,' said Ray.

'I hated cutting our evening short last night.'

'Not a problem.'

'Chaynnie mentioned the clinic was in the vicinity.' John pointed at the alley again, forcing Ray's eye line. 'It's practically spitting distance. You didn't see anything out of a window or hear any screams yesterday, did you?' he said, with a chuckle.

'Unfortunately not,' Ray replied with a tight smile, as alarm bells starting ringing in his head. *Something doesn't feel right, here. Or am I just being paranoid?*

'Can't blame me for asking. As you know, every little helps.'

'I'm sure you've got it well in hand over there,' said Ray, making a let's-head-to-the-car gesture.

'Here's a crazy idea. Why don't you come walk the scene with me? I'm not too proud to admit a Ray Leonard angle would be most welcome. What do you say?'

'I'm a bit rusty, John.'

'Gold don't rust, Ray,' John replied with his trademark warm smile. 'Plus the old magic was there in the pub yesterday, so don't give me that.'

'I'm bushed after the, you know, chemo.'

'Come on,' John said, gently corralling Ray with a long arm around his shoulder. 'It's en route to the car . . . and walking a blood-soaked alleyway will do you good. Just like old times.'

After Detective Inspector John Facey had a quiet word with the PC on log duty (no one should pass the cordon without ID, but few were impervious to John's charm), Ray stood on the perimeter of the crime scene. An awning had been erected the length of the alley, just in case the heavens opened – a wise precaution, thought Ray, rain can be the death of a crime scene.

'We're done,' said a young CSI, approaching them whilst removing her mask and protective glasses. Two of her colleagues were packing up equipment at the far end of the alley.

'Nicely done, Frankie,' said John.

'That was what we call a "what the hell am I doing with my life?" session,' Frankie laughed, despite the sentiment. 'Hi,' she said, looking at Ray whilst removing her blue medical gloves. Ray nodded, John did not make any introductions.

'Could be worse, you could be on clean-up.'

'True that. See you at the next horror show, Detective Inspector,' she said before leaving.

'Thanks again, guys,' John said as her two colleagues passed them, full-handed, saying their goodbyes.

Alone now in the alleyway with John, with the spotlights of the crime scene lamps shining down, the space was barely recognizable to Ray. In his mind the altercation with Dick took place in a shadowy nightmare, not this clinically bright corridor with all of its hideous grime revealed in unabashed glory. Even its rank odour was somehow sharper, more intense under the glare.

'It's the maid's day off,' said John, seeing the revulsion on Ray's face. 'I know you can't see because of the tarp, but there's no CCTV above. We're still going through the CCTV from the high street, but so far we haven't had any luck. There are two cameras out there. One is broken and the other looks away from the alley. This is one lucky guy. There are not many places left in this city where you can go unseen.'

Maybe my run of bad luck is coming to an end? thought Ray.

'Uniforms have done some door-knocking in the area. No one saw anything, and none of the surrounding shops have cameras that look out onto the street. However, a few of the people we spoke to were familiar with the victim. No one had a good word to say about him,' said John, 'one James Pentecost.' He pointed to the patch of dried blood at the alley's far end. 'The victim's final resting place after a knife wound to the chest. An ironic title, "victim", considering he'd spent most of his relatively short life creating them.'

So Dick was a James.

'Mr Pentecost was a Harringdon local, although he doesn't appear to have been of any fixed abode. Gainfully employed at a lumber yard until about eighteen months ago, when he was fired for stealing. Previous convictions include all the classics – drugs, theft and assault, but his PNC record pinged an old USI with a fourteen-year-old when he was seventeen.' John rattled off this pertinent information about James Pentecost's unlawful sexual intercourse with a minor without the aid of a notebook. His memory for detail had always impressed Ray. 'Now, considering all of the above, why do you think a man like that would come to a place like this, Ray?'

'You've answered your own question, John. All of the above.'

'Exactly! The real question is, which one? Drugs? Theft? Assault or rape?' he asked, tapping his pursed lips with his index finger in concentration. 'I think he lived a life riddled with bad choices and the last one he made was to follow someone into this alley and it cost him his life.'

'What about a professional hit?'

'I don't think so. He's too low-level. This is not a man who moves in those kinds of circles. Bluntly, no one is going to miss him. He just doesn't matter.' John walked a few steps away from Ray and crouched low to the floor. 'No. He followed someone into this alley and that person was more than he bargained for. I think this patch of blood here was the beginning of the end for Pentecost.'

Ray reluctantly made his way to John's side, coming to a

stop in almost exactly the same spot he had looked down at James Pentecost's buckled form yesterday, with his hand holding his bloodied mouth in shock.

'You see this?' asked John, pointing at a Pollock-esque piece of blood spatter. 'This blood was spat onto the ground by the victim. There were some horribly neglected teeth in and around it that have since been bagged. I was with Eloise at the post-mortem this morning . . . she was asking about you, by the way.'

'She good?'

'Same as ever. I am yet to catch her eating on the job, though.'

'I saw it with my own eyes, John. Cold baked beans straight out the can, I'm telling you,' Ray said, to laughter from John as he straightened himself to his full imposing height.

'Eloise showed me bruising to the chest, jaw and genitals,' began John, suddenly serious again. 'The jaw bruising definitely happened around this blood spatter area; he was hit with enough force to break his teeth. I'm guessing the chest impact happened at the same time, because the genital bruising and swelling I saw . . . well, he's had a kick to the bollocks I wouldn't wish on my worst enemy. You're not getting up from that in a hurry. And I think he did get up from the blow to the jaw. I think he had another go at the man he followed down here.'

John started to slowly walk in Ray's direction, giving him no option but to edge his way towards the spot where he had driven the knife into Pentecost's heart. John put his hand out before him and gripped an invisible knife pointed at Ray.

'I think Pentecost backed that man into a corner,' he said, coming to a stop over the dried dark red stain; Ray on one side, John on the other. 'This is where he made his move. Probably lunging with the knife, but our guy was ready for him. There's not a drop of another person's blood here so I think he successfully blocked Pentecost's effort –' He thrust the invisible knife at Ray. Ray made no movement. John retracted the knife. 'He blocked the knife,' he said again, making a nodding gesture at Ray's arm. He slowly extended the knife and this time Ray half-heartedly pushed John's arm away. 'Yes,' said John. 'Now, here comes the legacy-ending kick to the bollocks –' another gesture to Ray's feet.

'Really, John?'

'Just humour me.'

With a sigh, Ray raised the foot of his stronger leg (the right) about two feet from the ground over the spilt blood. John feigned a grunt and started to bring his hands to his crotch, 'Now, our guy saw his opening and stepped into Pentecost.' He paused, beckoning him to step through the blood towards him. Ray obliged. 'Excellent. With a kick that hard, Pentecost wouldn't even remember he had a knife in his hand. So, our guy used that to his advantage.' He took Ray's hand and encircled it around his own that held the invisible knife. 'There you go,' he said, before quickly thrusting it into his chest with a thud loud enough to startle Ray.

'Christ, John,' he said, a little breathless.

'Lights out. Game over,' John replied, looking at Ray with a grim expression.

Be calm. If he knew anything I'd be in an interview room by now, thought Ray, not enjoying the sensation of a tall man looming over him in the alley, once again.

'What do you think?' asked John, releasing his grip on him.

'I think it's one of many possible scenarios.'

John looked at him for a long moment. Then, 'Yeah, you're right. Lot of speculation. It's a work in progress,' he concluded with a shrug. 'It's fun to be back at it, though, isn't it? You can't tell me you don't miss this?'

'Nowhere I'd rather be, John.'

'Yeah,' his brother-in-law said, nodding for longer than was comfortable. 'All right!' He clapped his hands. 'Enough excitement. Let's get you home.'

As John walked towards the high street Ray took one last look at the bloody point where his own life and Pentecost's had fatally intersected. He concluded that in fact, there were *many* places he would rather be.

11

John's gaze was fixed on the road ahead, seemingly oblivious to the majesty of the last of the day's sun lighting a blanket of billowing red and orange clouds above.

Ray looked around the car and was impressed by the immaculate interior. He recalled ranting in the past to John about how dirty some of their colleagues could be, leaving drinks containers and food wrappers behind at the end of their shifts. Evidently, John had maintained Ray's aversion to disorder. In fact, he had taken it to another level.

'It's spotless in here, John.'

'When you left I was but the learner, but now I am the master,' he replied, in a peculiar voice. Ray looked at him blank faced. '*Star Wars*.'

'Oh, right. The space film.'

'Yeah –' John smiled, whilst keeping his eyes on the road – 'the space film.'

'How do you get that new car smell?'

'If I tell you, you have to promise to keep it a secret.'

'Scout's honour.'

With a big grin, John said, 'It's a brand-new car.'

They laughed.

As they did so, John's phone, which he had placed in the cup holder, began to vibrate, buzzing like an angry bee. Glancing at its screen his laughter came to a sudden stop. Ray saw the look of concern on his face.

'Everything all right?'

'Yeah . . . fine. Just work stuff,' John replied, and his face resumed its usual carefree demeanour. 'Hey, I was thinking, it's funny, isn't it – James Pentecost was clearly, beyond a shadow of a doubt, a grade-A piece of shit. Human garbage from snout to tail. He wasn't done hurting people by a long shot. Don't you think whoever put their heel on that cockroach deserves a medal not prison?'

'Medals aren't usually given for stabbing a man in an alleyway,' said Ray carefully. 'Regardless of how undesirable they might be.'

'You're right,' John said, bringing the car to a stop at some traffic lights, and turning to Ray. 'I'm just making the point that it's a big city. Big problems. That alley is a forensics nightmare. It's a petri-dish of human waste. Chances are we won't find a thing.'

Hearing John all but admit defeat was music to Ray's ears. The vice-like grip that had slowly been tightening around his body since John had greeted him outside the clinic began to release its hold on him. He breathed a huge internal sigh of relief.

John continued. 'And you know no cop is going on a crusade for Pentecost. I mean, stopping people like that is the reason why we became cops in the first place.' The lights turned green. He pulled off. 'Part of me thinks, yes, it's my job to catch the offender . . . but in the case of James Pentecost it looks like someone has already done that for me.' As John finished his thought he turned the car onto Ray's street. Pulling up close to his house, the unmarked car came to a stop. 'I already know what you're going to say.'

'You do?'

'Of course. The unwavering direction of Ray Leonard's moral compass is the stuff of legend at headquarters,' he said, aiming a wide grin at him.

'Flattering. Go on then.'

'You're about to say – *but what if the person who killed Pentecost is worse?*'

Ray attempted to mirror John's grin. 'Am I that predictable?'

'That's why they call me the Ray-whisperer.' They laughed. When the sound faded from the cabin John gripped the steering wheel and gazed down the avenue. After a short while he turned to Ray and gave him a long steady look. 'Rest easy, though,' he said. 'If the opportunity arises I *will* put Pentecost's killer behind bars. That's what we do, isn't it? As you used to say – *It's not our job to pass judgement. Our job is to catch the offender.*'

The vice turned a revolution back in the direction of panic and fear.

'Now,' began John, finding his easy smile once again. 'Why don't you invite me in for a cuppa?'

Ray exhaled. 'How about a glass of something stronger?'

After a quick wipe of his feet on the welcome mat, 'Where am I heading?' John asked, passing Ray as he held the door open for him.

'The sitting room,' Ray called after him, shutting the door, before following.

Entering his comfortable, well-kept sitting room the first thing Ray saw was John removing his suit jacket. The second was his log-burner, and the white plastic bag within, filled with the bloodied, incriminating clothes that he had worn the previous day, when he had killed James Pentecost. After a brief, panicked second in which he admonished himself and wondered how the chemo was affecting his faculties, he quickly turned to his brother-in-law.

'Second thoughts, why don't we sit in the kitchen? It's closer to the hard liquor,' he said, stepping between John and the log-burner with a strained, wonky grin.

'Oh. Yeah, sounds good,' John said. He picked his jacket back up off the chair he had draped it over and was about to follow Ray's gesture towards the kitchen when he stopped. 'What's this?' he asked, giving a quizzical look towards something behind Ray.

Before Ray knew it John was reaching down towards the log-burner.

'J . . . John,' he stammered.

'How is this here?' John asked, taking hold of the frame

of Chay's Year Nine school photo, which was positioned in pride of place on top of the log-burner. 'Chaynnie lets you keep this out in the open?' He laughed, taking in his niece in all her teenage glory. 'I remember this period. She'd have won a gold at the Awkward Olympics. Poor kid,' he laughed again and handed the picture to Ray but his laughter petered out when he looked up to the mantel-piece and saw more pictures of Chay with her mother, his dead sister.

Ray felt the hollow ache of loss that broke out on his brother-in-law's face. He deeply knew how it was. 'I put them up a while ago. They give me comfort. It reminds me of how lucky I was to have them both in this house. My little family,' he said, replacing Chay's picture exactly where it had been. 'It's going to sound crazy, but I was in here a few days ago and I swear to God I heard Odette shouting to me from the kitchen. I ran . . .' he made a sad laugh, 'but she wasn't there.' His voice broke. John reached out and gripped his shoulder. 'Christ, I miss her.'

'I know.' John looked to his sister, happy and smiling in Ray's small gallery. 'She was one in a million. And you two together . . . lightning in a bottle. I wanted that. I wanted that so bad with Angie. Wasn't meant to be.' He made a defeated huff. 'In those early days . . . I don't think I could have coped with my marriage ending without Odette's support . . . and I don't think I could have coped with losing my sister without you, Ray.'

'Same here.' It was Ray who now reached out a comforting hand to John's shoulder. 'Come on. Let's have that drink.'

John followed Ray into his immaculate kitchen.

'Whisky,' said Ray, opening the drinks cabinet next to the large dining table at the room's far end.

'Hello, what's this?' said John, surprise in his voice. 'This does not look like Mr "Everything In Its Right Place", Ray?'

As John took in the dining table, Ray saw his surprise disappear. It was not the lazy mess of bills and papers that it may have seemed at first glance, but files that contained evidence and various key points pertaining to the events of the twenty-eighth of September, two years earlier.

John draped his jacket over one of the chairs tucked under the table and Ray handed him a tumbler with two fingers of whisky in it.

'Thanks,' said John, lost in thought, reaching for a black-and-white picture on top of all of the gathered information. He picked it up and stared stone-faced at a partial image of a person stopped at traffic lights. Through the windshield, gloved hands could be seen gripping the steering wheel.

'Odette's killer,' said Ray, 'sat there at those traffic lights, driving her car. Those gloves have always bothered me. They look like ski gloves. They're bulky. Who would carry them around? Did he grab them in a hurry?'

John brought the picture closer to his squinting eyes. 'Yeah. Bulky gloves like that don't make much sense outside of winter.'

'Hmm,' said Ray, continuing his scrutiny of the picture over John's shoulder. Even though the time code on the picture indicated 20:41 (far past sunset) the sun visor was down, obscuring the driver's face. 'He's got the visor down. Gloves on. He's not stupid. And as you and I know, most robbers are. Yes, all her belongings were gone. Watch.

Jewellery. Handbag. But it just doesn't feel like a robbery to me, John. This is not some desperate lunatic who pounced on her. I'm sure of it. Where did their paths cross?' He looked hard at the picture.

The car was abandoned not far from where her body was found, still clothed in her nurse's uniform, in the high grass of the green belt on the outskirts of the city.

Ray breathed an internal sigh of relief that the picture of Odette with her skull caved in was not amongst his research files. John didn't need to see his sister like that again.

'Odette finished her shift at the hospital at eight,' Ray went on. 'From there it takes ten minutes to get to those lights. That's thirty minutes unaccounted for. I think she stopped somewhere along the way and that's where this man was waiting for her –'

'Ray –' said John, in a tired voice, gently placing the picture back amongst Ray's makeshift evidence board.

'There was blood in the boot,' he continued, oblivious to John's discomfort. 'Which means she was injured before she was placed in there. Why would he drive her to that location? If he was going to rob her he'd do it and then scarper.'

'Robberies go wrong all the time. Look at Pentecost.'

'He was left in the alleyway.' Ray reached for the picture. 'This man drove Odette to the fields. Why?'

'Ray . . .'

'Listen to me. What if for some reason Odette went to his house? What if something happened there . . . he'd want to get her as far away from his home as possible. It's the only thing that makes sense.'

'We've been over this a thousand times.'

'And that's how progress is made. Combing the data. Trying to find details we missed.'

'All right, what do you think we missed?' John asked with a sigh, leaning against the table.

Ray reached for the picture. 'I think he's middle-aged and medium height.'

'OK . . . what makes you think that?'

'Look at his hands on the steering wheel. Ten and two. That's how our generations were taught to drive. Youngsters nowadays are told nine and three because with modern cars and powered steering, if the airbag is deployed and your hands are at ten and two, they'll be blasted into your face.'

'Huh . . . I did not know that,' said John, with an impressed nod. 'And medium height?'

'Odette was five foot six. The driver's seating position was pushed back to a setting that would suit a man of around five foot ten or eleven.' Ray paused for a moment to analyze his own research. 'But of course he could have moved the chair to confuse us,' he said, shaking his head in frustration.

'I'm worried about you, Ray,' said John, his voice full of concern as he glanced at the papers on the dining table. 'Don't do it to yourself.'

'What am I supposed to do? Forget about it?!' Ray said, more forcefully than he would have liked.

'Of course not,' replied John with gentle patience, as he took a swig of whisky. 'The case is still open and that's the way it's going to stay as long as I have breath in my body. But it's not healthy to keep poring over it like this. We'll find him. Trust me, we'll find him and put him behind bars.'

'Prison? Is that what you would do with him?' asked Ray, unblinking.

'An eye for an eye, right?' He took the photo from Ray and looked down at it, breaking away from his brother-in-law's challenging stare. 'We're police. We put bad people in prison. No judgements, remember? As much as I would like to . . . I don't have the freedom to send him the way of James Pentecost.'

'I just want him caught,' said Ray, avoiding the Pentecost reference this time. 'I want him caught *now* . . . I've not got much time left, John.'

'No time? What are you talking about? You're going to be fine. You're hard as nails.'

'It's spread, John.'

'What?' he said, placing the photo back on the table.

'It doesn't look good,' said Ray, pouring more whisky into his sad wonky smile.

'*Bullshit!* I don't care how much it's spread. You're going to be fine.'

'I wish I had your confidence.'

A thought suddenly occurred to John. 'Have you told Chaynnie?'

'How can I? All she's been through and now I'm going to go and die on her too.'

'Don't fucking say that, Ray,' John said angrily, his eyes glistening. 'People beat this thing all the time, and you're one of those people. I know it. You're going to be fine –' At this point the angry bee started to buzz again from his trouser pocket. 'Sorry,' he said, as he removed the phone and gave it a quick swipe. Apparently the text he read was disconcerting enough to remove the expression of heart-ache that had been written across his face at Ray's grim prognosis.

'Work?' asked Ray, recognizing that same look he had seen in the car.

'Um . . .' John began distractedly, before realizing Ray was waiting for a reply. 'Shit. Yeah, sorry, Ray. Work.' With a sigh he knocked back the rest of his whisky in a single gulp. 'Isn't it always? I have to shoot off. Thanks for the drink,' he said, squeezing Ray's shoulder, 'of which there will be many more in the coming years. You're going to get through this, Ray. We'll get through it, as a family.'

13

Ray liked to ride the cross-town train. In his long career at the sharp end of the stick he had tended to meet only two kinds of people: victims and offenders. Both parties were at opposite ends of the worst of the human experience. This experience left a lot of police officers with the jaded view that that was all that happened in the world – people hurting, people being hurt. Ray never wanted to be that kind of cop, which was why he liked to ride the train whenever possible.

Heading to his chemo session he sat and quietly watched and listened to people as the carriage ebbed and flowed around him. Good, normal people, living their full lives happily unaware of the terrors he had seen. This was real life. Not all the times he had spent in interview rooms with monsters.

It was ironic to him that time on this train alone, surrounded by strangers, made him feel lighter; energized and alive. Chemo, on the other hand, the thing that was meant to keep him literally alive for longer, made him feel deathly. He had accepted the blood in his urine, the blood from his behind, the pain in his bones, because, through a combination of physical and mental strength, his training helped him cope. But now his strength was abandoning him thanks to chemo. He felt tired and weak all the time. Or perhaps tireder and weaker would be more accurate. He wasn't completely spent yet – just ask James Pentecost.

I still have plenty left to give, he thought, feeling the familiar rock and pull of the train as it decelerated into the next stop. The doors opened, people got off, people got on. A woman secured her pram and sat opposite Ray, a baby in her arms. She looked up and gave him a polite smile, which left her face as soon as she saw the crescent of his facial scar. She quickly brought her attention back to the sleeping infant. Ray was used to that reaction. It no longer bothered him as it had in the early days. Of course, such a vicious-looking scar was off-putting, how else would one react to it? A thought brought a crooked smile to his face, as he remembered the only person who had ever reacted honestly to it –

'*Ray, this is my sister Odette.*'

'*Pleased to meet you.*'

'*You too. Hell of a scar,*' she'd said, running her eyes along its jagged length. '*Very cool.*'

His smile slowly faded, as it always did when memories of Odette were infiltrated by the grim reality of what had happened to her. He felt the steady thud of his blood rising in his ears as the faceless form of the thing he hated most in the world materialized in his mind – the man who killed his wife. *I still have plenty left to give.*

'Hey!' said a shrill voice, bringing Ray out of his brooding. He looked over at the next seating section along and saw a pretty young woman rubbing her wrist.

'That hurt,' she said to an older, muscular man who had his tattooed arm draped over the back of her seat in a way that suggested they were a couple. He leaned into her with his scowling face and said something into her ear that Ray wasn't able to pick up. Whatever it was instantly cowed her; she shrank into her seat and stared at the carriage floor. Ray looked from her to the man, who was staring back at him with the same scowl he had directed at the woman.

Ray looked away. *Maybe they're not all good people.* The train started to slow. The next stop was his. The high-pitched squeal of metal on metal signalled the train's arrival. Ray stood up. He couldn't help but have one last glance in the direction of the couple. The man now had his tattooed hand on the back of the woman's neck, shaking her head with just a tad too much force to be described as playful. Over the sound of the doors beeping their opening warning, Ray heard the man growl, 'Come on, stop your pouting, you silly cow.' The doors opened. The people around him got off. The beeping started again. The doors closed – and Ray was still on the train.

'Excuse me,' he said, addressing himself to the woman and steadying himself by gripping one of the central support poles. 'I was wondering if you're OK?'

She looked up startled. 'Sorry?'

'I just wanted to make sure you're OK, because he doesn't seem very nice,' said Ray, pointing a finger at the big tattooed man next to her without actually looking at him.

The man removed his hand from the woman's neck. 'Have you got a fucking death wish?' he asked, loud enough for the surrounding commuters to take notice.

'A death wish?' said Ray, meeting the man's threatening glare. 'No. It's more of a promise at this point.'

'What?'

Ray ignored his confusion, turning his attention back to the woman. 'You can't be happy with this man? Tell me to go away if you are.'

She said nothing, biting her lip and casting her eyes down.

'*Bitch!*' her boyfriend hissed through an angry sneer. Then, to Ray, 'Best you fuck off, Scarface, before I have to get up from this seat. And you don't want that.'

'You don't know what I want,' said Ray, the first note of menace entering his voice. 'You don't know me. And *I know* you don't want to.'

The timbre of his voice seemed to plant the first seeds of uncertainty in the tattooed man. Ray noticed the sharp point of his Adam's apple bob in the man's throat. The surrounding commuters, who had been roused from their newspapers and iPhones, looked on, waiting for his response. Their expectation was not lost on him. His chest puffed up, stretching the tight fabric of his black T-shirt to its limit, and then he burst into laughter. 'Are you threatening me, little man?'

His laughter sounded forced to Ray.

With slow clarity, he replied, 'Yes. One hundred per cent. *I am threatening you.*'

The big man looked at Ray with eyes that finally registered danger.

'Huh, you're nuts,' he said, that Adam's apple bobbing frantically as he looked away down the carriage in an attempt to dismiss him. Ray read the words '*Six Foot Four of Bad News*' tattooed on his neck. He wasn't in the mood to be dismissed.

'Hey! Look at me.' After a moment's hesitation he met

Ray's cold stare. 'Remember this moment. Because this is who you are. Not what you see in the mirror. Not these tattoos and muscles. In here –' Ray leaned towards him and pressed a finger into his chest. It seemed to deflate under the pressure – 'this is who you are. Remember how you feel right now, because that's how *you* make people feel. It's not nice, is it? Change your life. Try being six foot four of good news.'

The man shrank into his seat and stared blankly at the carriage floor. Every inch of his skin was bright pink with shame. The woman looked between Ray and her broken boyfriend.

'He's not as bad as you think,' she said, in a pitying voice, placing a hand on his knee. As she did so, Ray noticed her fingers depress into the fabric of the man's jeans, moving unnaturally deep into an area that should have been met with resistance. Ray followed the line of the man's leg down to his ankle. Where a sock would usually have been observed, Ray saw a metal socket screwed into a prosthetic foot encased in a white trainer.

'Are you ex-military?'

'Yeah,' he answered, looking up into Ray's surprised gaze.

'Where did you serve?'

'Afghanistan.'

'Where?'

'Helmand.'

'Is that where you lost your leg?'

'In that very shithole.'

'Well, I'm sorry –'

'I don't want your fucking pity!' he spat, regaining some of his bolster.

'I wasn't offering it. I'm sorry that you've forgotten a soldier's values and spirit. Self-discipline. Integrity. Unselfishness. Humility. You remember, yes?'

'I do. That all went with my leg.'

'Many have come back with less. And some never came back at all.'

'They were the lucky ones.'

'No . . . they weren't.' Ray gave a long sigh. 'I wish you luck,' he said to the woman.

He turned back towards the door, preparing to disembark at the next stop. As he did so the only thing that could be heard was the rumble of the train rocking from side to side, weaving its way through the city, because every one of the surrounding commuters were staring at him in silence. If this had been a Hollywood movie the carriage might have erupted into applause. In reality, they looked at him fearfully. Maybe Ray didn't quite cut the figure of a man who practised self-discipline, integrity, unselfishness and humility.

14

'Who's this, Fish?' asked Lance Corporal Neil 'Mac' McCrindle, observing the young man holding a tray of food beside Lance Corporal George 'Fish' Chipton.

'Our sprog,' said Fish.

'Oh! So nobody,' replied Mac in his just-about-comprehensible Glaswegian accent.

'Name's Chris Yannick,' the young man said, a nervous smile framed in a clean-shaven face, every inch the sprog: pristine in sand-coloured working fatigues.

'What?!' barked Mac.

'My name is Chris Yannick,' he repeated, in a voice loud enough to be heard over the din of people eating and talking at the surrounding tables within the large galley.

'Christ, she's got a mouth on her this one,' Mac said, scooping a plastic forkful of mash into his mouth. 'Why don't you take a seat, sit down and shut up? Normally I'd tell you to put your fingers in your ears as you haven't earned the right to hear the awesome dit you're currently interrupting me telling the Multiple Commander here,' he said, nodding to the Sergeant sitting opposite him, 'but I'm feeling generous, so sit down, shut up, eat your scran and get ready to laugh your teats off.'

Fish lowered himself into the seat to Mac's right, the chair's plastic cool against his back and rump thanks to the deliciously cold air cascading from a network of ducting above. Yannick sat to the left of the Multiple Commander, Sergeant Ray 'Sugar' Leonard, who looked at him with a wink. 'Welcome to bandit country, Royal,' he said.

'Sir,' he replied with another nervous smile.

'Don't call me "Sir", I work for a living,' said Ray. Yannick nodded and stared into his meal.

'Where was I, Sugar?' asked Mac, who was a good five years older than Ray and should have been a Sergeant himself by now. But a problematic attitude and a reputation for an 'unfettered' disposition, had seen him plateau at Lance Corporal. In fairness, he didn't seem to care one way or the other. Which was exactly the issue.

'You were saying the hen-do had been drinking with the all-inclusive mindset,' Ray replied.

'Right,' began Mac, finding his thread again, 'so they're giving my missis the send-off she deserves. All the staples are there, the veil, L-plate on her back, a stripper hung like a Clydesdale. Although, apparently still not gargantuan enough to ward off Morag Watkins' maw, but anyways, they're having a good fucking time.'

'I can see it now . . . high society,' said Fish in his perfect Queen's English, raising a brow. His thin Niven-esque pencil moustache gave him the anachronistic quality of a gentleman from a bygone era and the air of a man much older than his twenty-nine years.

'English wanker,' said Mac, returning his smirk. 'It's an affair fitting of the woman who's landed the Moby Dick of Govan, yours-fucking-truly. Anyway, so Kim gets an array of presents from the girls —'

'Kim's your wife?' asked Yannick, absentmindedly breaking a piece of stale bread.

'*What the fuck has my wife got to do with you?*' hissed Mac, aiming a death stare at him.

'I . . . I was . . .' stammered Yannick.

'Why don't you make yourself useful and go get three wets for the grown-ups here.'

Ray reached out a calming hand and gently squeezed Yannick's forearm. 'Mac,' he said, prompting him to continue.

He ignored the prompt. 'And that's right, *three* wets, none for you.'

With the smallest of huffs, Yannick rose and headed for the tea station, or wets boat as the Marines know it.

'Double time, sprog!' Mac growled at his back. After a beat his vicious sneer suddenly transformed into a huge grin, revealing a row of spaced-out teeth you could store a handful of fifty pence coins between. (Fish, out of earshot, had once made the observation that Mac had teeth like a Territorial Army fighting patrol – one missing and a couple facing the wrong way.) In the next moment Mac reached over the table and with big, weathered hands shattered Yannick's plastic knife, fork and spoon into tiny pieces. 'He's gotta learn,' he said with a jolly chuckle.

'Ever the mentor,' said Fish, rolling his eyes.

'More like tor-mentor,' said Ray, with a disapproving shake of his head.

'There's no teacher like tough love,' Mac replied with a shrug. 'Now . . .' he began, before staring off into the middle distance, the lines of his brow deep enough to grow potatoes in. 'Christ, where the fuck was I?'

'Presents,' said Ray.

'Yeah, prezzies! Kim gets a load of presents from the girls: lube, pink fluffy handcuffs, whopping great big dildo, a twelve-pack of chilli-chocolate dicks, you know, the classics.'

'What's a chilli-chocolate dick?' asked Yannick, placing three cups before them on his return from the wets boat (he did not bring one for himself).

'What it says on the tin,' said Mac, without thanks for the tea. 'Chocolate in the shape of a dick infused with chilli . . . fucking delicious.'

'Soft centres?' Yannick asked with genuine intrigue as he took his seat.

'Fucking hell, sprog! Who am I, Professor of Chilli-chocolate Dicks?'

'What the hell?!' said Yannick, looking down at his bangers and mash, which now had a sprinkled topping of shattered cutlery.

'You're welcome. Don't leave your KFS hanging around in here,' said Mac, with a smile and a wink. 'Now, shut your yap! All right, so about an hour before sundown it's decided after my dear wife-to-be empties the contents of her stomach into the lap of the Clydesdale, it's probably best a small security detail escorts her home. Kim is of course so fucking sha-monkeyed she completely forgets the goodies . . . but luckily her mother is at hand to take responsibility of the forgotten bag of grot.'

'If I may ask, Miss Blyton, where is this story going?' said Fish, attempting to blow off some heat from his paper cup of tea.

'*Murder*,' said Mac, with a wicked grin. 'That's where.'

'Goodness gracious. Really?' said Fish, straightening in his seat.

'Really,' said Mac, knowing he now had them all in the

palm of his hand. 'So Kim's mum – Brenda, my beloved mother-in-law – eventually gets home to her gaff, totally shiters, no security detail required, I might add; she's a total fucking unit. Either way she makes a beeline for her bed for some much-needed head-down.

'The next morning Brenda wakes up with a hangover that would kill your average civvie so heads downstairs in search of relief. Now, gentlemen,' he said, meeting each of their gazes, 'we arrive at the point in this grizzly tale where I must introduce – Scampi. The family dog of some six years. I cannot overestimate the esteem by which this little Westie is held. In fact, forget dog, think son and brother who occasionally shits on the kitchen floor.'

'Copy that,' said Fish, laughing along with Yannick.

Ray wore a tight smile.

'To Brenda's eternal horror, upon entering the living room, there lies the light of her life – browners. Scampi's on his back with all four fluffy little legs pointing towards the heavens – dead!' Mac leaned back in his chair with a broad grin on his face, silently inviting comment.

'Surely not! Not Scampi! He's the only innocent in this entire sordid tale,' said Fish.

Yannick, who had just finished picking the last of his KFS from his food was the first to postulate cause of death. 'Did he not just die of natural causes?'

'Course not, dummy! As I said, he was only six years old,' replied Mac, with an arched brow, clearly enjoying himself.

'I have a theorem,' announced Fish. 'Did Brenda, a "total unit" as you mentioned, in her, what sounds like a black-out state, fall and crush little Scampi, perchance?'

'It's a fine theory, but no cigar. Not a mark on him,' said Mac.

The table was silent in thought for some time until Ray, finishing the last of his tea, said, 'I think Scampi was poisoned.'

'Poisoned?' said Yannick, incredulous.

'Go on,' said Mac, with narrowed eyes.

'Well, Kim forgot her presents, so the responsibility was passed on to Brenda. I'm going to assume when Brenda returned home she placed the bag on the first surface she saw ... probably the living-room couch. Scampi, a dog held in such high regard, of course, got the run of the house. So I think during his late night wanderings his nose got him killed.'

'*Holy shit*,' said Fish, mouth agog, 'the chilli-chocolate dongs!'

'What? I don't understand. What's chocolate got to do with it?' asked Yannick.

'There's a chemical called theobromine in chocolate. It can be highly toxic to dogs. It's rare for a dog to die from it. But as Scampi found out – it does happen. That's my theory,' Ray concluded, turning to Mac.

'Bullseye,' came Mac's curt reply.

'Incredible. A tip of the cap, Sugar,' said Fish, as Yannick looked to Ray with unbridled awe.

'You're right, *again*. The fluffy little fucker scoffed down a dozen of the choccy wangers. Full disclosure, I omitted the small detail that the entire living room was covered in shite. Scampi went via a *very* dirty protest,' said Mac, with a chuckle-infused sigh. 'It must be pretty nice knowing everything, Sugar.'

'Well, it doesn't do poor Scampi much good,' replied Ray with a shrug.

'Wow. Literally death by chocolate,' said Yannick, who was delighted when the table burst into laughter. Even Ray joined in.

'What did you say your name was again?' asked Mac, when they settled down.

'Chris Yannick.'

'OK. I'm McCrindle, hence "Mac". He's "Fish" as in Fish and Chipton. And the Multiple Commander here is Sugar,' he said, pointing a thumb across the table, 'because he's called Ray Leonard . . . get it?'

'I do. The boxer.'

'Good lad. My point is – what the fuck are we supposed to do with Chris Yannick?'

After a moment's thought, Yannick said, 'My middle name is Gordon, if that's any use?'

'Christ,' said Mac, looking to Fish and Ray in disbelief, 'is he taking the piss?'

'What?' said Yannick in confusion as he shovelled some mash into his mouth with the salvaged partial end of his plastic knife.

'What a cock-tease! Obviously, henceforth you will be known as – *Flash*.'

They laughed as Yannick looked on, perplexed.

'How old are you?' asked Mac, his voice now softer in a way that suggested he had been won over.

'Twenty-two.'

'Where are you arriving from?'

'Lympstone.'

'Straight out of the box to Kabul, the Vegas of

Afghanistan. I hope you've got your PAX insurance up to date?'

'I have,' he said with a grin.

'What's your specialization?' asked Fish, knowing full-well that new Marines don't have specializations.

'GD.'

'General Duties? That's not fucking special at all, is it?' said Mac, scratching his shaved head. 'Well, I'm a driver. Fish is a physical training instructor, and Sugar here is a PW, platoon weapons. All of which we are very special at. So my advice is to choose one that tickles your fancy before your fancy gets tickled for you.'

'I will.'

'Are you married?' asked Fish.

'Yeah. Laura.'

'Children?'

'Twins. Axel and Caprice.'

'Wait,' said Mac. 'You're Chris and Laura with two kids called Axel and Caprice?'

'Yeah.'

'That's the funniest fucking thing I've ever heard!' said Mac, through tears of laughter. When he stopped laughing, he handed him his used set of cutlery. 'You're all right, Flash,' he concluded.

15

'Maybe *The Matrix* is right? Maybe we are just batteries in a metal spider's arse,' said Luke.

'The what?' said Rose.

'*The Matrix*. It's a film. It thinks all of this –' he nodded at the small bare antiseptic-smelling space around them – 'is just a computer programme designed to exploit us humans as an energy source.'

'Energy source? I don't think you could power a TV remote with the energy left in me.' She gave a weak laugh, illustrating her point. 'I think not. We came from nothing. We go to nothing. We have a little window of consciousness . . . then we return to the never-ending black.'

'Ladies and gentlemen, let's hear it for today's motivational speaker – Rose Bisseker, everyone,' said Luke, clapping his hands, the sole appreciative member of her audience. 'Fantastic. Just great. T-shirts are available in the foyer.'

'There's no computer games. There's no never-ending darkness. There's Heaven,' Gog began in his quiet Welsh lilt, as he stared out of the room's only window. A dim rectangle today, the small courtyard below had been robbed of light by the clouds above it, which were the colour of hammered tin. 'I can't wait to see some of the people who've passed. I never knew my mam and dad.

It'll be lovely to meet them. They died in a house fire when I was a baby, see. It was Valentine's Day, so I was at my nan's.'

'Ahhh, man, I'm so sorry,' said Luke.

Gog gave him a thankful nod, before continuing. 'When they went my nan became my mam. She was a wonderful woman. It's been ten years since she went to see the angels. I still miss her every day. Can you imagine what it'll be like to see her again? See her smiling face. Give her a hug and tell her how much I missed her . . . what she means to me.' He wiped the beginnings of a tear from his eye with a big, calloused thumb. 'You know, according to my aunty there's a chance I might see her before I go to Heaven. She told me my Uncle Ichdyd –'

'Echhh-what?' Rose said, as if she had stepped in something foul.

'*Ichdyd*. You have to use the back of your throat.'

'I'll pass, thank you very much. There's not enough Strepsils in the world.'

'That's funny,' Gog replied with a hearty laugh, finding his cheer again. 'You're saying Welsh would hurt your throat.'

'Correct,' she said, rolling her eyes at Ray and Luke who looked on, enjoying the tête-à-tête.

'Anyway, my Uncle Ichdyd – he had cancer himself, funnily enough – he started seeing his dead mother just before he died.'

Suddenly their enjoyment ended.

'Hell no! Did they call in an exorcist?' Luke asked in horror.

'A what?'

'Someone to drag the demon out of your uncle.'

'Oh. No, no. It wasn't creepy or spooky –'

'The power of Christ compels you!' commanded Luke, fixing his fingers in a cross.

'She didn't hurt him or anything like that. She just stood there next to his bed and held his hand, told him everything was going to be all right.' That tear appeared in Gog's eye again. 'It made him happy. He was happy to see her. My aunty said he was de . . . deee . . . de-something, I can't think of the word.'

'Delirious.'

'That's it, Ray! She said he was *delirious*. But somehow she knew as soon as he said he could see their old mam, the person he had loved most in the world . . . he was good as gone. And she was right. He died not long after.' He unfurled his great paw. 'I'd like very much for Nan to be holding my hand now.' The room was quiet as he looked down achingly at his open palm. 'But if that doesn't happen to me,' he continued, 'no problem. I'll see my nan in Heaven. She'll be waiting for me. So, it's not all bad, you know, if this doesn't work,' he finished, gently tugging at his drip feed.

The room was filled with a thoughtful silence for some time until Ray said, 'I hope you're right, Gog.'

'Yeah, sounds lovely. But what if you don't believe in God?' asked Luke.

'Then you go where all the hopeless sinners go,' replied Gog.

'Benidorm?' said Luke, his eyebrows knitted together.

'Hell.'

'Oh. The bad place.'

'The lake of fire,' said Gog, and apologetic lines spread out from the corners of his eyes.

'So, brain cancer and eternal damnation. *Nice*,' said Luke, giving the room a thumbs up.

'It makes no sense to me. Can't you all hear what I am saying?' began Gog, his face reddening in frustration. 'Why wouldn't you want to believe in God and the Kingdom of Heaven? Who wouldn't want to go there? See all your friends and family again? Doesn't it sound fabulous?'

'No. I think I prefer perpetual darkness,' said Rose, sucking on her teeth.

'Rose! Why?' asked Gog, dismayed.

'The truth is, I don't like black people –'

'WOAH!' exclaimed Luke, as Gog's mouth dropped open. 'I thought this was chemo not a Klan meeting!'

'Careful now, Rose,' said Ray, an edge to his voice.

'Let me finish, *idiots*. I don't like black people, I don't like white people, I don't like Asians, Indians, the Welsh,' she said, stabbing a finger at Gog, 'the English. I don't like people. Full stop. And that includes my own family. My parents were unbearable towards the end. And the less said about Alan the better. I don't want any more of that, before death, or after, thank you very much.'

'Who's Alan?' asked Luke.

She paused before answering. 'He *was* my husband.'

'Oh. He died? Sorry, Rose.'

'Don't be.'

'Why don't you want to see your husband again?' Gog asked.

Rose opened her mouth but the words stopped in her

throat. 'I don't want to talk about him,' she eventually said, wrapping her arms around herself.

'What happened?' Luke pressed. But Ray gave him a look that said – *leave it*.

'Were you not listening?' Rose snapped at him. 'People. That's what happened to me. Hell is other people.'

'Do you not have kids?'

'Not on your nelly.'

'It's just you and little Alfie?'

'The way we like it.'

'But when you're gone that's it.'

'So what?'

'There'll be no one to carry on your line.'

'*My line?*' she said, mockingly. 'Who am I, the Queen of Sheba? Legacy is nonsense, my handsome boy. Didn't you know that? When you're dead, that's it. It's over. The world keeps ticking along whether you're in it or not and you don't get to look down from Heaven –' she rolled her eyes at Gog – 'and watch the whole thing play out like *The Game of Life*. When you're gone, you're gone. Why do you think we're all in this room clinging on to life for grim death? Sorry, gentlemen, but we all know the most likely answer – there is nothing after this life. This is it. It might be short, brutal and ultimately meaningless, but it's all we've got. As soon as I beat my last beat, roll me in a carpet and dump me in a canal. I really couldn't give a monkey's.'

'That's . . . so bleak,' said Luke, who looked shaken by her words. 'You don't know, Rose. Like Gog said, it might be some transcendental supernatural place –'

'What did I say?' mumbled Gog, scratching at his furry dome.

'– or a nihilistic nothingness,' continued Luke. 'No one knows. Whatever it is, we're all going to have to cross that bridge when we come to it. What I do know is I'm not scared. Death doesn't scare me. The thing that I can't get my head around, if everything sucks and humanity is a waste of carbon . . . why am I going to miss it so much? I hate that bit in the morning, that split second, where I wake up and I think I'm fine. But then I remember I've got cancer. I've woken up to a nightmare, you know.' He stopped to rub at his pale sunken temples before he exhaled a long breath and continued. 'But I'd still rather wake up to that than whatever comes next. I don't want it to end. I was just getting started. I'm young. I want kids. I want to fall in love. Don't I deserve that? Yes, I've got a shitty job but I'm not a bad person. So why am I being punished? It doesn't seem fair,' said Luke, looking at Ray.

'It isn't. Sometimes bad things happen to good people and vice versa.'

'*It's not fair.*' Luke's voice broke and tears brimmed in his eyes. 'I'm tired of every day feeling like the day my parents take down the decorations after Christmas.'

'I know. But don't think of it as punishment, think of it as something you're going to overcome. You *are* too young to have cancer. But your youth also means you're strong. You'll beat it. You'll be around to see your future ex-wife receive those massive alimony payments.' Ray smiled at him.

Luke laughed, and sniffed at his runny nose. 'Thanks, Ray.'

'What do you think comes next?' Rose asked Ray in a rare display of intrigue.

'I don't care. I'm not done living yet.'

16

As soon as Ray got into the car, he knew that something was not right. Chay was trying to pull off a carefree air that he at first assumed was for his benefit, but as the journey progressed the cracks began to show. Long, un-Chay-like bouts of silence, intermingled by very Chay-like moments of colourful language directed at fellow motorists, suggested to Ray (a father, and a seasoned detective) that all was not well.

'What's going on?' he finally asked as the long overdue pitter-patter of rain began to fall on the windscreen.

'What do you mean?' she said, flicking on the wipers.

'You seem a bit distracted. Annoyed, even.'

'I'm fine,' she said, two or three octaves above fine.

'Chaynnie?'

Surprising Ray, she suddenly pulled into the hard shoulder of the fly-over they were currently on. As the car came to an abrupt screeching halt she covered her face with her hands and burst into tears.

'Christ, Chay, what's wrong!?' he asked, his words almost drowned out by angry car horns and the sound of tyres cutting a path through the now heavy rain. She continued to hold her face, great heaving sobs hidden behind her fingers.

Ray lightly placed a hand on her shuddering shoulder. 'Please talk to me. What's going on?'

'I'm sorry, Ray. You don't need this,' she said, revealing her red puffy eyes.

'It's fine,' he said, grabbing some tissues from the back seat and handing them to her, 'just tell me what's wrong so I can help.'

Chay gave a bitter little laugh. 'It's nothing you can help with.' She went quiet for a long time. Ray waited patiently as the wipers squeaked back and forth on the windscreen glass. He sensed she was weighing up whether she wanted to share the source of her pain or not. 'A guy at uni . . .' she began, before her breath was taken away by another bout of crying.

'What did he do?' asked Ray, feeling the beginnings of a red mist descend upon him. 'Chay, what did he do?'

She tried to gather herself, taking a deep fluttering breath. 'A guy at uni, a nice guy. That's the crazy part, I actually do like him . . .' she said, wiping her running nose.

'OK,' he said, tentatively.

'He asked me out.'

Oh no! thought Ray. He immediately knew where this was going and his heart sank.

'What happened?'

'It was awful. I was so mean to him. Terrible. There were a lot of people around. It must have taken guts to approach me like he did . . . but I snapped, I embarrassed him. It's like I am looking down at myself doing it, pleading with myself to stop, but I can't. It just comes out. He'll hate me for it and then the ripple effect starts and everyone else will hear how much of a bitch I am . . . and they'll hate me too. And I don't blame them. I hate myself.'

'They don't know what you've been through.'

'I like him, but I want him away from me . . . it doesn't make any sense. What is it, Ray? Am I scared that he'll hurt me . . . or am I a bad person?' she said, beginning to cry again.

'You're *not* a bad person. Don't ever say that.'

Ray wanted desperately to reach out and hold her and tell her everything was going to be all right. But that wasn't something they did. Only Odette had been able to hold Chay in her arms; everyone else was kept at a distance.

'I'm so sorry, Chaynnie.'

He watched her cry, feeling utterly helpless, until she said, 'He gets to live his life, I can't move on.'

She wasn't talking about the poor kid who got the sharp end of her tongue earlier that day. She was talking about someone else. Ray's sadness disappeared, replaced instantly by a towering rage. His blood began to throb in his veins. His heart felt twice its normal size, straining against his ribcage. He turned away from her and tried to steady his breathing when he caught sight of his reflection in the passenger window.

Being there in the time he had left, when she had these episodes, wasn't cutting it. An understanding ear and the gentle voice of reassurance, year-on-year, had failed. She was never going to be able to live a full emotional life however loving and supportive he was. Something drastic had to be done. Something he had fantasized about many times but a voice inside him had always implored him to resist.

He listened now. He heard nothing. The voice was silent.

In the window's reflection, despite the steady stream of water delivered from dark clouds above, he recognized the look in his eye.

17

The rain had stopped. But dark clouds remained, adding an even greater sense of hopelessness to the brutalist architecture of the tower block that Ray stood before. He drew a deep shaky breath, thought of the series of events he was about to put in motion, and then slowly let it out. What he was about to do went against the grain of the man he strived to be. But it had to be done if Chay was to have a chance at happiness. If Ray were caught, he knew he would die in prison. The only saving grace being that the amount of time he could serve before cancer took him would be short.

He pushed open a pair of grimy glass doors, one of which featured a crack through its length, and stepped into the strip-lit waiting area of central station's Major Crimes Unit headquarters.

The front desk officer, who sat behind thick Perspex, recognized Ray immediately.

'Detective Inspector!' he exclaimed, straightening.

'Please, just Ray.'

'Oh . . . *Ray*,' the officer repeated awkwardly. 'Sorry to hear about your . . . retirement.'

'That's kind of you, Wayne.'

'How is it going? The . . . ahhh . . .'

'It's OK. You can say the word. It won't make it worse.'

'. . . *cancer*?'

'Well, it's hard to take the milk out of the tea . . . but I'm giving it a go.'

Wayne made a laugh that sounded laced with pity for a dying man. Ray took this to be the end of their cumbersome but well-intended back-and-forth and moved towards the door he wanted opened.

'Cheers, Wayne,' he said, as he was buzzed through.

He climbed the stairs (cancer-free, he used to bound up them. Today he felt thick and sluggish) to the major incident room, bracing himself for more of the same.

Thankfully the first person he saw as he entered the dated, open-plan office (he noted that its dreary grey carpet tiles were still in urgent need of replacement), was DS Ben Greylag. Ray knew Ben well enough to not expect any fluff and he did not disappoint.

'You're under arrest,' Greylag said, sitting at his desk with his feet up, reading a red-top.

'What's the charge?' Ray asked with faux concern.

'No visitor lanyard.'

Ray looked down at the empty space on his chest where the item in question should be. 'It's a fair cop.' He offered his wrists.

'Let's say a thousand hours' community service cleaning porta-potties and I'll overlook it just this once.'

'Well, I've learned my lesson.'

'Welcome back, Boss,' he said, with a mischievous grin, offering his hand. 'How was Sandals? I'm not seeing much of a tan?'

'Good to see you too, Ben,' Ray laughed, shaking his hand. 'Is he in?'

'Yup. In the goldfish bowl,' he said with a thumb directed

at Ray's old office. The nickname was in reference to the sparing amount of space the glass-walled office took up in the far corner of the incident room. Ray made his way through the labyrinth of haphazardly organized desks, nodding his hellos as he went. Arriving at the goldfish bowl, he leaned on its thin door frame.

Peering in, the space had hardly changed. Although he couldn't help but notice that the blinds that hung on the inside of the glass to provide privacy hadn't been dusted in an eon. John's car cleanliness had not made it this far, illustrated by the mountain of papers that were stacked precariously at his desk's edge. The man himself sat reclined, in deep concentration, scanning a file through a pair of stylish glasses that Ray had not seen before.

'Spectacles?' Ray said.

'Sooner or later old age humbles us all,' John replied, looking up with a grin.

'Old age? I have fillings older than you.'

John laughed. 'Come on in. What brings you to the fun house?'

'It's probably nothing,' he said, sitting in the creaking chair opposite. 'After being in the alley with you yesterday, I had a thought.'

'Oh?' John said, dropping the file onto his desk.

At a glance, Ray registered text too small to read on one side of the open file. On the other was a picture of the missing schoolteacher that John had mentioned in the pub – Jennifer Moody. Ray had seen her photo on the TV since. He pushed the thought aside. That was not why he came.

'I remembered a case from a few years back. A man was

stabbed in an alley not far from the one where Pentecost was killed. I'm not completely sure but I think the circumstances were similar. It might be worth taking a look at it.'

John's face lit up with an expression that landed somewhere between amusement and surprise, thought Ray.

'Really? Can you remember the name of the victim?' he asked, hitting the space bar to wake up his computer. He slid his glasses along the bridge of his nose, and then hit a series of keys before looking up at Ray.

'That's the annoying part. I've been racking my brains.' He scrunched his face in concentration. 'Try Henley. Owen Henley, I think.'

John worked the keys in a flurry. 'Nope. No Owen Henley.'

'Hennessy? Try that.'

After a moment. 'Hello. We've got a result. Here he is,' he said, scanning the screen. 'Hennessy. Owen. Born 1989. Looking at his disposal history, this is a bad man. Handful of cautions, robbery, theft. Mr Hennessy met his end in an alley between Lennox Road and Northfield Road. Yup, not far from Pentecost. He was pronounced dead at the scene. He died of multiple stab wounds to the chest and neck. The killer was never found. This case is starting to ring a bell,' he said, glancing at Ray over the computer. 'Hennessy was known to have gang links, so his death was assumed to be gang-related. This was seven years ago.' He removed his glasses with an apologetic frown. 'I'm not sure there's much here for us, I'm afraid.'

'Well, do I feel like an idiot. Sorry, John. As I told you –' he exhaled an exhausted yawn – 'I'm not at my best.'

'It's OK, Ray.'

'So bloody tired all the time,' he said, stifling another

yawn. 'You don't have any of that godawful coffee we used to have knocking around, do you?'

'We do. And I guarantee it's worse than you remember.' John rose, smiling. 'Although I should say, you once told me that a senior officer shouldn't be seen to be making drinks, but on this occasion I'll make an exception.' He winked.

'You're a good man,' said Ray at John's back as he left his small office and rounded a corner for the kitchen.

Ray quickly reached for the computer and turned it around. With relief he saw that John had not logged out of the Police National Computer.

All IT systems in relation to the PNC required passwords. To gain access all users were also required to have a current PNC compliance certificate. Ray's PNC access had been revoked the moment he retired.

He quickly abandoned the Hennessy transaction, returning to the main screen. He entered a name. By the time he glanced over his shoulder in the direction of the kitchen, the record he had come for was on the screen. He then located the AD page and was presented with a latest address.

57, Cordwallis Street, Salford, Greater Manchester.

He abandoned the transaction and re-entered Owen Hennessy before turning the screen back towards John's chair. As he did so, John appeared from the kitchen holding two hot mugs of coffee.

'As you're an honoured guest you can have the one cup that isn't chipped,' he said, handing it to Ray.

'Honoured indeed,' he replied, grasping it with both hands in an attempt to steady the trembling in them. 'You heading home soon?'

'I wish.' John sat and blew on the hot liquid. 'I'm working every hour God sends. Bloody alimony payments are killing me,' he said, with a tiered chuckle. 'Anyway, boo-hoo me.'

'I'm here for you if you need anything. You know that, right?'

John smiled. 'I know. Thanks, Ray.' He took a sip of his coffee before setting it on his desk. 'Now, why don't you tell me why you really came down here?' he asked, with an arched brow. 'You could have easily texted me your . . . hunch.'

Ray chuckled nervously. 'You've got me,' he said. 'You were right in the alleyway.' He took a gulp of the far-too-hot coffee. 'Christ, this is worse than I remember . . .' John didn't react, he just stared blankly. Ray continued, 'You were right . . . I miss it. Cancer isn't only scary, but it's also very boring. I miss the excitement of the job. The thrill of the chase. Catching the bad guys. I don't know, maybe I thought I could help. Silly old man. Coming down here like this. It's embarrassing. Forgive me, John.'

John breathed deeply, whilst shaking his head. 'You've got nothing to apologize for. As far as I'm concerned I'm sitting in your chair. You've got the keys to the kingdom, Ray. Come and go as you please.'

'Again, you're a good man, John.' Ray took another big gulp of coffee. 'Thanks for the cuppa. I think it's time I go as I please.'

18

'General Arthurs arrives at Kabul Airport at 17:00,' said Ray to the eleven men looking back at him in the swelter-ing heat of the Operations Room. Unlike the mess hall, the silver ducting pipes hanging from above were inactive as the big generator outside the semi-permanent tent had succumbed to the forty-five degree heat. 'He has a close protection team in tow but we felt it would be rude not to meet the General at arrivals with a nice bunch of flowers from the Marines.'

To some degree Ray felt like a football manager in the locker room addressing his team before the cup final. He recognized and shared the taut, nervous energy emanat-ing from them in a stew of sweat and testosterone. Excitement always accompanied the prospect of leaving the base and entering the field of play. Of course, the fundamental difference of the game they would play today was the stark reality of the fact that the other team wanted to kill them.

'We'll be heading out in thirty minutes. I want three teams of four in three WMIKs. Mac will drive with me on point.'

'You *Driving Miss Daisy* fuckers try to keep up, all right,' said Mac, to laughter, from his usual seating position at the back of the room.

'Yannick and Dowe,' said Ray gesturing to the pair,

'you're in the back of our vehicle. Yannick, are you happy to be our gunner on this excursion?'

'Yes, Sergeant!' exclaimed the young Marine, drawing chuckles from the surrounding members of Ray's Multiple.

'Fish and Bellamy, assemble your usual fire teams. Fish, I want you to bring up the rear. As Mac eloquently put it – *do keep up*. We move fast, we don't stop for anything, and don't forget this will be a new route to all of us, keeping in line with the necessity to vary our routes and keep the Taliban guessing. Any questions?'

Mac raised his hand. 'Can we stop for ice cream?'

'Any questions that aren't stupid?' repeated Ray. When the only response was laughter, with a wry grin, he went on. 'Then kit up.'

'Hell of a world we live in where they thought it was necessary to build one of these, Flash,' said Mac, as Yannick watched him slide into the driving seat of the sand-coloured WMIK, the Weapons Mount Installation Kit or, to the layman, a stripped-down Land Rover fixed with two large general purpose machine guns – or GPMGs – one on the passenger side, one in the rear. 'You're in the back in the gunners well.'

Yannick was now in full combat gear, as they all were after leaving the armoury, which included body armour, a helmet, an SA80 rifle and a 9mm pistol. He looked up at the rear of the WMIK's roll cage. The well, which took centre stage, offered the gunner a 360-degree arc of fire on a purpose-built rail at waist height. 'It's supposed to look terrifying. We go big to own the road and intimidate the enemy,' said Mac, seeing the look on Yannick's face. 'Don't overthink it, sprog. It's brown. It's sauce.'

'It's what?'

'The Brown Sauce Principle. They didn't call it Scat Sauce or Chocolate Thunder Sauce. They saw it was brown. And that's what they called it. Brown. Fucking. Sauce. Don't overthink it. You'll do fine.'

Yannick looked from Mac to the gunners well. 'Brown sauce principle.' He gave a stoic nod and said, 'Thanks, Mac.'

'That's Lance Corporal McCrindle to you,' he said with a gap-toothed smile.

'Yes, sir,' said Yannick returning the grin.

'Don't call me "sir",' came Mac's inevitable reply. 'Heads up, Boss incoming.' Peering into his wing mirror he watched Ray deliver the flap sheet, the manifest of all the people on the mission, to the Operations Room before striding across the dusty concourse that served as the fore-court to their makeshift base of operations in the heart of Kabul.

'Wheels up?' asked Fish, intercepting Ray en route to the lead WMIK.

'Good to go,' he replied, knowing by the look in Fish's eye he hadn't stopped him to exchange small talk.

'Did you have a think?'

'I don't see how I can't put him on report.'

'He's been out here at the coal face for a while. They'll never understand that.'

'He let a prisoner die, Fish.'

'I know. But isn't that why we're out here?'

'No . . . I don't think it is,' Ray said with a sad sigh. 'We need to get the General delivered safe and sound. Let's move out.'

Mac watched Ray give Fish a squeeze to the shoulder before he resumed his journey.

Fish turned and gave his driver, Shaw, a thumbs up and the rear WMIK roared into life, all three tonnes of it shaking the very ground beneath them. Bellamy received the same thumbs up and followed suit.

Arriving at the point vehicle, Ray climbed in. Yannick and Dowe were in the back, Dowe perched on the WMIK's absolute rear whilst Yannick held the machine gun with grim focus, and Mac had a look on his face that was uncharacteristically troubled.

'We good?' he asked.

Ray looked at his old friend for long moments. He needed him sharp. 'We're good,' he lied.

'Rock and fucking roll,' said Mac, turning the key in the ignition.

The sun was far past its apogee in a cloudless sky. Shadow pitted the massive chocolate-coloured mountain of rock that loomed in the distance; one of many jutting monoliths that kept watch over Kabul.

As Mac raced down a wide tree-lined street, swerving between traffic and trying his best to dodge enormous potholes, Ray's eyes flitted from one point of interest to another: rooftops, windows, doorways. They never stopped moving, constantly scanning their surroundings for danger. Every nook and every human they could see was a potential threat. What was in the saddle bags of that man's bicycle? What was under the produce on the back of that three-wheeler? Gripping the GPMG, he looked into his wing-mirror and noted with satisfaction that both Bellamy and Fish were keeping up nicely.

He also noted a motorbike – *how long has that been with us?*

Their greatest defence from attack was to keep moving, and to keep changing direction by taking a convoluted route to the airport. As if reading his mind, Mac swung the WMIK into a hard left, leaving the wide, well-lit street for a narrower shaded alley. He steered the WMIK through a series of breakneck corners with the skill and focus of a rally driver. Locals stood with their backs against the walls in surprise, watching the convoy tear past them like rolling thunder. As the deafening sound of the WMIK's engine reverberated off the brickwork either side of the alley, Ray's stare was fixed to his mirror. He was pleased to see the motorcycle had disappeared.

Looking ahead they were about to converge on an intersection. The alley opened up into a small square, creating a pinch point. A group of ramshackle market stalls acted as a central island for a makeshift roundabout, which was not ideal as Mac would have to slow down considerably. As the convoy braked, Ray was able to hear Yannick sweeping his GPMG from left to right, hedging his bets.

The convoy slowed, and all eyes in the square looked to them. A bearded man who stood next to a crate of produce shouted something at them Ray couldn't make out over the sound of their engines – then he threw something.

In horror, Ray followed the object arcing through the air until it landed in Dowe's hand at the back of the vehicle and, with a sigh of relief, he watched the Marine take a bite out of the apple and wave his thanks to the now smiling man. It was in that moment a loud crack rang out to their right. Yannick swung the GPMG in the direction of the sound, his finger on the trigger ready to open fire – and down the sights of the machine gun an old woman (oblivious) gave a hanging rug another almighty whack. Dust bellowed from its well-worn shag.

'Fucking hell!' said Yannick, blowing out his cheeks.

'First day on the job and he almost slots an old biddy for torturing a rug,' said Mac to Ray.

They both laughed as Mac guided the vehicle out of the square, moving through the gears to build speed once again . . . and then . . . the loudest bang Ray had ever heard, followed by darkness.

After an interminable amount of time he opened his eyes. Through the smoke and the dust that swirled around him he saw that the front end of the WMIK had been blasted through a wall and was now resting inert, its engine hissing and popping in surrender, inside a residential compound. He blinked his eyes in an attempt to focus them and saw a framed photo of a young family lying amongst the rubble on the WMIK's bonnet. He blinked his eyes again and then realized his left saw only black. He reached up and felt a soft warm wetness. No eye. With a groan leaving his dry throat he grasped at his face in panic . . . until he found an edge. Reaching beneath it, he pulled back the huge flap of skin that was covering his still present left eye. As his vision returned he quickly pressed the skin back upon the bone of his skull's cheek.

The sound of small arms gunfire nearby brought him back to the wider danger of his situation.

Someone yelled 'contact' followed by his and Mac's names – *Christ, Mac!*

With rapid shallow breaths he turned to his friend. It was immediately evident he had taken the full impact of the IED. The front left of the vehicle was gone, as were Mac's legs. The steering wheel was embedded in his torso. His face, the portion Ray could see just above the perversion of the steering wheel, was largely intact. His eyes were closed, his mouth slightly ajar – almost peaceful.

'Mac!' shouted Ray, reaching out to him before a lightning bolt of pain ripped through his left side. Looking down into his lap he saw a length of metal of indeterminable origin embedded in his thigh and hip. With his fingers shaking uncontrollably, he reached down to touch the sharp edge of the blood-soaked metal. The contact seemed to trigger his receptors and the metal started to radiate pain from the point where it bit into him. At the same time his face started to throb in agony. He fought to keep his lunch in his stomach as a wave of nausea swept over him.

'Sugar!' someone yelled again as more gunfire erupted. Friendly this time. He recognized the report. Ray turned in the direction of the voice back out on the street and was greeted by further devastation wrought by the IED within the Land Rover's rear roll-bar cage. Dowe was gone. Either the blast or the wall had sent him into the street. Yannick, his arm caught at an impossible angle between the compound's broken wall and the rail that supported the machine gun, hung limply from its twisted bloody mess. His helmet had been torn from his head and had taken most of his scalp with it, leaving his face a red mask of blood, making it virtually impossible to ascertain the full extent of his injuries. His closed eyes suggested it was over for the young Marine ... until they slowly opened and looked directly at Ray. He opened his mouth and, after a long stream of thick blood poured from it, he started to scream.

Ray woke with a start.

His knee had hit the steering wheel in his hasty exit from a dream he had had many times. Even now, twenty years later, his hands shook as he reached down to rub the pain from his knee. It took a moment for him to gather his senses and place where he was. Through the haze, an address he had committed to memory came back to him: *57, Cordwallis Street, Salford, Greater Manchester.*

Satisfied his knee was over the worst of the pain he returned his hands to the warmth of the pockets of his black bomber jacket. With the engine turned off, parked in the long shadow that reached out from the row of terraced houses on his right, the car's cabin had cooled significantly.

Ray! He might have left while you were sleeping! he thought, silently cursing himself that staying awake after a two-hour journey was now apparently beyond him due to the cocktail of drugs he was on alongside his chemo. The thought served as a reminder. He reached into his jeans pocket and popped a pill out of its plastic sheath into his mouth. The pill that helped stave off nausea was the easiest of the three to administer. The other two (hormone replacements to suppress testosterone, and bone strengthening to prevent complications that can occur with prostate cancer) were given as injections. Once upon a time, Ray had hated the sight of a needle. But after his injuries in Afghanistan he had become so used to seeing that thin shaft of metal disappear through his skin that he was now more than happy to administer his own injections.

He rubbed at his heavy eyes and re-focused his attention on the red-brick house fifty yards up the road on his left. Beneath its facade a narrow unkempt patch of grass and weeds filled the space between a low brick wall and the pavement. A short concrete path led to a front door that held a pane of stained glass in its weathered wood.

Three windows, their curtains drawn and framed in peeling black paint (one modestly big on the ground floor, two smaller pokey ones above), made up the rest of the house's bleak exterior. It looked exactly the same as it had forty-five minutes ago – utterly lifeless, thought Ray, noting the time he had been sleeping by the dashboard clock.

He had already walked the cobbled alleyway, strewn with broken glass and litter, that provided access to the rear of the property. All of the houses had the same set-up – a high red-brick wall with a wooden gate leading to a small concrete patio, which once contained an outside toilet and coal shed but was now a dreary space for storing bins. The gate was in an advanced state of disrepair. The wood had decayed to the point where he was sure he could snap it with his bare hands – although that would not be necessary as it had been left half open. Peeking around it he saw a plain white PVC door alongside a window (blinds drawn), which he assumed belonged to the kitchen. On the second floor, a frosted bathroom window provided just as little evidence of activity within. The back was as bleak as the front and equally lifeless.

As Ray sat low in his car seat, lamenting his forty-five-minute lapse in concentration and wondering how much longer he would have to sit there, the door to 57 Cordwallis Street opened, and Howard Fain stepped out.

19

Howard Fain looked very different to the last time Ray had seen him. A long time ago he had hidden in plain sight behind a clean-cut position of privilege and trust. Now, as he stood on his doorstep in a grimy tracksuit, lighting a cigarette, his hair greying and matted, he looked exactly what he was.

After a quick glance up and down the street, Fain took his phone out, crossed the road and started walking along the pavement. Ray put on a black baseball cap and got out of the car. With his hands tucked into his pockets and his head hung low he started to follow at a discreet distance.

Fain seemed to know exactly where he was going, barely looking up as he walked, smoked and stared at his phone. He turned up some narrow steps running between two houses. Ray stood on the other side of Cordwallis Street and watched him.

As Fain reached the top of the steps a large dog swung its big paws over a garden wall running parallel to the passage and barked viciously at him. Fain jumped back in surprise. After a moment to compose himself, he stood and stared at the dog – and then flicked his cigarette at it. Glancing off its muzzle, the dog barked and snarled in apoplexy as the embers of the impact faded away in the twilight. Fain laughed, turned his attention back to his phone, and continued on.

Ray made his way up the steps. The dog was still propped up on the wall. It made no sign of aggression towards him. He stepped closer and stroked its head and muzzle. The dog leaned into his touch. Ray watched Fain walking away hunched over his phone, already preparing his next cigarette. Turning back to the dog, he said, 'Good boy,' and continued on.

Ray followed his mark through a series of quiet side streets until Fain emerged onto a busier high street. Now sharing the pavement with pedestrians Fain tucked his phone away and walked with renewed purpose towards wherever he was going.

Passing the various shops, takeaways and businesses that had seen better days, Ray kept up with ease whilst blending in with the people around him. Eventually Fain stopped and checked the street for traffic. As his head swivelled from left to right, their eyes locked. Just for a moment. But they did lock. Ray hoped it was just through dumb luck that it had happened. He quickly broke the link, dropping his eyes beneath his cap's peak, and calmly sat down in a bus shelter a few yards away. Was Ray imagining that Fain's eyes had narrowed in recognition? Chancing to slowly look up, Ray saw that Fain was now crossing the road. He threw his spent cigarette onto the pavement before he entered a pub called the Ol Bottle. (Ray surmised that the Ol was not a welcoming familiarity: the 'd' had fallen off). As Fain disappeared inside he did not look back. Ray's line of sight moved to the pub's leaded windows. A warm glow shone out through the diamond-shaped lattice. He looked for the tell-tale sign of a shadow moving across the glass — a shadow someone might cast if they were looking out towards him. But despite a couple of tense minutes, he saw none. *Looks like it was just dumb luck after all*, he thought, relieved.

As daylight dimmed and night set in, Ray sat in the deep shadow of the bus stop (a smashed bulb above aiding his camouflage) and watched the pub. In the last fifty minutes, two people had left and two arrived. The leavers were a youngish couple who'd hurled drunken insults at one another as they staggered off towards whatever living-nightmare they called home. The two who'd arrived, separately, were a beer-battered ruddy-faced old-boy, and a short, scruffy, rotund man. Both had the look of men who had tried and failed at life.

A bus pulled into the stop. Ray squinted at the light cast out from the bus's interior. Its doors opened. A man and two women got off. No one got on. The doors closed and the bus pulled off, returning Ray to the shadows in its wake. Ray looked from the bus to the Ol Bottle and saw that Fain was standing on the pavement with two equally undesirable-looking men. They were all distract-edly smoking . . . apart from Fain, who was looking across the street at the bus shelter.

'Hello there,' he shouted.

20

Ray sat rooted in disbelief.

How?

Fain must have recognized him.

The plan was ruined.

What now?

He would have to improvise.

Ray began to stand up . . .

'Hiya, Howard!' called the man who just got off the bus.

Ray stopped.

'You're late,' Fain shouted back.

Ray sat back down.

'Yeah, yeah. Don't bloody start,' the man shouted as he walked across the road.

Leaning back into the shadows Ray felt his heart start to beat once again. Letting out an unsteady breath, he watched the man reach the other side of the street. Fain slapped him hard on the back and then offered a cigarette. With a yelp the new man accepted and then became one of the smoking gaggle of undesirables. Ray had been in the low-life business for long enough to recognize criminality; it showed in their furtive glances and world-weary attire. It was evident Fain was the alpha of the group. They listened to him with intense interest – *dogs captivated by their master's voice,* thought Ray, feeling his blood heat up in his veins.

Eventually, they finished their cigarettes and threw the butts into the gutter before heading back into the pub.

Ray got up and crossed the road. As he did so he took his phone from his pocket, brought it to his ear, hiding his scar, and began a conversation with nobody. Facing the street, with the pub at his back, he spoke animatedly into the phone. He turned and started to pace back and forth in the now chill night air and began to snatch glances through the window's glow.

Through the latticed glass, warped and distorted, he made out a pair of men sitting at the bar. One of them was the old boy from earlier. A couple of stools along, the short rotund man was talking to the barman.

His next glance found Fain in the pub's lounge area. He was sat around a table with the same three men he'd been with outside. The flawed glass seemed to offer a true window onto their gathering – a misshapen circle of gro- tesques. Ray couldn't hear what Fain was saying but the other men nodded their twisted heads in agreement.

His final glance saw the short rotund man arrive at Fain's table. On a tray he held four pints of lager and what looked like a gin and tonic. He placed the drinks on the table and slid the G&T in Fain's direction before taking the empty seat next to him. *A gin and tonic*, thought Ray. Even now, as low as he had become, he hadn't completely shed the skin of the reputable and successful *Doctor* Howard Fain. He took a sip of the G&T and then said something that seemed to come at the expense of the rotund man and they all laughed in delight. The sound of the laughter was trapped behind the window, but all the same, the sight of Fain laughing with abandon locked Ray's jaw like a steel trap.

21

Ray was cold. Unusually so, considering some of the winters he had endured in Afghanistan. He suspected it was his cancer that had ushered, with open arms, the chill into his bones. So, after another hour and a half of sitting in the bus stop Ray was relieved to see Fain walking out of the pub alone and heading in the direction of his home. The only deviation he made was to stop to pick up fish and chips. Clutching his supper in a plastic carrier bag, Fain walked down the steps towards Cordwallis Street, giving a wide berth to the point where the dog had sprung up.

From the bottom of the steps, Ray watched Fain walk back up the street and stop in his doorway, searching for the keyhole in the dim light of the orange street lamps. Finding the mark, he was soon closing the door behind himself.

Ray looked up and down the street – it was deserted and quiet, but for the faint sounds of televisions from behind drawn curtains. Ray stepped into the street and made his way to his car. Getting in, he slipped on a pair of surgical gloves, turned on the engine, and manoeuvred until he could reverse the vehicle into the cobbled alleyway. The car would be somewhat conspicuous, but if all went well the time it would be parked at the rear of Fain's home would be negligible.

Killing the engine, Ray got out and sidled up to the

pitiful excuse for a gate, still half open, and peered into the back of the property. A light was on behind the drawn blinds. Ray could hear the clatter of movement; a drawer opening, a plate being placed on a worktop.

Fain was in the kitchen.

Then the light was turned off and the small patio was cast into darkness. Ray waited for his eyes to adjust to the lack of light. Satisfied, he was about to step through the gap between the wall and the gate—

'*You can't park here*,' said a voice full of indignation.

Dammit.

Ray turned. In the orange glow of the streetlights was an old woman in a nightgown, hands on hips, stood at the mouth of the alley.

'Why not?' he asked calmly, pulling the peak of his hat low across his face.

'Can't park here.' She took a few steps towards him. 'It's bin day tomorrow and the truck needs access.'

'Oh right. Well, I won't be long. So no harm, no foul, eh?'

'Haven't seen you here before.'

'Just visiting a friend.' He nodded towards the gate and Fain's house.

'Who? Him in there?' She made a disdainful nod in the same direction. 'Didn't know he had any friends.'

'Yeah. It's been a while.'

She seemed to not hear him. She was distracted by something. He followed her gaze to his hands – *his surgically gloved hands*.

He quickly jammed them into his pockets.

Suddenly she seemed to be paying more attention to his face. And it looked like she didn't like what she saw.

'I best head in. Goodnight,' he said, then nodded and stepped through the gate.

'Yeah, OK, night,' he heard her say.

He waited a short time and then peeked around the brick frame of the broken gate into the alley. With her dressing gown pulled close to her narrow frame, the old woman walked across the street towards the open door of her home. Before she shut out the night air he saw her take one last long look at his car.

DAMMIT!

The car, the gloves, and just how much of his face had she seen?

He wavered. Seriously considering aborting. He looked at his car and then Fain's home . . . which brought back the image of his smirking face outside that pub.

This isn't over.

Ray forced calm back into his demeanour.

Pushing on, silently, he crossed the patio and placed his hand upon the cold metal of the door's handle. Pressing his ear to the door, he heard nothing from within. Slowly, holding his breath, he pushed the handle.

Resistance.

In a neighbourhood such as this, Ray had suspected it would be locked. It was an annoyance, a setback, but nothing that would keep him from his quarry. He squinted at the lock's cylinder in the gloom and ran his finger over it. It was a cheap lock (five internal pins, he estimated) set in a cheap door.

From his jacket's inside pocket Ray removed a narrow six-inch length of metal with three small peaks set into its last half-inch – a lock pick. The next item he took out was a tension rod, which the layman might confuse with an Allen key. He inserted the tension rod into the lock's core via the keyhole and pressed it downward until it was met with resistance. He then sent in the lock pick and gently started to lift up and pull out, repeating the process in a circular motion. In seconds the tension rod turned and the lock was nullified. He pressed his ear against the door once again and heard nothing. He pushed the handle and the door silently opened.

Closing the door behind him, he now stood in Fain's kitchen. Even in the faint light he could see the worktop was filthy. Dishes were piled high in the sink and the smell of rotting food soured the air.

The kitchen led on to a narrow corridor with stairs on the left and two doors on the right. All was steeped in darkness except for a flickering light that came from the open door at the far end. The sound of an audience laughing and cutlery connecting with a plate told him Fain was in there watching TV and eating his fish supper.

Ray walked towards the light. He stopped short of the room's entrance and craned his neck around the door frame. Fain was sitting in an armchair watching TV, facing away from him. From the plate resting on his lap he guided a forkful of chips into his mouth and laughed at something the talk-show host had just said to the actor he was interviewing.

Ray reached into his jacket and removed a gun. He quietly entered the room and pressed the gun's muzzle against the side of Fain's head.

'Hiya, Howard.'

Fain froze.

Unblinking, scared rigid, he stared at the TV set slack-jawed, as if his mouth was still waiting for the food that hovered midway. Ray edged his way to the spot directly in front of Fain whilst still pointing the gun at his face.

'Do you know who I am?' he asked, blocking the light from the TV. Fain was now cloaked in shadow, but Ray could still see the whites of his eyes as he looked from the gun to Ray's scarred face. Fain nodded and slowly lowered the fork back onto the plate.

Keeping the gun trained on his target, Ray dragged a chair from beneath a small dining table adjacent to the TV. Sitting down, with his free hand he pulled the cord on a lampshade that was on the table, illuminating a slovenly, depressing room. A filthy ornate fireplace contained a grate piled high with ash and cigarette butts. That was the chief source of the room's stale odour. The rest was a mixture of fish and chips and sweat.

'There you are,' said Ray, getting his first close-up look at Fain as he slumped in the armchair, his doughy body a contradiction beneath his tracksuit. *I don't need a gun to control this man*, he thought.

Along with his once black hair, Fain's looks had faded. Gone were the jawline and angular features that had conned so many into trusting him. There were still hints of the younger Dr Fain lingering beneath his puffy pale countenance but all they did was highlight the thin line between handsome and cruel.

Ray reached to the back of the TV and pulled its power supply out of the socket. In the silence that followed he could hear Fain's quick fearful breaths.

'W-what is this?' he said, looking at the gun that now rested in Ray's lap.

'A long overdue visit, I would say.'

'I don't understand,' he said with a tremor in his voice. 'Why are you . . . in my house?'

'Don't be stupid.'

Fain shook his head in confusion. 'I served my time. Four years.'

'Three years, eight months. You think that's enough, after what you did?'

'I paid my debt. I'm rehabilitated.'

Ray gave him a big lopsided grin.

'Let me explain something to you. You could work at a soup kitchen. You could train dogs for the blind. You could be canonized. None of that would matter because it's what you did twelve years ago that defines you.'

'*No!* I'm not that person any more.'

'Really? Nice company you were keeping earlier.'

Surprise registered on Fain's face. He looked down and licked his lips in thought for a time. 'I run a support group. I'm helping those men,' he finally said in earnest.

'They're going to have to manage without your support from now on.'

The blood left Fain's face. Cold sweat broke out on his

skin, which was now the colour of bone. With a quivering lip, he looked down and covered his eyes. Ray sat and watched him for long moments. Eventually Fain raised his head and opened his eyes. '*Please,*' he said, with a length of drool hanging between his mouth and his tracksuit. '*I was punished.*'

'Nowhere near enough,' replied Ray, standing. 'Get up.'

He made a high-pitched whine, then took the plate and its rattling cutlery and placed it on the side table next to his chair. His hand came to rest on the knife.

'The last man who pointed a knife at me didn't fare too well.'

He quickly retracted his shaking empty hand and once again placed it upon his leaking eyes.

'Get up.'

'Wait, *wait* . . .' Fain looked up at Ray as if he had just remembered something important. 'I . . . I saw in the papers what happened to Odette. I'm so sorry. It was a terrible –'

'There are many ways you can die tonight. Mention her name again and you can forget the humane option,' said Ray, low and menacing.

'This is insanity.' Fain's mouth hung open in disbelief. 'You can't do this. I know you're a cop.'

'I'm retired.'

'Doesn't matter. You're a cop. You can't do this. You're going to go to prison. You do know that, don't you? *You're going to go to prison!*'

'I don't think so. I won't be around long enough.'

'What do you mean?'

'I'm dying.'

'*D-d-dying?*' he said, stuttering in confusion. 'Of what?'

'Cancer.'

'What kind?'

'The kind that kills you.'

'I might be able to help!' Fain said, suddenly full of hope. 'I still know people. I'm a doctor.'

'*Was.*'

Ignoring him, Fain continued. 'I can help you! I still know some great people. I know some of the best oncologists in the country. I have connections. If you would let me speak to them I might be able –'

'Stop,' said Ray.

'Let me help you.'

'Bargaining? Don't be such a cliché.'

Fain's face transformed into an ugly sneer. '*I hope you haven't got long.*' He spat the words like acid through his clenched teeth, giving Ray a glimpse of why he went to prison.

'Maybe I haven't . . . but it's longer than you have,' Ray said, the vicious black shadow of his scar twisting in a mocking grin. '*Get. Up.*'

Fain stood, all indignation leaving his slumped frame.

'*Listen to me,*' he pleaded. 'I served my time. I'm not that man any more. I'm sorry. *I'm so, so sorry.* Is that what you want to hear? Because you have to believe I am. I hate that I hurt them.'

'*Hurt them?*' Ray looked at him with utter revulsion. It was hard to believe that this pathetic creature had once been a man of great charm and persuasiveness. A man who was trusted without question in the community. 'You *destroyed* them.'

Chay was almost ten when she had tried to protect her mother from another of her father's fits of unprovoked rage. That night, getting between her parents had put her in hospital for two weeks. A broken arm, ribs, and a cracked cheekbone had put her father in prison. Odette finally had her freedom, and Ray, first as a friend, and then as her husband, had been there to help her and Chay try to get back to a life without fear.

Ironically, it was Ray who had stopped John from capitulating to an urge to kill the man who, unbeknownst to him, had been terrorizing his sister and niece for years. John was never quite the same after those terrible events. Maybe only Ray could see it, but the light in him had dimmed; his edges had become sharper. *How could they not?*

'*I've kept away from them!*' Fain said through a choked sob. 'I could have tried to get in touch but I didn't. I left them alone. I hate what I did. I hate myself. I have to live with that.'

Ray placed his finger on the gun's trigger.

'No, Howard, you really don't.'

23

'I was up all night, vomiting.' Gog shook his head in irritation.

'Nausea sucks. You never know when it's going to hit,' Luke said sympathetically.

'Do my eyes and skin look a bit yellow?' Gog asked.

'No. You're OK. You're not quite a *Simpsons* character just yet,' he replied, with a sad smile.

Rose snorted. 'Yellow? What I'd give for a bit of colour! I'm like bloody Nosferatu. And I miss my hair . . . I had lovely hair.'

For a time, cancer took all four of them away to the sad place, until Gog said, 'I don't know if it's my cancer or the drugs . . . but my burps smell like farts. That's not normal, is it?'

Luke and Rose burst into laughter. Then Rose's cackling segued into a vicious bout of coughing.

When she eventually got her breathing under control, Gog said, 'You all right, Rose? You don't look too good today.'

'This coming from the man who looks like he should be on a packet of Monster Munch. I'm fine! I mean, I'm rid-dled with cancer . . . and I'm *bald* . . . but I'm fine.'

'Can we get back to the subject of mouth farts? My burps have been normal of late. I recently had a headache that could split granite. But my burps are good,' said Luke.

'It's probably the drugs they've got you on, Gog. Why are the side effects always negative? Mouth farts. Diarrhoea. Insomnia. *Why?* Just once I'd like to read the packet and see "Warning: possible side effects may include ESP, telepathy and telekinesis".'

'Some drugs do have good side effects though, Luke. Viagra wasn't made for . . .' Gog paused and glanced at Rose – '*boners,*' he said, apologetically.

'What are you apologizing to me for? You think because I'm old I'm embarrassed by sex? I've had more than any of you twonks combined. I'll have you know my generation discovered the G-spot in the fifties. What's yours ever done?'

'The fifties? How old are you!?' guffawed Luke. 'G-spot? Isn't that like the Loch Ness Monster or Big Foot. Am I right, Ray?' he winked, turning his attention to Ray.

Ray looked unimpressed and remained silent.

'What's up with you today?'

'I'm fine,' said Ray, looking down at the carpet that hid stains well.

'Not feeling well? Mouth farts?'

'I said I'm fine.'

'You've barely *said* a word.'

'*Luke* . . . I'm not in the mood for it, all right.'

'For what?'

'Bloody nonsense!' he snapped.

Luke blinked his surprise and sat in silence. But it wasn't for long.

'What's happened? Rough night?'

'You could say that.'

'You want to talk about it?'

Ray gave a mirthless chuckle. 'Not a good idea.'

'Why? Is it nonsense?'

'No. It's not.'

'Well shit, Ray. If you have something of substance to tell the group, we'd love to hear.' Luke glanced to Rose and Gog, who nodded their agreement.

'Forget I said anything,' Ray said, after what seemed like a second's hesitation.

'Evasive?' analyzed Luke. 'Now this is getting interesting. Come on, Ray. Spill the beans. If you can make the drudgery of this space a bit more bearable with a tale that requires an eighteen certificate, you have my discretion. What do you say, Gog? Rose? Shall we introduce a truth amnesty so we can hear what Ray deems to be a no-no for chemo?'

'What do I care? I'll be dead soon enough,' said Rose.

'It's not for me to judge –' said Gog.

'You see, Ray. No judgements.'

'– that's God's job.'

'OK. Apart from God,' replied Luke, his eyes fluttering sardonically. 'What do you say, Ray?'

Ray looked at their expectant faces, before lowering his head into his hand. For a long period he could feel their eyes watching him as he massaged his temples between his thumb and forefinger.

The list of people he was willing to confide in was a short one. His dead wife. A handful of men he had served with (one of whom was also now dead). The daughter of the man he had visited the previous evening, to a degree. And not forgetting his brother-in-law, whose profession, admittedly, currently limited Ray's desire for candour.

143

He looked up into their waiting faces.

Extraordinarily, these three strangers he had been randomly assigned to sit in a room to receive chemotherapy with were the only people he knew who could possibly understand what he was going through.

He made the smallest chuckle of disbelief, and said, 'I went to Salford to kill a man last night.'

After a moment to process what he had said, '*WHAT!? OK! Yeah, I'm sure you did,*' was their collective response, interwoven with a smattering of laughter.

Ray did not blink.

The room went quiet.

Luke's face lost all expression. 'He's not kidding.'

'I'm not.'

'Okey-cokey, campers,' announced Donna, breezing in via the door that blocked the small TV when it was open. 'How's everyone doing?' she asked as she started checking each of their stations.

'Oh, the usual,' began Rose, breaking the silence. 'Fed up. Uncomfortable. Depressed . . . and homicidal,' she said, looking directly at Ray.

'That's lovely,' replied Donna, far more focused on the job at hand. As she went about her business, they sat in silence once more, but for the sound of the small TV playing out its twenty-four-hour news cycle. A sharp-looking anchor was saying: '*Police are asking for information from anyone who might know the whereabouts of missing schoolteacher and mother of two Jennifer Moody. The last time Mrs Moody was seen . . .*' As the anchor continued the appeal, the missing woman's photograph filled the screen, young and attractive, smiling through a shock of strikingly bright red hair as if she hadn't a care in the world.

'This all looks fine,' Donna concluded. 'Buzz me if you need me,' she said, leaving.

The TV now showed a tearful man behind a desk flanked by two police officers.

'We just want her home. If anyone . . . knows anything . . . we just want her back . . .'

The screen went blank and Rose dropped the remote into her lap.

'He did it. The husband. It's always the husband,' she said, as all eyes turned back to Ray.

'Holy shit, Ray!' said Luke. 'I thought you were going to say you'd joined UKIP or you'd been flushing wet-wipes.' Gathering himself he continued. 'Who was the target?'

Rolling his eyes at Luke's turn of phrase, Ray answered. 'Howard Fain,' he said, disdain evident in his voice. 'My wife's ex-husband.'

'A crime of passion then.' Ray's death stare wiped the smirk off Luke's face. 'Sorry. This is serious,' he said with a raised palm. 'Did he deserve to die?'

Ray shook his head. 'Truthfully . . . I don't know. You tell me. He was a doctor in the hospital my wife worked at. They married. Howard was a violent man. He abused my wife for years. Then they had a baby, a girl. He put that little girl, Chay, my stepdaughter, in hospital. She was only nine years old. He went to prison for it, served his time. But she was hurt badly. Not just physically but emotionally. She still struggles with it to this day. And now I'm sitting here, the day after . . . I don't know if I've done the right thing by her.'

'You don't think she'd want him dead?'

'I don't know. I thought I did. But I don't.'

'What was your method of disposal?'

'That's not important,' Ray said.

'I think it is,' said Luke, fighting to suppress his excitement. 'We would very much like to know.'

Gog shook his big head in the negative. Rose, her bald wrinkly one, in the positive.

Ray acquiesced – he had come this far. 'I was going to make it look like a suicide.'

'Clever! Like, with a gun or push him off a –'

'Hold your horses!' Rose interrupted. 'Was? You said – I *was* going to make it look like a suicide. Did you or did you not actually kill the man?'

Ray rubbed the back of his neck for a time.

Finally, shaking his head, '*No*,' was all he said.

Rose looked amused. '*Ray*. This is a safe space,' she purred. 'If you killed him just come out and say it. There'll be no tears shed for that fiend.'

'Bad. Very bad,' said Gog, performing a small prayer towards Heaven, whilst Luke, a faint grin on his lips, watched Ray.

'He was alive when I left,' said Ray, more forceful.

'If you say so,' said Rose, still amused.

Luke asked, 'Does your stepdaughter know you went up there to–?'

'*No*,' came Ray's quick reply.

'What about Mrs Ray?' asked Gog.

'She was . . . she died.'

'Shit. Sorry to hear that,' said Luke.

'Is this something you generally do? You know, kill people?' asked Rose.

'Of course not. I just thought maybe I could make a difference before I die.'

'You wanted revenge,' said Rose.

'I suppose I did.'

'But you were a police officer? A Detective Inspector.'

'Yeah. But now I'm retired on death row my priorities have changed.'

'*Fuck me sideways!*' blurted Luke.

'What?' asked Rose.

'I just worked something out.' He started to laugh. 'Oh. My. God. I just worked something out!'

'What?!'

Ray already knew what he was about to say.

'He wasn't lying. He did kill that guy across the street!'

24

'That was self-defence.'

'Self-defence!? You chopped him up!' Luke said.

'Ray's a serial killer!' shrieked Gog.

'Keep your bloody voice down!' Ray ordered. 'I'm not a serial killer and I didn't chop anyone up.' He paused for a calming breath as they looked at him with a mixture of fear and excitement. 'I was caught short so I dashed into the alley. He followed me in and tried to mug me. He attacked me with a knife. Things escalated. I walked out of the alley.' His voice wavered. 'He didn't.' Ray looked down at the floor for some time before continuing. 'But if I think about it, and I'm honest . . . I've justified it to myself as self-defence, and it really was. He chose to follow me into that alley. He chose to take out that knife and threaten me. But I've been so angry about what I'm going through. What all of us are going through. I snapped. The truth is, I could have walked away, but I didn't . . . I put him down, he was still breathing, it was over. But I wanted him to get back up. In that moment he became this *thing* that wants to kill me, and I wasn't having it. I was going to kill that thing. I wanted to kill *him*.'

The room was filled with a long unsure silence, until Luke broke it. 'This is . . . *awesome*. This is the coolest, most badass thing I've heard since you told us you went to kill your wife's ex.'

'It's really not.'

'Ray, you're the Terminator.'

'Ray's going to Hell,' added Gog.

'What's it like?' asked Rose, who had been watching Ray with an intense look on her ancient face.

'What's what like?'

'Taking a life.'

'A terrible thing . . . in hate.'

'What do you mean, in hate? Isn't that the only way to kill?' she asked.

'No, it's not. Human beings are naturally resistant to killing other human beings. Instinctively we know there is value to all life. As a soldier, obedience and duty play a big part in taking someone's life. But we're also taught to feel compassion and respect for the enemy. That way it's a life that has value. That's a life worth taking. The life of some-one you hate is worthless. But it's extremely rare to meet a person like that.'

'You were a soldier?' asked Luke.

'I was a Marine.'

'Is that how you . . .' Luke pointed to his own very prominent cheek bone.

'Yeah.'

'What happened?'

'Kabul, Afghanistan. An IED – an improvised explo-sive device – detonated beneath the vehicle I was in.'

'*Fucking hell*,' whispered Luke.

'Yeah. I was one of the lucky ones.'

'Who wasn't so lucky?'

'Marine Chris Yannick. He was twenty-two. Lance Corporal Neil McCrindle . . . my friend,' he said, with a far-off hollow look in his eyes, 'who I was going to ruin.'

'Ruin? Why?'

'He let a prisoner die. I was going to report him.' He shook his head. 'I was a lot younger then. I saw everything in black and white. No grey areas. He would have hated me for what I was going to do. I'm glad we were friends when he died. I wonder what he would have made of my trip to Manchester.' Ray let out a dark chuckle. 'I left not long after my injury. I wanted to return to active duty. But my hip . . . if you can't walk with heavy kit on your back, that's it. I was discharged. Then I became a cop.'

'And now here you are,' said Rose, 'telling us about things that would see you in prison. Why?'

'Why not? Prison isn't quite the same negative deterrent when your life expectancy has been dramatically shortened. I thought if anyone could understand what I'm going through it's the people in this room.' Ray hesitated briefly before concluding, 'And . . . it feels good to share. It feels like a release.'

'Hmm,' was all Rose said, accompanied by a little nod.

'Well, that, and Luke said there's a truth amnesty,' Ray added with a wonky grin.

'Ray fucking Leonard. Total badass,' said Luke, returning the grin. 'What about the police? Are you worried about them?'

'Fain is still alive –'

'His memory is, at least,' said Rose, stroking her wrinkled chin.

Ray ignored her and continued – 'and I don't think there's anything that connects me to Pentecost.'

'That's the guy in the alley?' Luke asked.

'Yes. The guy in the alley.'

'Such a badass,' Luke repeated. 'So, who's next on the hit list?'

Shaking his head in a tired kind of way, Ray said, 'There's no hit list.'

He was speaking the truth – there was no hit list. But only because he didn't have the name of Odette's killer – *yet*.

'Fair enough. Either way the amnesty stands. None of this leaves the room. Am I right G-unit?'

'My nan always told me off for telling tales. She'd give me tanners.'

'Tanners?'

'Tan your hide,' said Gog, shifting uncomfortably in the creaking leather of his chair.

'Very Dickensian. Rose?' Luke prompted, seeing the far-off distracted look in her eye. 'Rose?'

'I can keep a secret,' she said finally, as if hearing him for the first time.

'What's wrong?'

'I was just thinking about Ray's wife and daughter.'

Ray turned to her in surprise.

'I know a little bit about what they went through.'

25

Ray, Luke and Gog sat like three statues, all aware that the slightest disturbance might scare her off. They held their breath as Rose stroked her forearm beneath the cotton of her cardigan.

'I told the doctor I'd fallen down the stairs,' she began. 'This was way back before that kind of excuse became a cliché. We lived in a flat. We didn't even have stairs,' she said with a bitter snort. 'Alan sat next to my bed, stroking my hand with a concerned look on his face. The doctor said they should keep me in overnight as a precaution because of the bump on my head. *My Angel,* Alan said, *what am I going to do with you?* Then he kissed my cheek before he left, saying he'd be back for me the next day.'

They sat in silence. From the corner of her eye she could see that the look of concern he had worn at her bedside in the hospital yesterday was gone. Instead, he now drove far too fast, and with that expression of perpetual anger that had taken up residency on his face a few years back. Coincidentally, it had appeared at exactly the same time they had discovered that Rose was barren.

Alan loved to drive. His car was always immaculate. When he wasn't driving it he stored it in the garage that accompanied their council flat. He'd spend hours in there shuffling around the car that was far too big for the garage, polishing it till it gleamed. Rose privately thought to herself that the big car made Alan's five-foot-five build seem even smaller as he sat there gripping the steering wheel with his ridiculous leather driving gloves.

The bumps in the road made her ribs and head throb. But she had become more than adept at coping with pain. Her focus was on the peculiar weight of the plaster around her forearm in her lap. It was the most odd sensation.

Once the car was *tucked away*, as he liked to put it, they climbed the steps to their eighth-storey flat and entered. The air inside was hot and oppressive as their side of the building faced west, looking into the summer sun all day long. Much like the car, their modest living space was spotless. Just how Alan liked it – *A clean house is a happy house.*

'Where do you think you're going?' he asked, hanging his coat as Rose turned in the direction of their marital bedroom.

'I thought I'd have a lie down.'

'I think you've been lying in bed long enough. Waited on hand and foot. What about me? In case you hadn't noticed I haven't had a hot meal in two days.' He stepped aside, clearing a path between Rose and the kitchen.

She looked down and held the plaster around her arm. 'But . . .'

'Come on.' He nodded at the kitchen. 'Don't be so bloody dramatic.'

He had always had a bad temper, she thought, as she made her way to the kitchenette, but his fuse had been long when they'd first met. Gradually it had become shorter and shorter. Now a fork amongst the knives in the cutlery drawer could send him into a fit of rage – *It's not rocket science!* he would yell.

She took a frying pan out of the cupboard and placed it on the hob. Using her left hand, the action felt strange and clumsy. With difficulty, she lit the hobs beneath the frying pan and a large saucepan full of oil. Then, with a spike of fear, she realized that she would not be able to peel potatoes to make the chips to accompany Alan's steak. She would have to use oven chips. Alan hated oven chips. The half-empty bag that had been in the freezer forever was a testament to that – *They taste like bloody cardboard!* But what could she do? Were oven chips a greater or lesser crime than burning the collar of one of his shirts whilst ironing? The very thing that had put her in the hospital two days ago?

She stared out of the small window that looked out onto their narrow balcony and saw the sun beating down on her hanging basket of flowers. They looked withered and sad. She filled a jug with water. As soon as she felt its weight in her left hand she knew she would not be able to save the flowers from the heat on her own. After a breath of trepidation, she headed to the living room.

'My hanging basket could do with a watering. Would you mind, love?' she asked, as her husband sat in his armchair reading the paper.

He peered over his reading glasses. 'I can't get a minute's peace with you, can I?' he said with a huff. 'Fill a jug.' She retrieved the jug from the kitchen. Alan had risen and was now tucking his tie into his shirt. He opened the door to the balcony before snatching the jug from Rose and picking up his foot stool.

The basket, which had been installed by the previous tenants, was hung too high for Alan's diminutive stature. The foot stool just about gave him the extra height needed. He stepped onto it and with the aid of tiptoes he was able to pour the water into the beleaguered flowers.

Rose stood shielding her eyes from the sun, watching him.

'They look dead to me. Bloody waste of time, if you ask me,' he said, straining in the act of balancing on his toes and pouring the jug.

The balcony's low wall had a rail mounted upon it. Rose noticed the rail didn't even come up to Alan's hip, the way he was stretching.

She looked from Alan's hip back to the rail – and then from the rail back to Alan – and her heart started to thump in her chest.

She took a step towards him. She reached out the hand she had been using to shield her eyes.

Just a push.

'Yeah, all the water in the world isn't going to help these,' he said, oblivious to her proximity.

She took another small step. Her trembling hand was inches from him. The jug was almost empty. It was now or never. One quick push and it would all be over. No more bullying. No more violence. No more living in fear. No more Alan.

'Bloody waste of good water. Dead as a dodo,' he said as the last of it left the jug.

She blinked her way out of what had felt like a trance.

What was she thinking? What had come over her? This was not her. 'Will oven chips be OK?' she asked, lowering her hand.

'Oven chips!' Clutching the jug, he turned angrily. '*For fuck's sake, Ro–*' It was then that the stool slipped from under him. He fell backwards. Rose instinctively reached out to stop him, but it was already too late. As his rear cleared the rail, he looked at Rose with unnaturally huge eyes. His free hand (he still held the jug) flailed, hitting the rail with a metallic clang. As he disappeared from view, he screamed – '*ROSE!*'

By the time she looked over the balcony he had already travelled four of the eight storeys towards the paved courtyard below. He gave a final unintelligible scream that was abruptly silenced by the dreadful never-to-be-forgotten sound of flesh and bone impacting on concrete. Strangely, she could never recall the sound of glass shattering, even though the jug was at his side in a million jagged pieces.

'I'm so sorry, Rose,' said Ray, breaking the silence that followed her terrible tale. 'That bastard.'

Luke and Gog looked on, heartbroken.

'He was a bastard to me. But to the outside world he was the perfect husband. I know, more clichés. Whenever we were around family or friends he made out that I was the best thing that had ever happened to him. He loved me. He adored me. He didn't care that I couldn't have kids. That's what everybody thought.

'But as soon as the front door shut, the air around him would change. He'd suddenly become this put-upon man who worked, paid the bills and kept me fed. He could do anything he wanted with me because I was a burden who brought nothing to our relationship. I deserved my beatings.'

'I can't believe there are people like that in the world!' said Gog in vexation.

'They're not people. They're monsters. Like a lion snatching its prey from the herd, they take you away from real people . . . people who love you,' Rose whispered, with a haunted look. 'I knew he would eventually kill me, and I still couldn't kill him first. If he hadn't fallen off the balcony that day, I wouldn't be here now.'

'Well, thank God for oven chips,' Luke said with a sad grin.

Gog and Rose laughed.

'Who doesn't like oven chips?' Gog added, incredulous.

Ray asked Rose, 'What did the police say at the time?'

'I thought you might ask.' A wry smile spread across her old face. 'How do you think it went?'

'Sadly, evidence of the abuse you suffered might have made it hard to prove your innocence.'

'You're right. But they couldn't prove I did it. And I couldn't prove I didn't. Even now, all these years later, where I live I'm still known as the crazy old woman who murdered her husband.' She took a moment to think, before continuing. 'Maybe, within these four walls, under the protection of the truth amnesty . . . maybe you three will be the first to believe I didn't?'

'You're telling the truth,' said Luke quickly. 'No doubt in my mind.'

'I believe you, Rose,' added Gog.

'Me too,' said Ray.

'Thank you,' she said, with the glimmer of a tear in her eye. Learning about the abuse she had suffered, and that tear of vulnerability, seemed to shrink her. Rose suddenly looked so weak and small that surely there could be nothing left for cancer to take? Any smaller and she would be gone – reduced to nothing.

26

Three days later, just before his regular chemo session, Ray was sat opposite Dr Burnel. It was easy to forget himself and slip into his familiar, irrational dislike of doctors, Ray mused, as he watched Burnel, who had an intense look on his face, silently mouth the words he read in a file that was open upon his desk.

Doctors like Burnel had consistently delivered bad news to him over the years. But Ray reminded himself that it was not their fault. An IED and cancer were mainly responsible, and the less said about Dr Howard Fain the better. And Burnel, with his neat hair and Clark Kent glasses, his shirt sleeves rolled up and that expensive-looking tie he wore held in place by a stylish silver clip, looked more like a banker or some colleague of Luke's than an oncologist, Ray fancied.

'Mr Leonard,' he began.

'Call me Ray.'

'Ray,' the doctor said, as he removed his glasses. 'How are you feeling?'

'Tired. But OK. All things considering.'

'Yeah ... yeah, sure,' Burnel replied, nodding vigorously. 'So, I've taken a look-see at your blood work and imaging . . .'

Here it comes, thought Ray.

Burnel took another quick glance at the file before

meeting Ray's worried glare. 'Frankly ... your chemo-therapy and medication is having an extremely positive effect. I'm really happy with these numbers,' he said, with a tap of the file. 'We aren't out of the woods just yet but what I've seen is definitely very encouraging.'

Ray looked at him, dumbfounded.

'Oh,' he finally said. 'I wasn't expecting that.'

'This is good news,' Burnel said with a warm smile. 'Let's just keep doing what we're doing. If we keep heading in this direction ... well, let's see. But as I said, I'm very happy with where we're at, Mr Leonard ... Ray.'

'Well, OK,' Ray replied, as a wonky smile formed on his face. 'Thank you. Thank you so much.' He rose.

'You are most welcome. Just keep doing what you're doing.'

With that wonky smile still stretching across his face, Ray shut the door with its sign that read 'Dr Elliott Burnel' and stood in shock in the corridor. The door opposite him opened and a nurse exited. He quickly raised his shaking hand to cover his giddy grin. She gave him a nod before heading off down the corridor. As she walked away he fought the urge to punch the air and shout – *Yes!*

Burnel's words came back to him and his cheeks reddened at the thought. 'Just keep doing what you're doing.'

If only he knew.

27

'I popped one of my nausea pills earlier and it was broken in half,' said Gog, full of concern.

Ray and Luke stared back at the Welshman in confusion.

'That's a great story, Big Man,' said Luke. 'It had it all. And I never saw that ending coming. What a twist.'

'Behave, Luke. I mean, will it still work?'

'Will what work?'

'The pill?'

'Let me get this straight.' Luke scratched his brow. 'You're asking, will a nausea pill still work if it's broken in half?'

'Yeah.'

'Yes, Gog. It will still work.'

'But it's broken? When something is broken it doesn't work any more,' replied Gog, looking a bit pleased with himself.

'Yeah, but a pill's not an iPhone, is it? You break one of them in half it's not going to work,' said Luke, with a grin for Ray who was checking his watch.

'She's late,' he said, nodding at Rose's empty chair. 'That's unusual.'

Luke glanced at his watch. 'The two-fifteen from Hell must be running late,' he chuckled.

Ray and Gog did not share his humour.

Luke's smile faded a little. 'Hmm. Yeah, she's never late.'

They called for Donna and after voicing their concerns the nurse rushed off. Ten minutes later she returned looking flushed.

'Any news?' asked Luke.

'We've called her home. No answer. We're sending someone.'

'*Shit*,' Luke replied.

'Bloody hell,' said Ray, shaking his head at the empty chair. Donna met his eyes and he could see that this was something she had experienced many times before.

'She's dead,' said Gog.

'*Gog?!*' said Luke, throwing his arms up.

'Everybody calm down,' Ray advised. 'She *could* be running late.'

The silence that followed spoke volumes.

In Ray's mind's eye he saw a little Jack Russell curled up in Rose's lap, unable to feel the comforting warmth of her touch. He placed his hand over his eyes as he felt the cool flow of the drugs that were fighting to lengthen his life enter his bloodstream. With them came a sense of guilt. He had been so happy to hear the drugs were working, but maybe they hadn't worked for poor Rose?

'Christ alive . . . who died?'

Ray lowered his hand. Rose stood in the doorway. They all looked at her flabbergasted as she removed her coat and adjusted her purple bandana.

'*Where have you been?*' Luke demanded, startling her as she sat.

'None of your business, pretty boy,' Rose snapped. She looked from one face to the next. 'What's wrong with you lot?' Only Donna now sported a big grin as she went to work rolling up Rose's sleeve. 'What's wrong with them?'

'I think they missed you,' said Donna.

She looked to them again and they were all now smiling back at her.

'I have to go and speak to my colleague,' said Donna, patting Rose's hand. 'Play nice and stay hydrated.'

Once Donna had left, Ray said, 'We were worried about you, Rose.'

'Well, don't be. My idiot cabbie went the wrong way.'

'As long as you're here safe and sound,' Gog added, with shiny eyes.

'Oh!' Her face suddenly lit up. 'Now I get it. You all thought I was dead. That's it, isn't it? You thought I'd succumbed?'

'For a second. But then I remembered your pact with the devil,' said Luke, beaming. 'I'm glad you're still with us.'

'Gentlemen, you'll know when I'm a goner because I'll come and visit you in the dead of night. You'll wake up screaming and I'll be there floating over you.' She extended her skeletal claws and hissed at them through her yellow teeth. Seeing their collective colour drain she burst into a cackle, followed by the usual coughing fit.

'That,' began Luke, who looked genuinely fearful, 'is the single most terrifying thing I have ever heard.'

They laughed.

In the lull that followed, Gog asked Rose, 'Where did he take you?'

'What?'

'The taxi-man.'

'Oh. That berk. He went left when he should have gone

right. I ended up down by the arches. Stinking horrible place. Bloody graffiti everywhere.'

'You don't like street art?' Luke asked, already knowing the answer.

'*Street art?!* Is that what you call it? It's ugly. All of it. Hideous. It brings everything down with it. To me I see no difference between a four-year-old scrawling crayon on a kitchen wall and the twenty-four-year-old man-child spraying his stupid name down at the train tracks.'

'Or woman-child,' Luke offered.

She tilted her head in pity at him. 'Word to the *clueless*. It's only men who cock their legs, you silly boy.'

'All right.' Luke straightened, accepting the challenge. 'What about Banksy? He's a national treasure.'

'Gutless.'

'Gutless?!' He laughed.

'Where's the courage going out in the dead of night –' she pressed her index finger to her thumb and made two *psst-psst* sounds – 'spraying your strong political views on a wall before slinking back into the shadows where no one's allowed a comeback? Politicians are arseholes but at least you can see their arsehole when they're talking out of it.'

Ray looked from Rose to Luke in a way that suggested he had been won over.

Seeing the look, Luke said, 'She does make an interesting –'

'The only spray on walls that I'd like to see from these "street artists",' continued Rose, 'is the spray of blood from the firing squad.'

'Aaaand there she is,' said Luke, lowering his face into his palm.

'What?'

'That's a bit much, Rose,' said Gog.

'Come on, you pansies! Are you telling me you've never fantasized about offing some of the most annoying people out there? I know Ray has,' the old woman said, regarding him with a wicked twinkle in her eye.

Ray gave a tiny head shake of annoyance.

'OK. I'm picking up what you're putting down,' said Luke, wriggling with excitement in his seat. 'Putting aside the obvious murder, rape, paedo lot . . . who would you off? You know – hypothetically.'

Gog turned to him in confusion.

'Not real. Just for fun,' Luke clarified.

'Got it. Well, as it's just for fun . . . motor-bikers,' said Gog.

'What's wrong with bikers?' Luke asked.

'All that revving. One person shouldn't be allowed to make that much noise on the high street. It's ob . . . umm . . . ob . . .'

'Obnoxious,' said Ray.

'That's the one. It's horrible. Makes my ears hurt.'

'All right.' Luke laughed in delight. 'Death to everyone on an engine with two wheels. What about you, Ray?'

Ray distractedly ran a thumb along his scar, deciding whether to play ball or not. Finally, he said, 'Can I order an air strike on every local council in the country?'

Laughter ensued.

'Fantastic,' said Luke, giving Ray one of his 'my hero'

looks. 'Death from above for all those squandering tax-payers' money.'

'And you, Luke?' Ray asked.

After a short ponder: 'Billionaires.'

'That sounds a bit rich coming from you,' Rose said.

'I know. The ol' venture capitalist over here. Look, I'm rich but I'm no billionaire. I've been around a few and they're always the most selfish people in the room. And that's not necessarily a bad thing if your life goal is to be the richest person in every room. You need the greed. Elon Musk, or as I call him, Tech Trump, is a great example. I respect the cash, he earned it. But what does he do with it? Launches pointless metal dicks into space. That's just frivolous. I'm not down with that. Why not do something meaningful for humanity. How about – I don't know – *cure cancer*?'

'Bit of a vested interest there, I think,' said Rose.

'Obviously. But also for the billionaire.'

'In case they got cancer?' asked Gog, scratching his big dome.

'Well, yeah. But I was thinking more from a PR angle.' They looked back at him, lost. 'Think about it. The billion-aire could say and do all the dumb shit they wanted and every time someone called them out on it, the PR machine could say, "Yes, Elon has behaved like a deplorable fuck-wit, but let's not forget – he did cure cancer."'

'That's a mulligan for life,' said Ray.

'Exactly. It's genius,' Luke replied. 'But it'll never happen. So, let's just line them up with the street artists.'

'If only it were that easy,' said Rose, longingly. 'But it's not . . . is it, Ray?' She turned to him. 'You can't just wish for it. If you want to rid the world of scum, you have to get out there and do it yourself, yes?'

'Rose . . .' Ray shook his head in a tired manner. 'Whatever I've done recently, due to what I can only assume to be luck, has gone unanswered. For that I'm thankful. So my days of being . . . *proactive* are over.'

28

Chaynnie had classes that afternoon so Ray had caught the train home after his session. As he sat reading in his living room, under the watchful gaze of Odette from the mantlepiece, he felt more relaxed and positive than he had in a long while. Burnel had said, 'We aren't out of the woods just yet', but Ray dared to imagine that he might be getting close to their edge . . . and then the doorbell rang out.

'Howard Fain is dead.'

'*Dead?*' said Ray, who now had an answer as to why John had a grin on his face as he had opened the door to him.

'The bastard topped himself,' he replied, as Ray ushered him off the doorstep and into his kitchen.

'When? How?'

'I got a call from local CID in Manchester.'

'Really? George Dunnock?'

'Retired. Nick Sutter.'

'Sutter?' Ray made the word sound as if he were describing soured milk. 'Nick? I thought he was on the Major Incident Team?'

'He was on MIT, until he pissed everybody off. He's now a DI in CID. He declined to share the hows and the whys of Fain's demise, but he did tell me he'd been dead for two days. A "concerned" colleague from the warehouse he worked at found him.'

'That's . . . extraordinary.' Ray's mind reeled. *What is going on? This is bad,* very *bad.*

'Hard to believe Fain ever had the decency to book himself an early ticket to Hell? But there you have it. Ding-dong, he's gone,' said John, dragging a chair from under the table that still had Ray's sheets of notes scattered over it.

'Yes, humility was never a burden for Howard,' said Ray, flipping the switch on his kettle.

'You don't seem as happy as I was expecting. I mean, I wasn't expecting you to be doing cartwheels. But –'

'I'm the doing-cartwheels-on-the-inside type, John,' Ray said with his back to his brother-in-law as he opened a cupboard.

'Well, that's true.'

'Coffee or tea?'

'Coffee, please.'

Ray prepared the beverages.

'Did he leave a note?'

'Apparently. Again Sutter wouldn't tell me what was in it. Thanks,' John said, taking the mug. He drank. 'Now that's what a good cup of coffee should taste like.'

'It's just instant.'

'God dammit we need to get some better coffee at the station.'

'Yes, you do,' Ray agreed. He then took a gulp of his tea and leaned against the kitchen worktop in what he hoped looked like a casual manner. 'So, what *do* we know?'

'Well, at first I assumed Sutter was calling as a courtesy. He's aware of my grim connection to Fain. But then he mentions this mysterious stranger.'

Here we go.

172

'Oh,' Ray replied, grinding his teeth in the knowledge that this would not have been an issue if Fain hadn't decided to take it on himself to finish what Ray had started.

'An old dear who fancies herself as the neighbourhood watch said she saw someone parked in the alley behind Fain's house a few nights back.' John took another swig of his coffee. 'Are you sure this is instant?'

'I am. What about this mystery man?'

'Man? I didn't say it was a man . . . *got you!*' he exclaimed, before he burst into laughter. 'I'm kidding. Obviously it was a man.' Ray forced a chuckle. 'She actually spoke to him.'

'Did she?'

'Yeah. He said he was there to see Fain. Told her he was a friend.'

'Hmm . . .' Ray felt his heart begin to race.

'Does sound a bit suspicious, doesn't it? A friend parked in the alley visiting late at night.'

'Could she describe him?'

'Sutter wouldn't say. Either way, for me, the most important take-away is that that piece of shit Howard Fain is no more.'

'Do you think Sutter will try and find this man who was parked in the alley?'

'I don't know, could be tricky. How good a look did the old dear get? Does she know the number plate or the make of the car? What's the CCTV situation on Fain's street?' *There's nothing* – Ray thought. 'That's a lot of ifs, buts and maybes. But my guess is Sutter smells something off. Working on MIT, murder was his bread and butter . . .' John paused and tapped at his lips. 'Sutter's a mean dick-head, but as you know, a good cop. He has experience and he does things properly. He'll probably find this guy just to tick him off the list of possibilities. Personally, I'd slide Fain into the file marked *who gives a shit*. But I'm angry. Sutter on the other hand will look at the whole thing with his usual *I have nothing else going on in my life* intensity. You do know why he was calling me, yeah?'

'Because you're a person of interest.'

'Exactly right. But I told him – I haven't been to Manchester in a long time and definitely not in the last couple of days. Which is a fact easily confirmed.' He took a sip of his coffee, watching Ray over the rim of the mug. 'He mentioned you.'

A knot of acid started to burn in the pit of Ray's stomach. *This is extremely bad.*

'What did he say?'

'He said, there are a few people who will be overjoyed to hear of Fain's death and one of them is Ray Leonard. He then followed that up with the oh-so tactful question – has Ray been sampling Manchester's night life of late?'

'And what did you say?'

'I laughed and told him that my brother-in-law is currently going through chemo for prostate cancer. Sutter said he was really sorry to hear that. Asked me to send his best wishes and hopes for a speedy recovery.'

'What a lovely thought.'

'Yeah. I'm not sure he has those.'

For a few long moments Ray and John regarded one another. John finished the remainder of his coffee and placed the empty mug on the table. 'Out of interest . . . *have* you taken a trip to Manchester recently?'

'Are you asking me if I killed Howard Fain, John?'

'I'm just making conversation,' he said, in an inscrutable tone.

'On Odette's grave,' said Ray, placing his hand upon his chest, 'I did not kill Howard Fain.'

After another protracted silence between them, John said, 'That's good enough for me,' finding his easy smile once again. 'I'm not sure it's going to be enough for Sutter, though. I know the last thing you want right now is a surly Manc bothering you, so I'll do what I can to keep him at arm's length. But there's only so much I can stall him before it just looks like I'm protecting my brother-in-law,' he said with an apologetic shrug. 'I'd expect a call from him if I were you.'

'I can't think about that right now,' said Ray, whose face remained grave. 'I'm more concerned about telling Chay.'

29

When Ray had moved in with Odette, he'd decided to keep the bachelor pad that he had called home before he'd met her. He reasoned that it would be handy and convenient for them to have a bolthole in the heart of the city. But, rather prophetically, one of the main reasons Odette had wanted Ray to keep hold of it was for Chaynnie. *It'll be perfect for her if she decides to go to university*, she'd said.

Ray remembered her words now as he walked past the university and took a right onto Luxembourg Street. Skirting the university's large modern structure of glass and steel, the street soon transformed into a green space of grass and trees and private parking surrounded by a fence. Beyond it was an imposing white building, with the words Luxembourg Tower written above its entrance.

After making his way through a gate and along a path, Ray now stood in front of the building's entrance. He swiped a fob over a pad and the door opened. Entering one of the two lifts in the tower's small foyer he pushed the button for level twenty, the top floor.

He looked at his reflection in the lift's mirror as the counter above his head increased in number. If there was something beyond this mortal realm, he thought, Fain was surely there, laughing at his unenviable situation. For a moment after Burnel's promising news, Ray had felt re-invigorated, but now, after John's visit and hearing that

Sutter was investigating Fain's 'suspicious' death, he thought he looked gaunter and paler than ever, as if he were fading away – regressing into the woods. Even the jagged crescent of his scar seemed to have dimmed from an angry purple to a more muted pink. Was Burnel's prognosis premature? Ray shook the thought from his head – telling it to take a ticket and stand in line. Yes, potentially dying was a problem . . . but so was living, if a surly Mancunian working hard to put him at the scene of a crime he hadn't committed was anything to go by.

The lift stopped and he got out. But before Ray had reached the bell to 106 the door of the flat opened and Chay stepped into the hallway holding a small bag of rubbish.

'Oh! Ray. Hi. What are you doing here?' she asked, walking the short distant to the rubbish shoot. 'I thought you were anti-unannounced visits?'

'I . . . ahh.'

The shoot clanged shut and Chay turned back to Ray empty-handed. Seeing the look upon his face her smile faded. 'What's wrong? Are you OK?'

Much like he had done with his chemo group, Ray decided not to share his positive news from the meeting with Dr Burnel with his daughter. The ride in the lift with his reflection had reaffirmed the idea that he shouldn't count his cancer-free chickens before they hatched.

'Let's go inside.'

'You're freaking me out, Ray. What's going on? Are you OK?' she repeated, as she closed the door behind them. To Ray's immediate left a set of stairs led to two bedrooms and a bathroom above. The ground floor was a simple yet elegant open-plan kitchen-cum-living-room. A modest couch in the middle of the room faced a wall-mounted television. A small table, with study books and a laptop on it, was placed against one wall. Large French windows spanned the room's far end and opened up onto a balcony Ray and Odette had enjoyed sitting out on. He observed the deep red sun in the distance, rapidly cutting its way through the city's omnipresent layer of smog.

'I'm fine. It's . . .' he began, and then realized, in her company, this name hadn't been said out loud in years. 'Howard Fain is dead,' Ray said. 'He killed himself.'

Chaynnie opened her mouth to speak, but all that came out was a short gasp. Silently, she made her way to the couch and sat.

'You OK?' asked Ray, as he sat next to her.

'I don't know,' she replied without emotion. Ray watched her stare blankly at the floor, trying to process what he had told her. 'So that's it. He's gone,' she finally said.

'Yes.'

'How?'

'I don't know. Greater Manchester Police got in contact with John. They can't give out all the details at this point. But he is gone.'

'Jesus . . .' she said, with her gaze still levelled at the floor. 'Why? Why now?'

'I don't know,' he lied.

'I'm just . . .' Chaynnie paused to rub at her face. 'I'm just trying to work out how I feel. Should I be sad?' she asked, angst and confusion creasing her face.

'You can feel any way you want, Chay.'

'I don't think I *feel* anything.' Ray could see that her

hands were shaking. She turned and looked into his eyes. 'I should be happy, right? Happy he's gone, after what he did to me and Mum?'

'Is that how you feel?'

She paused again. 'No. I feel exactly the same.'

'That's OK. It might take some time to sink in.'

'Yeah. Maybe.' She stood and walked to the windows. 'And maybe not,' she said, looking out at the view, arms folded. 'He might be gone . . . but it still happened, didn't it? He still did what he did. I've tried so hard to bury the past. But it's always there. I still remember that period so clearly. Hiding in my room. Under the bed. In the cupboard. Covering my ears to block out the noise. I can still hear it now. Mum crying and screaming. I was so confused and scared . . . I wanted it to stop. And when I tried to stop it . . .' Her voice trailed off.

Ray had never heard her speak like this about what happened.

'It took a lot of courage, Chay,' he said to her back as she stood motionless, looking out at the setting sun.

'When he was sent to prison . . . believe it or not there was a part of me that felt guilty. I hated him with all my heart. But I've never wished death upon him. How do I feel now that he's gone? I feel exactly the same. What he did to me . . . I can't get beyond it. It's always there because it changed me. It's part of who I am. *He* is a part of who I am,' she said, as her shoulders began to shake.

'There's bad people in the world, Chay. And one of them was your father. You're not him. You proved that when you tried to protect your mother. You were a great kid and now you're a great woman, despite what that man

180

put you through. *You are not your father,*' he repeated, as he stood up.

She turned, with tears streaming down her cheeks, and ran into Ray's arms.

Odette was the only person who had been able to hold Chay in the years since Howard had left his mark on her. But now, as she cried huge, gut-wrenching sobs into his shoulder, for the first time Ray was able to comfort her as he had always wanted to – like a father.

'It's OK. You're all right,' he said, gently rubbing her back. 'I know it's a cliché. But time is a great healer. When you're going through it you can't possibly imagine a time where it won't be on your mind . . . but I promise you, Chay. That time will come.'

'It's already been a while, Ray,' she said, with a muffled sniffle.

'I'll be here for you. As long as it takes.'

She eventually peeled her wet face off Ray's equally wet shoulder. He handed her a tissue. 'Thanks,' she said, with the smallest of smiles, as she started to dab at her eyes.

'So, I'm officially an orphan, I suppose . . .' She stopped, suddenly realizing what she had said. Ray looked back at her, unable to conceal his hurt. 'I'm such an idiot. Sorry, Ray.'

Hurt or not, he couldn't deny she was right. Ray had, for his part in Fain's death, left her fatherless and motherless. 'I didn't mean it like that,' she implored. 'You know how I feel about you.'

'It's OK, kiddo.'

'You're my . . . my Ray.'

'I'm whatever you need me to be.'

Pushing aside his hurt feelings, it was not lost on Ray that the fact Chay had openly spoken about what had happened and had let a man hold her was undoubtedly an emotional breakthrough. *Maybe some good would come from Fain's death?* he thought, until a bitter seed started to bloom.

If he were to be arrested for killing Fain, any prospect of an emotional recovery for Chay would surely be lost. How could Ray be the man he wanted to be for her if it were revealed that he was a murderer. He would be just one more violent man in her life that she could not trust. If the net closed in around him, not only might he lose his liberty, but also the only thing in the world he loved – her.

30

Later that evening, Ray walked along Gilmour Avenue towards his home. As he reached into his pocket to retrieve his keys, a car door opened on the other side of the street and a man got out.

'Ray!' the man shouted as he dashed across the road towards him.

'You're a bit far off your patch,' he replied, pushing his keys back into his pocket.

The other man ignored the observation. 'How are ya, Ray?' he asked.

Beneath the streetlights, his unkempt hair and five o'clock shadow gave the appearance of a man at the end of a long hard day. His suit jacket was crumpled. His tie askew. One might think it was a result of sitting and driving for hours (which no doubt he had). But Ray knew him of old. He had always looked like this. Ray suspected it was an affectation to lull people into a false sense of superiority. The only thing that gave the game away were his eyes – they were sharp and clear and informed anyone who took the time to look into them that it was a mistake to underestimate DI Nick Sutter.

'I'm doing OK, thanks, Nick.'

'Fucking cancer,' Sutter said in his thick Mancunian accent. 'Must be hard work. In and out of hospital. All them drugs.' He reached into his pocket and took out a pack of cigarettes. 'I imagine you're around a lot of needles at the moment. I hate needles. How about you?'

'You get used to them.'

He nodded and put the cigarette in his mouth. Ray watched him spark up. 'You want one?' Sutter said.

'No.'

'Christ. Look at me offering the guy with cancer a bloody fag. Daft bastard,' he said, exhaling a cloud of smoke. 'I have to say, though, you don't look like you're ready for the hospice just yet. You still look like you can handle yourself. John made out you were at death's door.' He took a quick drag. 'No, I still wouldn't like to bump into you in a dark alley,' he finished, with a penetrating stare through the smoke.

'I'd invite you in but . . .' Ray nodded at the cigarette.

'Nay bother. This is just a flying visit. It's what I call an informal whites-of-their-eyes chat.' He paused to literally study Ray's eyes. 'One police to another.'

A car that had been slowly making its way along Gilmour Avenue came to a stop behind Sutter. The driver sat in shadow and waited with the engine idling. *What's going on here?* thought Ray. *Has Sutter come with backup?*

Suddenly someone spoke from behind, startling him. 'Hey, Ray. How's it going?'

He quickly turned . . . only to see his neighbour securing her gate. 'Hi, Ashley,' he replied, forcing a smile. 'All good.'

She slung her handbag over her shoulder and crossed the pavement towards the waiting car. She smiled at Sutter. 'Evening.'

He took another quick drag. 'All right, love,' he replied, forgoing the smile.

'Have a great night,' said Ray.

'You too,' she said, getting into the back seat. She closed the door and the car pulled off.

'You seem a bit on edge, Ray?'

'What can I do for you, Nick?' he asked, not taking the bait.

'John mention I called?'

'He did.'

'You've had a bit of a run of it, with your missus and the big C an' all.' Ray fought and succeeded in keeping his cool in the face of hearing two of the worst things that had ever happened to him referenced so flippantly. 'So I imagine you popped the cork off a bottle of champagne when you heard the news? Good fucking riddance, eh?'

'Something like that.'

''Ere, 'ave a look at this.' Sutter put his cigarette in the corner of his mouth and retrieved his phone before hitting its screen in a flurry of taps. ''Ere,' he said, handing it to Ray.

It was a picture of the back of a partially torn envelope with some writing scrawled on it. 'Zoom in,' Sutter prompted.

Doing so, Ray saw the two words of Howard Fain's poorly scrawled suicide note.

IM SORRY

'That's a real fucking tearjerker, that,' said Sutter, with a laugh. 'Back of a gas bill, Christ. What a mess. It's definitely his writing, though. Got me thinking maybe it were done under duress?'

Ray looked closer. 'I think doctors are famous for their terrible handwriting.'

'Funny you should say that, cos the last prescription Fain filled out was for himself. You heard of pentobarbital?'

'It's a barbiturate. It's used for anaesthesia or as a sedative.'

'Gold star. There were a bit left in the syringe in his hand.' He dropped his cigarette and ground it out. 'The Yanks use it to put bad people to sleep. It's not available at Boots, but probably not hard for an ex-quack to get his hands on some.'

'I wouldn't have thought so,' said Ray, looking up from the ashen scorch mark on his pavement.

'Bit strange he jabbed himself in the neck, though.' Sutter scratched at an unkempt eyebrow. 'You would have thought the arm . . . but no, a needle to the jugular. Strange that, eh?'

Ray shrugged – now realizing why Sutter had mentioned needles earlier.

'But saying that, I suppose a doctor would know that's the most direct route to the heart. Did ya know that?'

'Makes sense. It's literally closer.'

Sutter ignored Ray's glib reply. 'So, we've got a drug he knew how to use and a suicide note telling us he's sorry for the terrible things he'd done. To borrow from our Yank cousins – looks like a fucking slam-dunk.'

There was no question asked for Ray to answer so he stood with his hands loosely at his sides, relaxed and confident, not defensive.

Sutter, unfazed, lit another cigarette. After a deep drag he turned and looked down the empty street. 'So, what do you think about this guy hanging around the back of Fain's house?' Sutter knew John would have told him. 'The old girl across the street spoke to him. Said he were dressed in black. Had a hat on, the peak covering his face. I asked her, could you tell if he were black or white? She said what she could see of him looked orange in the streetlights. Whadda ya reckon, Ray? Do you think an Oompa Loompa did it?' Sutter laughed at the thought. 'Said he were a friend of Fain's. But here's the funny bit. She thinks this guy were wearing rubber gloves. The kind a doctor would wear. That's strange again, ain't it?'

Ray said nothing as Sutter took a drag.

'Eh, what car do you drive?'

'Mercedes E-class,' Ray replied, feeling his Adam's apple fat and sluggish in his throat.

'*You are not going to believe this,*' said Sutter, exaggerating each word as if Ray were a pantomime audience. 'That's the make of the car the old girl thinks the guy in the alley were driving. What a coincidence.'

'It's a popular car, Nick.'

'Is that it?' he asked, nodding to a black Mercedes parked at the kerb.

'It is.'

Sutter read out the number plate. 'I wonder if it activated ANPR on a recent trip up North?'

'Why don't you ask me what you came here to ask me, Nick?' Ray said, tiring of the dance.

'OK.' Another quick toke. 'Did you kill Howard Fain?'

'I did not,' he replied, calm and even.

'Oh, I think you did. Night before he died you were there, weren't ya? How'd you say it in army lingo – a recce?'

'I'm a cop. I believe in the rule of law. Fain went to prison. He served his time.'

'Where were you on the night of the twelfth and thirteenth?' Sutter asked, changing gears.

'Home alone.'

'Can anyone corroborate that?'

'I wouldn't have been alone if they could.'

He gave a tight, humourless laugh. 'How about a security camera? You got one of them?' Sutter looked around Ray at his house. 'They're all the rage nowadays.'

'Never felt the need for one.'

'Of course not. You take care of your own security, don't you, Ray?' the detective said with an unpleasant grin, throwing his cigarette into the gutter. 'You're in a tough spot. Cancer has a way of shifting priorities. Existential crises and all that. You were a soldier; you've killed people before. Probably enjoyed it. And I bet it's not a skill that's easily forgotten. Here's what I think happened. I think you got in that car —' another nod to the Mercedes — 'and drove to Salford. I think you put on some gloves, cos all us cops are swabbed and printed on day one, then you forced Fain to write a shitty little note, and jabbed a fucking needle in his neck. How does that grab you?'

'It doesn't.'

'Fucking grabs me.'

'Got any proof?'

Ignoring the question, Sutter leaned in. 'I'm not unsympathetic, Ray,' he said conspiratorially. 'I get it. I mean, who wouldn't want to kill the man who . . .' He brought his nicotine-stained fingers to his chin in thought. 'What did he do to your kid again? Beat her up . . . or diddle her or summat?'

Ray felt his scar tighten. He stepped to Sutter, immediately silencing him.

'If you use one more word that makes light of what that man did to my daughter, this jaunt from Manchester to come see me will have a very different conclusion to the one you had in mind.'

Sutter started in sudden shock and fear, looking into Ray's fire and brimstone glare. Until slowly . . . a smile started to spread across his face and his eyes found their clarity once again. 'There he is. There's the man who killed Howard Fain. Fucking deadly.'

Ray stepped back full of instant self-loathing. He had been drawn into Sutter's trap.

'You're wrong,' he said, drawing in a deep breath. 'I'm the man who won't be insulted outside his own home.'

'I were insulting your daughter, Ray. Not you. You got very angry because of the offensive words I were using. God forbid anyone actually hurt her . . .'

'I did not kill Howard Fain.' It was all he could think to say.

Sutter nodded in an I've-got-the-measure-of-you fashion. 'You did this job for years. You're familiar with that feeling. That feeling when you absolutely know it's the guy who's standing in front of you. *He did it*. You'd bet the fucking house on it.'

'I have had that feeling. But I always had to prove it,' Ray said, turning and reaching for his house keys. 'Goodnight, Nick.'

31

'He had a change of heart and decided to finish what I started.'

Rose, Gog and Luke nodded their understanding, which was followed by a long pause. The TV was muted so all that could be heard was the muffled babble of the clinic beyond the door to their small treatment room.

'What?' Ray finally asked.

'Sooo . . .' Gog began, reaching up to scratch his head. 'You went to his house to do him in . . . didn't . . . and then he did it for you the next day?'

'Yes,' said Ray, frowning. 'That's exactly what happened.'

The three of them exchanged awkward glances.

'What?'

'I have to say . . . it does sound a bit . . . far-fetched,' Rose said, wincing.

'Yeeeaaaaah,' Luke added. 'You *literally* told us you were going to make it look like a suicide, Ray.'

'*Yes*,' he replied, forcing himself to keep calm. 'But I didn't. He actually *did* kill himself.'

'Hey.' Luke shrugged. 'We're not here to judge. You killed the guy, you didn't kill the guy – who cares?' He turned to Rose and Gog. 'Goodbye, horrible, horrible monster man. All's well that ends well,' he concluded with a clap of his hands.

'*Hey!*'

They looked at Ray.

'I did not kill Howard Fain.'

Luke held up his hands. 'All right. OK,' he said, calmly. 'We're listening. Tell us exactly what happened.'

With the gun's muzzle pressed into his forehead, Fain screamed, high-pitched and terrified, '*NOOOO!*'

'Turn around and put your hands behind your back. We're going on a trip.'

Ray had already scouted the area and had found a secluded woodland not far from Cordwallis Street. Properly motivated, the distance could be easily walked. But that need not be a concern for Fain, who would be chauffeur-driven in the boot of Ray's car alongside a hold-all that contained a length of rope.

Fain turned, the gun tracing the outline of his skull as he did so, and put his shuddering hands behind his back. It was now time to use the electrical tape and cable ties in his pockets – and Ray would have, if his eyes had not come to rest on Fain's mantelpiece.

'How do you have that?' The thought that he had a similar set-up in his own living room did not escape him. '*Why?*'

Fain, whose bloodshot eyes had been clamped shut, due to the gun still pressed to his skull, carefully followed Ray's line of sight.

'I kept it on my desk at work,' he said, panting like a snared animal. 'Personal effects.'

Ray reached for the lone picture in the middle of the dusty mantelpiece.

They were outside a theatre. In the background, up a

short flight of steps, there was a set of golden doors. Above them, Ray made out the bottom half of a sign that read '*The Wizard of Oz*'. It must have been in the winter because they were all wrapped up in big coats. Fain was in the middle. One of his arms was wrapped around Odette's shoulder. The other was filled with a six- or maybe seven-year-old Chay. They all smiled happy warm smiles.

'Why do you have this?' Ray asked, quiet and distant.

Fain dragged his sleeve across his face. 'They stopped loving me. I never stopped loving them.'

Ray looked back to the picture.

He had never seen them all together.

Odette had spoken of her guilt and shame during and after that time and Ray could see it now in the photograph. The warmth of her smile faded before it could reach her eyes, deep and brown, almost black – they gave her away.

Ray thought of how Odette might react to what he was doing. How might she have looked at him? Would he have seen shame and disappointment? The gun he held suddenly felt impossibly heavy. The items in his pockets seemed brutal . . . *evil*.

She would not want this.

He fought the thought. *She's gone, she would never know.*

But the little girl on the other side of the picture . . . if Ray went to the woods tonight – she might know. There were no guarantees that Ray's plan was watertight. There were a lot of variables, the woman in the alley tonight to name but one. If the authorities worked out it was him then Chay *would* know.

How might she react? Revulsion? Hate? Would her stepfather killing her biological father really fix what was broken in her? Another thought nagged at Ray: was Fain truly rehabilitated? Might there be a chance of reconciliation between him and his daughter in the future. She had lost her mother. Could Ray rob Chaynnie of her father too?

It was then that Ray realized who he was there for – *himself.*

He lowered the gun.

Fain sensed that the picture had changed something. He lowered his arms and turned to face Ray. He could see that the gun was now at his side.

'Thank you,' he said, with sobbing relief.

'Shut up.'

Ray placed the picture back on the mantlepiece. He regarded Chay's innocent smiling face for a time. 'Thank the little girl in the picture. The one you put in hospital . . . she just saved your life.'

Fain looked at the photograph. His lip started to quiver again. He bowed his head and tears fell to the floor.

Ray put the gun back beneath his jacket and started for the door.

'I promise I won't say a word,' said Fain, barely above a whisper.

'I don't care what you do, Howard.' He gave the rank hovel one last contemptuous glance. 'Nobody does.'

And that was how he had left Odette's ex-husband, Chay's father, the once great and respected Dr Howard Fain, quivering in fright, broken and alone.

32

'So he really did kill himself,' said Luke, goggled-eyed. 'Are you glad?'

'Still ambivalent,' replied Ray.

'What does that mean now?' asked Gog.

'Uncertain.'

'If your stepdaughter can find peace from his death then at least he did something right – offing himself,' said Rose.

'Maybe. The scars are still there. But it's my hope that they'll fade in time.'

'They will,' said Rose.

Ray nodded his agreement but the gesture clashed with the lines on his brow.

'There's something else,' said Luke.

'Yeah . . .' Ray ran a hand over his face. 'A neighbour saw me.'

'Oh,' said Luke, with a note of doom. 'Do you think she could identify you?'

'I don't –' Ray began, until a pair of voices on the other side of the door brought their conversation to a stop. Through the meshed glass they could see Donna and another nurse talking animatedly. They caught the latter end of Donna's sentence '. . . *and then I said, thanks but I'm watching my figure*', which resulted in the other nurse bursting into laughter before they moved on.

All eyes turned back to Ray.

'I don't think she could make out my face,' said Ray, tracing a finger along his scar. 'But she did notice I was wearing surgical gloves.'

'Fuck a duck!' said Luke, his mouth full of cringing teeth. 'Nothing says murderer more than surgical gloves worn outside of an operating theatre.'

'Yeah. It's bad . . . and she knows the make of my car.'

'Bloody 'ell, Ray. This is going from bad to worse,' said Rose, throwing her hands in the air. 'So she saw the gloves. She might have seen your face. And she can identify your car. Bloody amateur hour!'

Ray had no comeback for that.

'But did she get your licence plate?' asked Luke.

'I don't think so. But anyway, there are two ways to track someone's movements in a car. Mobile phones and ANPR. That's Automatic Number Plate Recognition. You've probably seen the signs telling you that you're in a ANPR zone.'

'Oh yeah. I've seen 'em,' said Gog.

'Well, I left my phone at home, and I switched number plates with a similar-looking car before I drove to Manchester. I returned the borrowed plates when I got back.'

'Well, now we're talking. Not so amateur,' said Luke, with a look for Rose. 'That's some Jack Reacher shit.'

'Pretty standard knowledge that any cop would have. DI Sutter included. He's not stupid. Rightly so he's picked up my scent. I'm a suspect,' he finished, bleakly.

'Bollocks,' Luke tutted. 'What are you going to do?'

'I think I've done enough,' he concluded, shaking his head in despair. 'All I can do now is hope for the best.'

'Well, at least he's dead,' said Rose, in search of a silver lining. 'That's something, yes?'

Ray considered her words, searching himself for an honest reply. 'You know what? I'm not ambivalent. Uncertain,' he added, with a glance at Gog. 'I am glad he's gone.'

'Ray,' began Gog, with a sad shake of his head, 'all I would ask is you seek forgiveness.'

Ray gave a world-weary sigh. 'Yeah? And where would I find that?'

'In the welcoming embrace of our Lord and Saviour Jesus Christ.'

'Here we go,' muttered Rose.

'You're talking dark deeds,' Gog continued, unabashed. 'Shine a light on them, Ray. Seek forgiveness.'

'Forgiveness?' scoffed Rose. 'If you ask me, the man deserves a bloody medal.'

'It's a sin to kill no matter what you think about it, Rose.'

'Your so-called God is killing *you*, you silly boy,' she said with raspy indignation. 'If you're right, and there is a God – he gave you cancer!'

'I have faith in his plan. God will either give me a miracle and heal me –'

'Yes, and an onion under your bed at night will cure bowel cancer.'

Unflustered by Rose's sarcasm Gog continued. 'Or I will see him in the Kingdom of Heaven, soon.'

'Miracle? Kingdom of Heaven?! Listen to yourself! No wonder you have the wrinkle-free brow of the truly ignorant.'

Gog either didn't understand or chose to ignore her.

'Come on, Rose,' said Luke. 'We're all trying to get

through this the best way we know how.' Instead of what should have been a customary barb for meddling in her affairs, to Luke and Ray's shock, the old woman gave a small nod of contrition. 'Anyway, if wrinkles equated to intelligence then you must be the most intelligent person who ever lived.' Luke giggled. Rose did not. 'Plus, my balls would be making better decisions. Am I right, big man?'

Gog did not react to Luke's quip or Rose's unprecedented partial apology, because he was looking out of the room's window with a misted-over look on his smooth face.

'There's a lot of history where I come from, back in the Valleys. Good history, important. We helped build the world we live in. Did you know the roof of the White House, over there in America, was made in South Wales?' Gog asked, without taking his eyes from the window's non-existent view. The group looked on, unnerved by a reflective Gog. They shook their heads. 'It was. Pontardawe in late eighteen-something-or-other. Welsh coal melted the steel that made that roof,' he continued. 'That's something to be proud of. There was a lot of that in the Valleys back then, *pride*. And then, when I was a kid, the mines started to close. You're probably thinking – good. Who would want to go down a filthy, dirty, dangerous pit to mine that horrible stuff anyway?' Gog turned from the window and met their eyes. No answer was forthcoming. 'No one,' he said, looking back to the window. 'That's who, *no one*. It was terrible work. It took so much courage to go down there. To go far beneath the ground, tons and tons of rock above you, waiting to crush you, bury you where you can never see your family again.' He paused to run a hand over his bristly bowling-ball head. 'No man went down there lightly. But they went down there together. They were together in their struggle. Equals. My grandfather spent years working away in the dark and then he died from emphysema. It's sad, but he died surrounded by a family who loved him. Hundreds and hundreds of people turned up for his funeral to show their respects. That's what you did back then, everybody knew the sacrifices those men who went beneath the ground had made. When the mines went, all that self-respect, that feeling of community went with them. The men of the Valleys had to find a different way to show they were hard men.'

33

Dennis, a triangle of pints between his hands, made his way around the various chattering groups of weeknight drinkers towards his two friends who were sat at a shabby table in the far corner of the bustling, smoky bar of Pontydale Social and Working Men's Club.

Raising his voice to be heard over the sound of Oasis's 'D'You Know What I Mean', blaring out of a TV encased in a metal frame that was bolted into the nicotine-stained ceiling, Dennis said, 'Get 'em down 'ew,' placing the lagers on the table

'Ambassador! With these pints of flat lukewarm piss, you are really spoiling us,' said Icky, taking a greedy gulp, spilling some on his top that stretched over his large belly.

'You're a gentleman, Den,' said Gog, the drink disappearing in the clutch of his giant hand.

Icky flicked his Zippo and lit his cigarette in one deft motion.

'Christ. Choose one. Fat or smoking. You can't do both,' Dennis said, lowering his lean muscular frame into the seat opposite as Icky lit up.

'I look at it as a money-saving exercise. I'll be dead by the time I'm fifty, which means I'll save about thirty years' worth of money I would have spent living until I'm eighty.'

Dennis took a second to think. 'I must be getting drunk because that sounds like it makes sense.'

The friends laughed.

Three big men, sat at the next table along, looked over. The biggest of them by far (wearing a vest so all could enjoy the sight of his massive, pockmarked, spray-tanned shoulders) looked with just one eye as the other was hidden behind a swollen purple and black welt.

'Oi! If you wanna smoke, fuck off outside,' he said in a deep voice from a petite mouth.

Their laughter stopped.

'That shit wafting over here is getting on my fucking nerves.'

'That's fair enough,' said Dennis, with a polite pinched smile.

'No bother, Carl,' said Icky, stubbing out. 'I could probably cut back a bit anyway.'

Carl's heavily sculpted brows furrowed. 'I don't give a fuck what you do just don't smoke next to me,' he said, turning back to his table.

The danger had passed.

Dennis and Icky breathed a sigh of relief.

'Nasty-looking black eye that, Carl,' said Gog.

Dennis and Icky performed a mirror image of a palm to the forehead.

'Yeah?' said Carl, over his shoulder. 'You should see the other guy. He'll be shitting through a straw for a month.' The two goons with him laughed with excessive gusto.

By now the whole bar had heard about Carl's spat the previous evening with a 'Lump' from an adjacent Valley. Apparently, in the chippy, the Lump had made a disparaging comment about the size of Carl's head. Carl had retaliated by squirting vinegar in the Lump's eyes before attempting to put his head through the glass cabinet that housed the fish, pies and pasties.

Judging by the state of Carl's eye, it hadn't been a completely one-sided affair.

'You need a good steak,' said Gog.

'What!?' Carl scoffed, as if Gog had said the stupidest thing ever uttered.

'A steak,' replied Gog, unfazed. 'You should put one on your eye. That's what my nan says.'

'Good advice. I'll get a prescription off my butcher,' Carl said to more laughter from his table.

Carl Howring had always been mean. But it didn't take a degree in Psychology to identify the root cause of his anger. Carl's leaning towards wickedness originated from a deep insecurity about the size of his head. As a kid he was gangly, there wasn't a great deal of meat on him, but even so – there was no escaping the fact that his head was unusually small. A fact not lost on his peers who ribbed him mercilessly.

One day Carl decided to do something about it. He went to a gym with the intention of getting ripped. And he did exactly that. At first the natural way, and then – after seeing the results anabolics brought to some of the other gentlemen pumping iron – the unnatural way. The effects were immediate and staggering. Carl became huge and he revelled in the change of attitude this brought towards him. He had never been feared before – and he discovered he loved it.

There was just one small, minor detail Carl had overlooked in his realized quest to become a man mountain, and it was the very thing that brought about the nickname whispered far and wide. Carl's preposterous muscles now made his head look even smaller. *Ironic* was born.

Suddenly, a commotion at the entrance stole the attention of both tables. A group of women had come barrelling into the bar, and it was clear from their raised voices, drinks had been imbibed elsewhere.

'Lads! Lads! Lads!' shouted the most animated and glamorous of the group.

'All right, Taz!' bellowed the room's mostly male patrons as they made their way to the only table that remained empty in the now at-capacity bar.

As Taz and her friends settled into their secured area, and splintered off to the bar for drinks, Carl's chest became engorged to bursting point. His arms rippled with veins that carried enough blood to transfuse a Blue Whale. His head, now perched upon truly colossal shoulders, looked like a peanut on an ironing board.

'Wa's 'appnin' girls?' he said, attempting charming, but achieving threatening.

'Carl,' came their lukewarm response.

The girls quickly turned their attention to the neighbouring table. 'How're you boys doing?' asked Taz, but the enquiry was directed at Dennis.

'Good, thanks, Taz,' he replied with a warm smile.

'You girls are looking a bit sun-kissed,' said Icky, with a nod of appreciation.

'Just got back from Corfu. Bloody brilliant,' said Taz.

'What's Corfu?' asked Gog.

'What's Corfu?!' replied Taz, in amused surprise. 'I think you mean where's Corfu, Gog? It's an island in Greece.'

'Ahh, there you are then,' said Gog, edified.

'You'll have to excuse him, girls,' began Carl. 'He almost drowned in the sewer when we were kids. He was technically dead for ten minutes.' More laughter from Carl's goons.

'Come on now, Carl. That's not true. The doctor said it was less than that,' replied Gog, matter-of-fact. Carl's table laughed again. Dennis and Icky shifted uncomfortably in their seats.

'What were you doing in the sewer?' Taz asked Gog, but Carl answered for him.

'He was looking for Teenage Mutant Ninja Turtles, the fuckin' div!' he said, to more laughter.

'Come on, Carl . . . go easy, is it?' said Dennis, bringing their laughter to a sudden halt.

'Feeling brave after a few pints are we, Den?' Carl said, icily. 'I'd shut it. Unless you wanna get battered in front of the women 'ere?'

Dennis held Carl's gaze for as long as he dared before looking down at his pint.

'Let's get this party started!' said Taz's friend as she placed a tray of drinks on their table. Her happy drunk smile disappeared when she saw the tension on the faces of the surrounding tables. 'What's happened?'

'Just sit down, Steph,' replied Taz, nervously.

Gog, after seeing his friend spoken to in such a manner, felt the ember of a fire ignite in his stomach.

'I'll tell you what happened, Steph. Carl here's being a bit of a show-off.'

'Show-off!?' Carl aped, to goon laughter.

'Yeah . . . you're acting like a *big head*.'

The laughter stopped.

Pints were suspended in mid-air.

Cigarettes paused mid-drag.

'What did you say to me?' A challenge – *I dare you to say that again.*

'You're not being nice to my friends,' replied Gog. 'I don't like it.'

The expected explosion did not come. Instead, as he lowered his pint, Carl's face broke into a half-smile, half-sneer.

'There's the guy I was hoping to see this evening. We've been circling each other for a while now. What do you say we find out who the hardest man in the Valleys is?'

'I don't want to fight you, Carl.'

'Of course you don't. You'll lose.'

'I don't want to fight.'

'*Fucking pussy.*'

By now, the bar was completely silent. Someone had even turned the volume down on the TV.

'Why don't we just calm down, gents?' urged Dennis.

'Dennis . . . I said, SHUT YOUR FUCKING MOUTH!' Carl yelled, without taking his gaze off Gog. 'It's you or him, Gog. Either way someone is getting a fucking hammering.'

The ember started to expand.

Gog's chair screeched on the plastic floor tiles as he raised himself to his full six-foot-seven height.

'*Gog –*' Dennis began, but Gog silenced him with a raised hand.

'Outside.'

34

'Okey-cokey, campers! Let's get you unplugged,' said Donna, breezing in with her merry way.

'Whoaaah!' said Luke.

Followed by 'Just a bloody minute!' from Rose.

'What?' The nurse stopped in her tracks.

'Sorry, D. We were just in the middle of something,' said Luke.

'Be that as it may, you're at the end of your session, so-o . . .' She continued to perform the task she had come to do, beginning with Gog. He looked away as she pulled the needle from his vein. 'There you go.'

'Thank you, Donna,' he said, rubbing at the little plaster she had covered the tiny hole with.

She made her way to Ray. 'How goes it?'

'I'm OK.'

'Good,' she said, taking hold of his forearm. 'I gotta say, this is an unusual group.'

'How so?' he asked.

'Every time I come in here you're all chattering on about something or another. It's nice to see. All the other groups pretty much sit here in silence.'

'Trust me, I've tried sitting in silence. It doesn't work.'

'You're the strong and silent type, aren't you, Ray?' She flashed him a mischievous grin before she moved on to Luke's station.

'He's what I would call an economical linguist, Donna. Am I right, Ray? Why use fifty words when one will do?'

Ray nodded.

'Or none,' laughed Luke.

'One of the things I like about Ray, when he's speaking,' began Gog, 'you never hear him swear.'

'Thank you, Gog. I always thought of swearing as a tool. Use it too much and it becomes blunt.'

'Wow,' said Donna, as she removed Luke's needle. 'Did you just come up with that?'

'Umm . . . yes,' replied Ray, bashfully.

'That's excellent,' Donna replied, then, turning back to Luke, 'How are those headaches?'

'That medication is helping,' he said, relief written across his face.

'I'm glad,' she said, squeezing the younger man's upper arm before moving on to her next patient.

'Yep. Ray says shit like that all the time,' Rose said, as Donna went to work.

'How are you feeling, Rose?'

'If I were a dog they'd put me down,' she said, tearing off the plaster Donna had just applied to her arm.

'Lovely. Look, I need the room in about fifteen minutes. So you can finish . . . what *were* you talking about?' Donna asked, turning to Ray. 'Ray?' she prompted. He seemed to not hear her. 'Ray?'

'Sorry, Donna. Miles away,' he said finally, coming out of his reverie.

Luke answered for him. 'Sorry, D – the first rule of Chemo Club is –'

'– you don't talk about Chemo Club. Got it.'

'You know *Fight Club*?' Luke asked, impressed.

'Yes, Luke. I'm over the certificate age of eighteen. I've seen *Fight Club*. Fifteen minutes,' she said over her shoulder, breezing out of the door.

'Is it me, or is Donna kind of hot?' Luke said.

Ray gave Luke a roll of his eyes and turned to Gog. 'Please continue.'

The car park that served the high street was opposite Pontydale Social and Working Men's Club. Gog looked across the road at the crescent of people who had gathered there. The orange streetlights above muddied their features but even at a distance he could see their eyes wide in anticipation.

Carl, now bare-chested, stood in their centre. 'Come on!' he shouted in Gog's direction, pounding a fist at his heaving pectoral muscles.

Gog, his supporters in tow, took a deep breath and started to cross the road. In the brief time since the fight had been agreed word had travelled fast. From all directions people were heading to the car park.

Gog stepped into the crescent.

Carl was now at the opposite end with his broad back to Gog. His goons shouted incomprehensible grunts of encouragement at him, slapping his chest and shoulders at the same time.

'He looks angry,' said Gog, turning to Dennis and Icky.

'You're going to have to get angry too,' said Dennis.

'I am.'

'Good. Don't hold anything back. You can take this guy.' Dennis's words were reassuring but his face betrayed his true feelings.

Icky looked up at Gog with an expression not dissimilar to Dennis's. 'Yeah. Go get him, big man.'

Cars had turned in and blocked the road and their headlights shone onto the area where Gog and Carl would fight. Horns beeped in excitement as rabid faces stared out of rapidly steaming windows.

'Hold on to this for me, will you?' Gog unclasped his watch and handed it to Icky. He gave a tight nod as he accepted the heft of it in his hand.

At that moment, the gathered crowd produced a collective gasp. One bystander in particular managed to convey the horror of what was about to happen with a high-pitched scream. Gog turned just in time to see Carl's last couple of rapid strides as he charged towards him before he felt a fist impact his teeth.

Pain blackened his vision and silenced his hearing for a time. When it passed, and the roar of the crowd returned, he found himself on his back with Carl on top of him. Reflexively Gog's hands grasped and held whatever was closest to them. That served to stop what would have been a torrent of blows. Carl switched to the only unrestricted weapon he had. His forehead struck the same point of impact his fist had moments ago. Gog's incisor came away, a useless white stone in a mouth full of blood.

Carl pulled back for another attack. Gog turned his head to the side, blood gushing from his mouth, and pushed Carl with all his might, raising him a few inches too far for his head to connect. Above him he could see the angst-stricken faces of his friends amongst the crowd, screaming for him to get up.

Their desperation rallied him.

The maelstrom of liquid fire in his stomach began to spew great towers of magma once again. Carl felt Gog's hands tighten, vice-like, around his wrists. The few inches Gog had raised him to protect his face suddenly turned into a foot and a half. With a tremendous roar, Gog threw his attacker across the tarmac. Carl landed with a dense thump, tearing skin off his exposed shoulders and back.

But with extraordinary agility for such a big man he was quickly back on his feet and charging Gog, who in the meantime had only managed to raise his great bulk onto one knee. Carl swung his boot in the hope of adding his foot to the list of things to make contact with Gog's head that evening.

In the nick of time, Gog's well-placed forearm deflected what might have been lights-out contact. The resulting almighty *thwack* produced a groan from the crowd and knocked Carl off balance. Gog used that moment to get back on his feet and press the advantage. But again, Carl was just too quick. In a heartbeat he found his centre and redoubled his efforts.

As Gog tried vainly to protect himself from the barrage of blows that seemed to have no space for recovery between them, the screams of the crowd, the beeping car horns and the frightening toll of a bell rung by hard fists, in the centre of his brain everything blended together in a hellish soup of fraught confusion.

'Stop! *STOP!*' he screamed through swollen bloody lips.

But his cries were swallowed up in the surrounding cacophony.

He had to make Carl stop.

With his left arm covering his face for protection, Gog took his right arm and reached back as far as it would go. He balled his fist into a pink boulder and swung it as hard and as fast as he could. He felt his knuckles make impact with something hard . . .

The crowd went silent.

Gog took his arm from his eyes.

Carl stood before him swaying gently, arms loose at his sides. His mouth hung open and his eyelids fluttered rapidly, nothing but white to be seen underneath. Gog's blow presented itself as a long bloodless slit cutting a path through his eyebrow.

Carl fell to the ground.

The crowd, who had been holding their breath, erupted.

35

Luke and Rose whooped cheers of triumph. Ray politely clapped with an impressed grin.

'Fair play,' he said.

'Champion of the World!' Luke cried, as he swung a punch at the air. 'Sweet dreams, Ironic!'

'Took him down a peg or two, I should think,' said Rose, with a look of pride in Gog's direction.

'That's quite a story,' said Ray.

But Gog showed no joy at its conclusion. Instead, he looked at the big, calloused hand that had delivered the winning blow, and said, 'I fractured his skull, which caused blood clotting and bruising. From that night he's been physically and mentally disabled. Brain damaged. Carl can't walk on his own, he can barely talk. He can't even eat, he's fed through a feeding tube. He lives in a care home now.'

'Nooo,' said Luke, deflated, swallowing his joy. 'That's terrible.'

'I'm sorry about that, Gog,' sighed Ray.

'Am I missing something?' Rose asked, confused. 'Did we not want that pinhead to lose?'

'Not to the extent where he became a fucking cauliflower, Rose!' Luke glared at her, incredulous.

'He wanted to fight. They fought! What happened can happen. It wasn't Gog's fault,' said Rose.

'I was just showing a little empathy for what he went

through. I wasn't suggesting it was Gog's fault.' Luke turned to the Welshman. 'I wasn't.'

'Well, the police thought it was. They sent me to prison.'

'Fucking hell. This story is a roller coaster with a brick wall at the end of it,' Luke said, kneading his sunken eyes.

'How long?' asked Ray.

Gog raised two thick fingers.

'How long did you serve?'

'Thirteen months. Broke my nan's heart. I should have listened to her but I didn't and then I was in prison,' he replied, hanging his head in shame. 'That punch gave Carl a life sentence . . . and I was out so soon.'

'Obviously you didn't mean to hurt him like that. There's no way you could have known that was going to happen. It wasn't your fault,' Luke repeated, placing a hand on the giant man's shoulder.

'I hate what I did to Carl. And I'm sure he hates me for it . . . or if he could he would. But I don't hate him for what happened to me. I'm grateful to him.'

'Grateful?' Rose echoed in disbelief.

'Yes . . . prison was the best thing that ever happened to me.'

Ray smiled a knowing smile. 'Did you find something in there, Gog?'

'Not something . . . someone. God found me in that deep dark hole. Jesus said – I've not come to call the righteous but sinners to repentance. He replaced hatred and bitterness and gave me faith and gratitude in my heart. When I left it wasn't just prison that made me better, but God did too. There's not much to do inside, you see. The days are long and empty,' Gog said, staring into space as if remembering that time. 'Nan packed me a Bible. She said it would keep me company. Bless her, I had no intention of reading it. But one day I picked it up and I never put it down. I was a captive audience for God's word, you could say. I never thought I would go to prison and I certainly didn't think it would be the place where I found peace . . . but it was. That guilt for what I did to Carl would have destroyed me if not for God's promise of forgiveness. But even when our sins are forgiven it's important we still remember them. I still visit Carl and help him in any way I can.'

'You're a good man, Gog,' said Ray.

'You are too. But the things you've been doing . . . you can't hide your sins from God.'

'If there is a God I'll cross that bridge when I come to it.'

'Every moment falls under God's judgement. I'm worried about you now, Ray.'

'Don't be.'

'I'm worried what else you might do.'

'Gog . . .' said Ray, the beginnings of annoyance creeping into his voice.

'We have to leave. Fifteen is almost up,' said Luke, in an attempt to placate both Ray, Gog and Donna.

Ray took a breath. 'I appreciate your concern for me, Gog. And yes, it's probably warranted. I've done some . . . out of character things lately because I wanted to make a difference before I'm gone. But if I don't get arrested for Fain's death then all I want to do now is beat my cancer and be a father to my stepdaughter. That's all I care about. I'm done with all the other stuff, I promise you.'

And in that moment Ray truly believed it.

36

They gathered on the pavement outside the clinic. This was the first time they had been a group outside the confines of the chemo room (Ray had always been the first to leave their sessions with the quiet purpose of a bullet train). For a few lingering moments they regarded one another in this strange new harsh light-of-day environment.

'Well,' began Luke, 'I feel like I'm seeing my teachers out of school.' He pulled the thick long black coat he wore close to his thin body even though it was not cold.

Gog laughed. 'I know what you mean. I saw Mrs Birch at the local baths when I was a boy. Handsome woman. She was there in the pool in a swimming costume. Made me feel very peculiar, it did.'

'Poor Mrs Birch. It must have been quite off-putting seeing an eight-year-old homunculus dribbling at her in the pool,' said Rose, but her traditional scowl had genuine warmth woven into it.

'Behave, Rose,' grinned Gog.

'And with that, I'm off. Until next time, gentlemen,' she said, averting her gaze towards the road.

'That's my ride.' Luke gestured to a spotless Range Rover. The man in the driver's seat made a little wave. 'That's my guy, Billy.'

'Wow! Cool car. Looks expensive,' said Gog.

'You can't take it with you.' Luke shrugged.

'Tell that to the Pharaohs,' quipped Rose, with her eyes still searching the road.

Luke chortled, before he asked her, 'Rose, do you need a lift?'

'A kind gesture and please thank your poncey driver on my behalf. But I think I'll stick to my usual conveyance.' Right on cue a black cab appeared amongst the passing traffic. Rose placed two fingers between her thin lips and blew a surprisingly loud whistle. The car immediately pulled to the kerb. 'That's how you whistle,' she said, with a wink for Gog.

Before any of them could react she was in the back of the taxi and off down the high street.

'Curiouser and curiouser,' said Luke, watching the car disappear from view.

'Indeed,' Ray agreed.

'And then there were three. Just the wolf pack. What do you say, chaps? Fancy a bender? Billy will take us anywhere in the city.'

'Why do they call getting drunk a bender?' asked Gog. 'Funny word, isn't it?'

After a short ponder, Luke said, 'You know, I've never thought about it. But now you say it . . . yeah, it's a bit weird. What the hell is a bender?'

Both Luke and Gog turned to Ray.

Ray looked to the street for his own get-out clause of Chay parked and waiting but she was not there. With a sigh of resignation, he replied, 'Bender was the nickname given to a sixpence, an old coin that was used for about four centuries. The metal in the coin was made in part out of silver, which meant it could be easily bent. So, they started calling it a Bender. Twopence was enough for someone to drink in a tavern all day. Sixpence, well, that would get you thoroughly inebriated. Hence the term – going on a Bender.'

'This. Fucking. Guy!' Luke shouted loud enough to startle a passing woman who was pushing a pram. 'You're in the presence of greatness, madam,' he added, as she hurried on.

'That's amazing, Ray,' agreed Gog. 'How do you know that?'

'Things just stick in there. It's just stuff. It doesn't make much of a difference.'

'Well, it's enhancing my dark days,' said Luke. 'Now what do you say about that drink?'

'We're not supposed to drink a lot of booze. I think I'm just going to go home and have a rest,' said Gog.

'Come on, G-Unit! Why should my cancer have all the fun? I can kill brain cells with the best of them. Let's get fucked up! Ray?'

'I can't today. Another time?'

'I'll hold you to that,' Luke said, disappointed. 'Do you need a lift? Where do you live?'

'I'm down in Fullworth.'

'No way. That's not far from me. Where exactly?'

'Twenty-three Gilmour Avenue.'

'I know it.'

'Thanks for the offer, Luke, but my stepdaughter should be here soon.'

A car, coming to a full stop on double yellow lines, sounded its horn. The driver raised a hand in their direction.

'Who's this guy?' asked Luke.

'My lift, apparently,' said Ray, with a frown.

'That's not your stepdaughter.'

'No, it's not. I have to go.'

'All right,' said Luke, offering his hand. 'Take it easy, Ray.' Ray took the younger man's hand, followed by the Welshman's, noting the contrast between Luke's sharp, cold hand, and Gog's massive warm paw. He turned to depart but Gog held him firm.

'"Refrain from anger and turn from wrath. Do not fret, it leads only to evil. For those who are evil will be destroyed, but those who hope in the Lord will inherit the land." David, Psalm thirty-seven.'

Ray looked into Gog's big doe-like eyes and found himself smiling back into them even though he was growing weary of all the righteous concern.

'I'll keep that in mind,' he said, patting the giant's hand. Gog released him, and Ray made his way to the waiting car.

'This is becoming a bit of a habit.'

'A taxi courtesy of the taxpayer is not to be sniffed at,' said John, through the lowered window.

Ray got in and the car pulled off.

'Who's Count Dracula and King Kong back there?'

'They're in my chemo group.'

'How's that going?'

'Fine.'

'Good,' John said, before he turned off the radio. 'I spoke to Chaynnie. She seems to be doing OK.'

'She's stronger than she knows.'

'What that girl has been through . . .' He shook his head. 'Hopefully now he's dead she can get on with her life.'

'Hopefully.'

'Has Sutter called yet?'

'Last night. He was waiting outside my house.'

'He came to see you?' John replied in shock.

Ray nodded.

'Hmm.' He couldn't hide the concern on his face. 'What did he say?'

'He thinks I killed Fain.'

'He just came out and said it?'

'He did.'

'What's he got?'

Ray told him.

When he was finished John said nothing, choosing instead to concentrate on the road.

They sat in silence in the car's sparkling interior for a while. Ray watched John from the corner of his eye, waiting for him to explain the reason for this unannounced pick-up. But his brother-in-law stared ahead, his chiselled features inscrutable as he navigated the road in a seemingly directionless meander. 'This isn't the way –' began Ray, but John cut him off.

'Did Odette ever talk about our uncle, my mother's brother, Ken?'

It took Ray a moment to register the unexpected question. 'Umm, yes . . . she spoke of him fondly.'

'You would have liked him. He was a great guy. More of a father to me than an uncle. Unfortunately he died of cancer. Prostate. Twenty years ago – back then they hadn't made the advances that we have today,' he said, a disclaimer for Ray, it seemed. 'Anyway, he was a one-off. He truly didn't give a shit, zero filter. If anyone had a problem with him he was more than willing to accommodate them. An outspoken black guy, in this country, back then – that took balls. He taught me a lot; he always treated me like an adult even when I wasn't one. It would properly rub my mother up the wrong way. She would spend an entire afternoon just tutting at him and shouting – Kenroy! She didn't know the half of it. I remember when I was a kid he threw a bag into my lap, "Sex education," he said with a wink. I looked into the bag and saw an unlabelled VHS tape and a battered old *Razzle*.' John laughed to himself. Ray also laughed but truth be told he was starting to feel uneasy. *Where was this going?*

'One evening, close to the end, Ken came to dinner. It broke my heart seeing this giant of a man so withered and small. But he never let it get him down. He used to tap his head and say – I can still think big.' John smiled at the memory as he brought the car to a stop next to a grassy common. The view through the windscreen in front was filled by a row of tall townhouses set behind some even taller chestnut trees that made up the common's perimeter. Ray was not familiar with the area.

'He never lost that sense of humour,' John continued, looking out at the common. 'He was still outrageous, and Mum still spent the entire evening tutting and shouting "Kenroy!" while we were all sat around the table.

'I remember, about halfway through the meal, he had barely touched his food, but he did have a little swig of his wine here and there. Mum went to top it up, he put a hand over his glass and said – It goes straight through me. You wouldn't believe what this chemo is doing to me. My pee is the colour of Fanta.' John turned and looked Ray in the eye. '*Bright orange.*'

Ray's world went silent. It felt like the car's cabin had

suddenly become a small, pressurized capsule that threatened to crush him. *Pentecost*, he thought in despair, *the puddle between the recycling bins.* He saw the incriminating orange stain in his mind's eye.

'What happened?' John asked with a steely gaze.

If only he had dropped a refuse sack on top of it.

'What happened, Ray?'

'You already know. You got it right in the alley. All of it.'

'Why didn't you call me?'

'If I'd called you . . . well, you know what would have happened. I couldn't let that man take away the time I have left.'

John looked out the window at the townhouses, ran a hand over his hair, and blew out his cheeks. 'Jesus, Ray.'

A thought suddenly occurred. 'If you've known all along, why haven't you taken me in?'

'No prints on the knife, and as you know urine is an extremely unreliable way to identify DNA. Especially urine that's been lying in an alley that's a petri-dish of human waste. It was useless. But either way – *take you in*?' John repeated it incredulously. 'You think I was going to arrest my brother-in-law, my sister's husband, for James Pentecost. Not a fucking chance.'

'I don't know what to say.' Ray gave a tight relieved smile that was not reciprocated. 'Thank you, John. I'm sorry that I've put you in this situation.'

'Don't worry about me. Nobody's going to find out. I promise you.' John looked to the townhouses once again. Ray could tell there was more. Something else was weighing on him. After a protracted silence, John continued. 'There is one thing that's been bothering me.'

'And what's that?'

'*Fain*. I can't believe you would lie to me, swearing on my sister's grave as a cover –'

'I would never use Odette's –'

John held up a hand to silence him. 'I know you were there. I just know it, and so does Sutter. Tell me what happened, Ray. Did you kill him?'

'I did not.'

'But you were there?'

Ray looked away in shame. 'I snapped, John,' he said, in a hollow tone. 'Chay's been struggling recently . . . I snapped. I went to his home. I was going to kill him. But I couldn't do it. I swear to you he was alive when I left.'

'Tell me exactly what happened. Don't leave anything out.'

In the way only Ray could, he proceeded to tell John the finer details of his trip to Salford. The licence plates swap, the recced woodland area, the gathering at the Ol Bottle pub, the old woman in the alley, picking the lock, Fain begging for his life, the picture on the mantlepiece – everything.

John listened, enrapt.

When Ray had finished, a smile teetered on John's face. 'I knew you were there.' His smile broadened. 'That's what that visit to the station was all about. You wanted his address.' Ray sheepishly nodded. 'I should have known. No one in their right mind would ask for a cup of that coffee.' He gave a bittersweet chuckle. 'Sounds like you've been on a bit of a rampage recently. Look, as far as I'm concerned Fain and Pentecost can rot in Hell together. Case closed.'

Ray looked back at him dumbfounded. 'I don't know how I can ever repay you.'

'No need,' John said with a wave of his hand, bringing the discussion to a close. 'But Sutter, though, he's a whole different ball game.' His smile disappeared. 'He won't sweep Fain under the rug. The injection site on the neck? The "stranger" in the surgical gloves? Black Mercedes? He's close to making it officially what he wants it to be – a murder investigation.' His eyes darted about as if connecting the dots. 'I can see why you're a suspect. And it still feels off even though I now know the whole story.' He grimaced.

'I know.' Ray looked down into his lap. 'I've messed up, John. At every turn. I wanted to do good, punish the man that hurt our family . . .'

'I'll do what I can with Sutter.'

'I don't want you getting mixed up in this,' said Ray, with a hard edge returning to his voice. 'You've done enough.'

John turned back to the townhouses and his face instantly became grave. 'Maybe there's one last thing I can do for you,' he said.

Ray followed his line of sight.

'What's going on, John?'

He kept looking ahead as if he hadn't heard him.

'*John?*'

He gripped the steering wheel, his knuckles paled.

'Jennifer Moody.'

'The young schoolteacher?' said Ray. 'No leads?'

'Yeah. We spoke to the usual suspects, family, friends, known associates – but nothing, she's vanished,' he began. 'I don't need to tell you that when a happily married mother with no previous physical or mental health conditions goes missing . . . it looks bad, really bad. We were drawing a blank right up until recently when I was with the husband at their home, doing my best to assure him we were doing everything in our power to find her. As I was leaving, I noticed a stack of unopened letters. At first, I assumed he was too distraught with worry to bother with them. But then I noticed the name the letters were addressed to was different. I asked the husband who they belonged to and he explained they were for the previous owner. Turns out the Moodys had only lived there for nine months. Apparently the guy they bought the house off had moved not too far away and his new house was on Jennifer's work route. She had intended to drop their post off but hadn't got around to it. I thought, why not? I'll head over there and give him a once over. What's one more dead end?'

'What's his name?' asked Ray, as his pulse began to quicken.

'Peter Brooks.'

37

'When a stranger knocks on your door in the late evening, and let's say that stranger is me, black and six foot two ... well, the face staring back is generally peering around the door with a look that says – I'm going to call the police.'

'I hear you,' said Ray.

'Not Peter Brooks. The moment this guy opened the door I knew it was him. At first glance he looked absolutely unremarkable. Sixty-ish, average height, little soft around the edges. He has one of those beards that men of advancing years grow. It makes him look like a guy who wants to tell you all about his passion for model railways. He's plain white bread. If he was stood next to you in the queue at the coffee shop you wouldn't look twice. A real hide-in-plain-sight type.

'But the one thing he couldn't hide was that arrogance that *all* of these guys have. He swung the door wide open and just stood there with his hands tucked snuggly in Grandpa's brown fucking cardigan. Defenceless, big welcoming smile on his face without a care in the world. He was fearless.

'I explained why I was there and he changed the shape of his face to mimic concern before he invited me in without asking to see my ID. We sat in his drab living room. What do you do for a living? I asked. He says, I sell insurance. What kind? Life. I know. Terribly boring, but I tell you what, I'll outlive most rock stars. I imagined him practising the line in front of a mirror. I pressed on. Just you here? He says yes. So, you moved to an even bigger house on your own? I come from humble beginnings – it's always been a dream of mine to have some space, he explained, utterly unflustered.

'I took him through the details of Jennifer Moody's case. He said all the right things at the right time – how terrible, such a lovely family, I do hope she turns up, what is the world coming to?

'Joe Bloggs would have been convinced. But I could see that there was a normality to him that was forced. The whole thing felt like a carefully cultivated mask that he was looking out from behind.

'I thanked him for his time and left. Walking down his path, getting into my car, I couldn't see him but I knew he was watching me. Made my fucking skin crawl.'

'I'm not questioning your judgement,' said Ray. 'But what evidence do you have to support these feelings that he's kidnapped and killed Moody?'

John reached into his jacket pocket. 'This,' he replied and withdrew a clenched fist. He offered it to Ray. He extended his hand and John dropped 'this' into it.

Ray stopped breathing.

'I remember she got you a watch for your birthday and you wanted to do the same for her. You asked me if I thought she'd like it. Did I think it was as good as the watch she got you? I remember being confused by the engraving. Sugar?'

Ray turned the small steel-cased watch over.

He released a slow painful breath. Grief was crushing his windpipe, constricting it to the eye of a needle.

'Odette thought it was funny they called me that in the Marines, so she started using it . . . when it was just me and her,' he said, running a finger over the words. After long moments of staring at the engraving, 'Where did you find this?' he asked in a whispered growl.

'There,' said John. Ray followed the direction of John's finger and his eyes came to rest on the last townhouse in a row of four beyond the tall chestnut trees. 'I broke in.'

Despite the rage growing within him, Ray raised an eyebrow.

'Look, I had no evidence,' John said. 'Peter Brooks seems clean as a whistle. I couldn't find anything on him, and he hasn't done anything out of the ordinary – I've watched him go to work, come home. Nothing to justify a search warrant. But Brooks killed Moody. I'm sure of it. And I thought that if he did, there's a chance he also killed –' He couldn't bring himself to say her name. 'And I was right. You're holding the evidence.'

'A trophy,' said Ray.

'There's more like it in there.'

'You broke in? When?'

'Day before yesterday.'

'And now I'm holding key evidence. So this is definitely off the books.'

'Just you and me.'

He looked back to the watch.

'Middle-aged. Average height,' said Ray, thinking of gloved hands on a steering wheel and the position Odette's car seat had been left in. 'It's him.'

'Like you called it,' John replied. He then pointed to a solid wooden door connected to the right-hand side of the house. 'There's no alley at the rear so I used the side door to the garden and broke in through the back. When I found the watch . . . I thought for a second that I'd wait for him to come home from work. End him there and then. But I realized I was spiralling. Spur of the moment like that, anything could happen. It needed to be planned, done right. I started thinking about you. I knew you'd want to be part of it. I know how hard you've been trying to find the man who took her away from us. This guy needs to be put down, Ray. There's no way he gets to lie in a box for the rest of his life reliving his sick fantasies over and over. Let's you and I go in there and do what needs to be done.'

Ray turned from John and stared long and hard at the townhouse – the home of the man who had killed his wife. Despite John's wise thinking to put a plan in place, he fought to quell the urge to exit the car, walk across the green, enter the house and tear Peter Brooks limb from limb. Capitulating to impulses had not been favourable to him recently, he reminded himself.

What was the right thing to do? He should have walked away from Pentecost. He shouldn't have gone after Fain. As a result of that poor, reckless decision, Sutter now had him in his sights. Plus he wasn't even sure if Fain's death would actually help heal Chay in the long term? Would Brooks' death make a difference?

The answer came quickly – *yes, yes it would.*

The void that this man had created in their lives, the wound that would never heal, Chay would want an eye for an eye. Who wouldn't?

'I'll take it from here.'

'Not a chance.' John balked. 'We go in together.'

'No.'

'She was my sister –'

'I said *no*, John,' Ray ordered, stopping John's protest in its tracks. 'You've played your part. You've done enough. I don't want you anywhere near this. It's me. It has to be me.'

'*Ray* . . .' His face screwed up in anguish before he let out a frustrated huff. 'You can't mess around in there. Think Pentecost. Get it done quick. Don't let a word come out of that snake's mouth. Don't take any chances.'

'I know what I'm doing.'

Ray clenched his fist around the watch. He had come to a decision and he was sure that this time it was the right one. Go to prison, avoid prison, in sickness or in health – Peter Brooks was already dead.

38

He opened the wardrobe and looked at the rail that still held Odette's clothes. Her scent had faded from their fabric but he could still remember which were her favourites and what she looked like wearing them. He passed his hand over a pink summer dress she had worn to a picnic in the park. She had wanted to bring extra bread to feed the ducks, but Ray had explained that bread wasn't a natural food source for ducks and geese. They were far better off being fed peas or sweetcorn or oats. She had laughed and asked where was this level of concern when he had ordered the crispy duck from their local Chinese.

Ray smiled at the memory. Despite the hell that she had been through, Odette had always had a way of reminding him that life needn't be so serious. He pushed the bulk of her clothes to the side and revealed a safe set into the wall. Turning its dial in four quick movements, he opened the door and reached inside it, and gripped cold steel.

For the want of a better term – this gun was a family heirloom, given to him by his mother, by way of his father. It might have been eighty years old but it had been kept in perfect condition. Even though Ray was sure the ammunition was dry and preserved, before his trip to Salford, for peace of mind, he had taken the gun deep into a deserted woodland and fired a single round into a conifer.

Looking at it, feeling its solemn weight in his hand, Ray

thought how peculiar it was that this model of firearm, which had killed so many people in two dreadful wars, would conjure up memories of his parents.

Ray, an only child, had been a surprise. The day he came into the world his father, Morris, was fifty-two, and his mother, Nancy, was forty-one. He was never meant to have them for long. Fifteen years later, Morris died of a brain haemorrhage on a plane returning from a holiday in Spain. Ray would have just over a decade longer with Nancy. She died in his twenty-sixth year (which meant his parents were the same age when they died) from ovarian cancer ... yes, cancer was already in the family. Ray felt lucky that his mother had lived long enough to see him join the armed forces, inevitably following in his father's footsteps. She was immensely proud.

All these years later he still missed her terribly. His mum had been the most caring, nurturing person, gentle and kind to a fault. Even as a young boy he could see that his father relied on her greatly to pull him out of a periodical malaise that could last for days. Ray hadn't understood why his father would disappear into himself like that until one night not long after his tenth birthday.

He had woken needing the loo. Setting off for the bathroom, avoiding the creaks on the landing as he passed his parents' bedroom, he heard a noise from downstairs. To him it sounded like a wounded animal ... something or someone in pain. Nervously, he made his way down towards where the noise came from. Peering into the living room, he saw his father sat in his comfy chair bathed in the light of the TV, which was just showing static at that late hour. In the dim light he could see in one hand his father held a glass of whisky, and in the other – a gun.

'*Dad?*' he said without thinking, fear controlling him.

Morris turned with as startled a look as the whisky would allow. He dragged his sleeve across his wet eyes. The action brought the gun inches from his head.

'Kiddo,' he said, attempting a sloppy smile. 'What are you doing up?'

'S-sorry, Dad. I . . . I heard a noise . . .' They looked at one another in the half-light for a long moment. 'Are . . . are you . . . all right?' It felt odd for Ray to ask his father such a grown-up question.

'Umm . . . yeah.' His dad blinked some sense back into his face. 'Yeah. Of course. I'm fine,' he concluded, stronger now, sounding more like himself.

'OK . . . goodnight,' Ray finally said, turning towards the stairs.

'Wait a minute. Come here.' Ray stood rooted to the spot. 'It's all right. Come sit with me.'

Ray made his way into the room, his feet cold on the threadbare carpet, and sat on the settee opposite his father.

'Have you seen one of these before?'

Ray looked at the gun resting flat in the palm of his father's hand. He had not seen one that looked like this before. He shook his head.

'It's a Luger pistol.' His dad tossed it into the air and, with startling speed and accuracy considering the half-empty bottle beside him, its grip landed perfectly in his fist with his index finger resting above the trigger along the weapon's side. 'It was designed by an Austrian named Georg Luger. A revolver has a chamber that spins.' He placed his finger on the trigger and looked along the gun's sights at the flickering TV screen. 'The Luger has a stationary chamber. Makes it lighter, reliable, more accurate.' He lowered the gun and made it flat in his palm once again. 'I took it off a dead German. A Nazi.' He looked up from the gun. 'They teach you about the war in school yet?'

Ray nodded. Whether this pleased his father or not he could not tell as his gaze was fixed back upon the gun.

'Yeah. *He was a Nazi*,' he repeated, his voice now distant and strange. 'But . . . he was also a scared young man. Terrified. Just like I was.' He sipped at his whisky. 'I took this from him, not as a trophy, but as a reminder that what happened was real. I didn't want time to cloud what I did . . . what I became. When I hold this I can see the moment he left this world – at my hands – as clear as day.'

Ray had no idea how to respond.

His dad smiled in a way that suggested he knew and that was OK.

He placed his glass on the side table.

'Do you want to hold it?'

Ray looked at the gun, his eyes full of fear and excitement. 'Yes,' he said, breathless.

His father checked the safety lock at the gun's rear. Satisfied, he handed the pistol over.

Ray was immediately surprised by its weight. His father had said the gun was light but considering that the only gun Ray had ever held was his Challenger cap gun, the real thing felt frighteningly heavy – deadly.

'It's known as the Luger or Luger P08, but its full title is the Pistole Parabellum,' his dad went on. 'That comes from the Latin phrase, *Si vis pacem, para bellum*, which means "If you wish for peace, prepare for war."'

39

That was the only time his father had ever spoken to him about the war. It would be years later, after Morris's untimely death, when Ray next saw the gun. When Ray became age appropriate, his mother gave the Luger to him.

Now, as Ray sat on a half-empty bus, his head hung low on the back row (wearing the same outfit he had worn for his house visit with Fain – black bomber jacket, black baseball cap), he recalled her words. *It's a horrible thing. I don't know what to do with it. Maybe you do?*

He could never have known then that it would be this . . . or did he? Why else did one keep an untraceable secret gun, but for occasions such as this? A shiver ran along his spine. He took a focusing breath and forced himself to drop his self-indulgent pondering. There was a job at hand and it would not go the way of Howard Fain. He had intended to kill Fain, serve him justice, but his resolve had faltered the moment he had seen that picture on the mantlepiece.

There would be no such reprieve for Peter Brooks.

John had stressed that regardless of his appearance Brooks was an extremely dangerous man who Ray should give no quarter – *make it quick*, he had said.

Quick. Slow. Ray didn't care as long as Brooks took his last breath tonight.

After alighting the bus, Ray walked away from the

streetlights and into the blackness of the grassy common. Almost invisible, black on black, he removed another pair of surgical gloves (*caught gloved-handed?* he thought, his lips curling against his teeth as he pushed aside the annoyance the gloves produced) from his pocket and put them on as he stood watching the last townhouse beyond the chestnut trees.

The house was made up of three storeys. On the ground floor, a door at the top of a short run of stone steps was situated between windows that looked out onto a stout olive tree and a metal gate and railing that separated the house from the outside world. Curtains prevented Ray from seeing in. But the brief movement of a shadow past the glass in the door told him someone was home.

He made his way to beneath the chestnut trees. He was about to cross the street when a shooting pain ripped through his pelvis and lower back. It forced him into a crouching position. He screwed his face and stifled a wail with a fist to his mouth. He had had some discomfort in that area before now. But this was new – severe. He was buckled.

'*No. Not now . . . no-o-o . . .*' he pleaded, through long quivering breaths. He stayed crouched in that way for a time until whatever it was twisting his bones started to slowly release its grip.

Eyes still closed, he reached for an old Marine adage. '*Pain is weakness leaving the body.*' He breathed deeply in through his nose and out his mouth until the terrible sensation became a memory.

Whatever it was, this was not the time to give it consideration.

Ray rose and moved out from beneath the chestnut trees. Tentatively, willing his body to work with him, he crossed the street and stepped onto the pavement two doors along from Brooks' townhouse. He then began a slow amble that took him past the home of his quarry. John had broken in so Ray had to assume there were no security cameras. But he still felt the need to check. Maybe there were security lights in operation at night? After a few furtive glances he was happy to confirm that neither devices seemed to be present.

To the left, the house was connected to the neighbouring property. To the right, butting up against a high wall that defined the property's perimeter, was the wooden side door John had used to gain access via the garden at the rear.

Calming the pounding in his chest, Ray took an internal inventory of his body, searching for weakness, twinges that might expand to something more debilitating. There were none – although he did feel his strength had been depleted by the episode. Enough to postpone his meeting with Peter Brooks?

Not even close.

As casually as possible, he opened the wrought-iron gate. Thankfully, greased hinges meant the action was carried out in silence. With the same casual manner, he passed under the curtained windows into the welcome relief of the shadowy area that housed the wooden side door. He then took hold of a ring connected to a latch and turned it. In both directions it was met with resistance. It was secured from the inside. After a brief unsuccessful survey for footholds that might help him scale the door, he stepped back and looked into the street. A car passed by, followed by another, but there were no people around. He looked to the front of Brooks' house.

'*Plan B.*'

He reached into his jacket for the Luger and walked towards the front door. En route a quick glance into the light saw no shadowed movement from within. He gingerly mounted the steps and looked through two narrow strips of frosted glass in the upper half of the door into the light of the foyer. He raised the gun and reached for the door's brass knob. Holding his breath, he slowly turned it.

Locked.

No big surprise, thought Ray.

It was too bright and too exposed to pick. There was only one option left to him – ring the doorbell.

Ray rehearsed the scenario in his mind. Ring the bell. Wait for Brooks to open the door. Barrel him into the house at gunpoint. Kill him. There was only time for one pass of the plan as he had now been standing in the doorway for a conspicuous period.

He held the gun behind his back and pressed the doorbell. A long silence followed the bell's last ring. Nothing could be heard from inside the house; even the empty street behind him seemed to hold its breath in anticipation. For a moment, Ray began to question whether he had actually seen that shadow inside. Maybe it had been a trick of the light? Passing car lights, perhaps? He was about to push the bell again when the sound of footfall on wood brought his attention back to the door.

A shadow grew in the door's panes. With one and a half

inches of wood separating them, Ray watched a man, his features a jumbled mess in the frosted glass, unlock the door. As the door swung open, and with the sound of blood pounding in his ears, he felt his hand tighten around the gun's grip.

But despite his intention to charge Brooks the instant he opened the door, Ray couldn't help but capitulate to the need to give a face to the faceless man who had haunted his dreams. He had to see the last thing Odette had ever seen before she was taken away from him. He had to look Brooks in the eyes.

He hesitated.

With a broad welcoming smile, Peter Brooks said, 'Hello.' And then thrust something into Ray's chest plate.

Ray's central nervous system exploded in a hail of sparks. Rooted to the spot as his brain violently shook in his skull, 50,000 volts coursed through his body like wasps under his skin. The circuit-breaker popped inside him and mercifully the world faded to black.

40

Ray blinked his way back into consciousness. The blurred outline of a figure stood before him in silent regard. Slowly, Peter Brooks, the man Ray had been hunting for the last two years, came into focus.

'Welcome back, sleepy head,' Brooks said, in a voice that was surprisingly pleasant – warm and fuzzy, the kind that could sell a funeral plan to the over-fifties. 'I thought I was going to have to throw a bucket of water over you.' Despite the sentiment he smiled kindly through the hole in his dense salt-and-pepper beard.

A shaded bulb above cast the outer reaches of a windowless room of concrete into shadow, but it shone down brightly on Brooks, hiding his eyes in a pair of black featureless pits that raised the hairs on the back of Ray's neck.

'What am I going to do with you? Tricky.' He ran a hand through his beard. 'I think we're past the let bygones be bygones stage. Very tricky,' he concluded with a tut.

Ray's body ached from the taser shock but that was the least of his immediate worries. He couldn't move. He was held captive in a metal chair. The blood in his hands throbbed stagnant below straps which were fastened to the chair with ferocious bite into his bare skin (the bomber jacket, hat and surgical gloves were gone). His ankles were secured in a similar fashion to the chair's legs. But by far the worst aspect was the leather strap across his forehead, compressing the back of his skull against mercilessly hard steel. His eyes were the only part of him that could move freely and they did so with a rising panic he found difficult to master.

'I know. Sorry it's a bit dramatic. Bit OTT. But there's a reason they use this set-up in all the films . . . it bloody works.' Brooks laughed politely at his own quip as he started to unbutton his cardigan. Removing it, he draped it neatly over his arm. Ray read the white printed words on his black T-shirt – *Lady Killer*. Seeing this, Brooks said, 'My nephew got it for me.' He shook his head coyly. 'And he has no idea. How funny is that?'

Ray did not answer.

'I suppose I'll have to update my wardrobe to *Gentleman Killer*.' He paused for a laugh that did not come. 'No? Come on, that's funny.'

More silence.

'You don't say much, do you?' With a shrug he turned and walked into the shadow. Now hidden from view, he was just a voice from the black. 'I suppose I'll have to lead the introductions – I am the promise of horror.'

With all the strength Ray could gather, coupled with a guttural growl, he pulled at the wrist straps. For long, agonizing seconds the veins in his arms and neck throbbed in exertion . . . but alas, it was no use. Although, he noted, the right strap did feel slightly looser than the left.

'You're going to hurt yourself doing that,' his captor said, pushing a surgical tray on wheels out of the shadows. It rattled its way across the concrete until it came to a stop inches from Ray's right hand. Its lower shelves held gauze, needles and medicines. A plasma pack hung from a rod fastened at its side. Seeing the hanging sack, Ray thought, with grim irony, that there were worse places to be sat than his chemo chair.

From there, his eyes came to rest on the only item upon the shiny top tray – a leather bundle.

'Normally my subjects would give anything to leave. But here you are desperate to get in.' Brooks reached into his pocket and held up his mobile phone. 'Hidden cameras. You can't be too careful nowadays. There're some nutters out there.'

What? thought Ray, fighting for clarity in his recently electrified mind. Had they been newly installed? Or had Brooks actually seen John break in? That might explain the taser and the heightened security. Evidently he had been lying in wait this time.

'You anything to do with that good-looking cop who came here?' asked Brooks, as if reading his mind. Ray said nothing. 'Is that how you found me? Hmm. Maybe I'll have to pay him a visit. I would like to see that face again. I always thought only the truly handsome can pull off clean shaven,' he concluded, stroking his beard.

It took all of Ray's willpower not to react to the threat towards John. Brooks stood watching him beneath the spotlight, staring through those twin black holes. After an unnerving amount of time he walked back into the shadows.

Ray's vision had started to adjust to the room's light and shade. With his head and neck fastened, his eyes strained to the left and saw a large floor-to-ceiling metal cabinet. Its contents he was *not* eager to see. Straight ahead, at the far end, Brooks stood before a small, high, narrow table.

Actually, no. It wasn't a table. Partial light from the far right of the room, from what looked like a set of stairs that went up, cast just enough light for Ray to see Brooks open the lid of a record player.

'Bit of music will lighten the mood.'

He pulled a small lever and the needle dropped. For a moment, the sound of crackling and popping was intertwined with Ray's laboured breathing before music started to play.

Brooks stood with his back to Ray, silently swaying to the music. In that moment Ray worked his right hand frantically. He was positive that it was becoming looser the more he worked it.

'*The very thought of you, and I forget to do. The little ordinary things that everyone ought to do . . .*' Al Bowlly sang. As he did so, Brooks drew the Luger from his waistband and quickly moved towards Ray.

Ray gave a start as Brooks pressed the muzzle to his scarred cheek.

'You wanted to come into my home and blow my brains out?' he said calmly, seemingly not put out at all by the prospect. 'You're a little beaten-up, aren't you?' he observed, tracing the line of his scar with the gun. 'Who are you?'

Ray was silent.

'I can only assume I've upset you in some way? Perhaps someone you love was there one day and gone the next?'

At that Ray wrenched at the arm straps again. '*You bastard!*' he spat through clenched teeth.

'So that's it. You're here for revenge.' Brooks retracted the gun. 'And how's it going?' he asked, with a soft joyless laugh.

He walked back to the record player (just as Glenn Miller's 'Moonlight Serenade' began) and placed the gun and his phone on top of it.

When his back was turned Ray worked some more on the right strap. He felt the blood begin to flow in his hand once again. It was definitely becoming looser.

Brooks re-emerged from the shadows and this time he was carrying a small video camera mounted on a tripod.

'Perhaps my most recent subject, Moody? Is she something to you?' he asked, distractedly positioning the camera so it was pointed at Ray. Following more silence from his captive he looked up at him. 'I'm going to get my answers. So, we can either have a bit of a gossip, or we can get straight to the part you really won't like. What's it going to be?'

Ray needed more time to work on the wrist strap. He needed to keep Brooks talking even though the thought of it made him sick to his stomach.

'Her name was Odette.'

'And who was she?'

'My wife.'

'And how did our worlds collide?'

'Two years ago . . . you murdered her.'

'*You're going to have to be more specific*,' he said, singing the words.

'She was a nurse. She left work one evening. You took her,' he said, numbly, 'drove her car to the outskirts of the city and left her in the high grass.'

Brooks stared back at him in quiet thought. Fine creases deepened into shadow on his forehead.

'No. Doesn't ring a bell.'

'*YOU FUCKING SON OF A BITCH!*' Ray roared as his body thrashed against the straps again.

Once Ray had settled into spent misery, Brooks said, 'You've got a really nasty temper there. I used to be the same until I discovered Jazzercize. Have you tried it?'

Ray looked back through a mist of pure hate.

'No? Well, it works . . . it's a lot of fun and a great way to stay in shape.' He blew out a breath. 'Look . . . your wife is in the past. Let's focus on the present.' He passed a tender hand over the camera. Ray looked into its lens as a little red light started flashing. 'It's important to catalogue my work. People will want to see what I create in this room. The perfect agony of it all. They can't get enough of it, can they? Everywhere you look – film, TV. The news. Murder, kill, rape, slaughter. Endless violence played out to a captivated, salivating audience.'

He reached for the leather bundle and unrolled an array of knives, ranging from small and precise to large and hacking, that glimmered in the light. The last item to be revealed, as the bundle flattened, was a compact metal hammer – the kind used for bone procedures.

Withdrawing a scalpel from its sheath, Brooks held it up and examined its deadly edge.

'Funny, isn't it? In any other room this scalpel might save a life.' He turned and looked into Ray's sweat-soaked wide-eyed gaze. 'Not in this one.'

He gave the scalpel a last look of admiration, returned it to the leather wrap, and then bent down to examine the camera's shot.

Ray desperately wriggled his right hand. His wet wrist was tantalisingly close from slipping out of the strap.

Brooks looked up from the camera lens.

'I was planning on having a quiet night in, a word jumble and a glass of wine, but here you are, the impala offering the lion its neck. You can get anything delivered to your home nowadays,' he concluded, with a broad smile. The needle scratched its way to the next track, 'Midnight, the Stars and You' by Ray Noble. 'This is just heaven,' he said, giddily heading to the record player to turn up the volume.

Ray pulled with all his remaining might at the strap. He felt as if it were just a fraction of an inch from slipping off. His only chance of escape was about to come. He needed to make it count. *Slash hard, deep and fast*, he thought, as a voice hissed into his ear.

'*How are you coming along with that strap?*'

Brooks had circled around to appear behind him. Ray froze.

'You didn't think it would be that easy, did you?' He grabbed the strap and pulled it tight, equalling the left's painful grasp. 'I made the right one loose on purpose. And look how close my instruments were to your hand. Such a shame.' He looked at Ray as a mother might look at her child who had missed the potty. 'You could have opened me up like a bloody geyser.'

Leaning in, he brought his face inches from his now fully incapacitated prisoner. '*Ye-e-esss. There it is.* I can see the light of hope fading away in your eyes. You finally understand that this is the place of your death. This is where the curtain comes down,' he said, relishing every syllable of every word, his mouth wet and hanging open, hungry for Ray's torment. 'I'm no amateur. Unlike your wife, you're not in the presence of some ham-fisted dullard. I don't dump bodies in the high grass, I transform them here in my black theatre.'

'But . . . b-but . . . *the watch?*' Ray sputtered.

'The what?'

'You had my wife's watch.'

'Watch?' His mouth snapped shut. 'I don't know what you're talking about. This is becoming quite tiresome. *Don't ruin this for me.*'

For the first time, close up, Ray could see the man's eyes. They were green and piercing despite the gloom. Something in them stared back at him. With a building sense of horror, he finally understood – *truth*. Brooks was telling the truth. He had not killed Odette.

Which meant . . . *No. God, no. Please, no. It can't be true?*

Ray's chest cracked open. Cold air poured into the gaping chasm of his despair and shattered his heart into a million grief-stricken pieces. Brooks was not the man who had killed Odette. He was the man who would kill Ray. Chay would have lost both of her fathers and Odette's killer would never be brought to justice. His failure was complete.

Brooks saw Ray's eyes glassing over, 'Now, now!' he said, clicking fingers in his face. 'Stay with me.' Ray blinked in shock and the tears began to roll down his pale cheeks. 'I need you present! Do you understand?' He grabbed and held Ray's face. 'This is my moment. *See me, or I'll cut your eyes out!*'

Ray forced his eyelids open and saw multiple blurred snarling images of Brooks through his tears.

'Good. Now let's have some fun, shall we?' Brooks took a breath. Finding his calm, once again he reached for the scalpel. 'There is a question that has sat at the centre of my being for as long as I can remember. How much of a person can one cut away before they die? In the beginning, I admit, I found the frustrating answer to be – not much. But that was a long time ago, and practice makes perfect. My last subject,' he said with a wistful look. 'Spectacular. I peeled and chopped until there was nothing left, and she was with me every step of the way. Incredible woman. What do you say? Are you equal to her stamina?'

Ray blinked away the last of his tears.

Brooks was right. All hope had abandoned him. What remained in its place was pure desolation. He was broken. It was time to accept that this really was the end. He mentally said goodbye to Chay, and told Odette that he would be with her soon. Then he pushed their images from his mind. This was no place for them. He took a shallow, shaky breath and met the killer's gaze.

'Let's find out.'

'That's the spirit.' Brooks' tongue traced the edges of his lips as he leaned into Ray. 'Now, let's start by reopening old wounds.' He guided the scalpel towards Ray's cheek. Bracing himself, Ray felt the metal of the chair's edges dig into the palm of his hands.

Suddenly, an almighty crash brought the scalpel to a halt a hair's breadth from slicing open Ray's jagged crescent scar. Brooks quickly turned in shock to see his record player and its stand upended in a heap on the floor. From there, he slowly moved his eyes to a massive black shadow.

The shadow spoke. 'I'll use this if I have to.' The Luger, gripped in a big, shaking hand, caught the edge of the light. 'You all right, Ray?'

'Thank God,' he replied in dazed astonishment.

'Yeah, you might be right, there,' said the massive shadow in a voice that was shaking as much as his hand.

Brooks, who had been frozen statue-like with his body pointed at Ray, turned to fully face the unwelcome intruder. 'You're a big boy, aren't you?' he said, noting his intruder's huge head turned at an angle against the low ceiling.

'Gog, shoot this guy dead,' said Ray.

Brooks calmly returned the scalpel to its sheath and then walked his fingers to the bundle's biggest blade. Extracting it with an adoring look, he flicked its steel and the axe-like cleaver sung a deadly metallic ping. With a sigh of pleasure, he turned his attention back to Gog. 'You've never held a gun before, have you?'

'To be honest with you, no. But like my old nan used to say – there's a first time for everything.'

'*Gog! Pull the trigger!*'

'No sense pulling the trigger if the safety's on,' said Brooks.

Automatically, Gog turned the gun in his hand to check if he was correct.

'*GOG!*' Ray screamed, as Brooks lunged, swinging the cleaver with terrifying speed in the Welshman's direction.

What followed was the second loudest bang Ray had ever heard as the report of the gun sounded against the basement's concrete walls.

Then all was silent.

Brooks stood motionless under the ceiling light. After what felt like a long time the silence was finally broken by the cleaver falling. He reached out a hand to steady himself against the camera and tripod, but both toppled over to join the cleaver on the ground.

'I'm . . . shot,' he said in a stunned voice, as his legs buckled. '*I'm fucking shot!*' he shouted in an unfamiliar high-pitched squeal, grasping at his thigh and curling into a fetal-like ball.

'It just went off,' said Gog loudly, through the ringing in his ears.

'Kick the knife away from him and untie me.' Gog kept looking down at Brooks' writhing form. '*NOW, GOG!*'

'Yeah,' he said, with a shake of his head. 'Yeah, righto.' He kicked the cleaver and got to work on Ray's straps.

Released, 'I'll take that,' said Ray, rubbing at his wrists and forehead. Gog handed him the gun as Brooks moaned between various uttered expletives in the middle of an ever-expanding pool of blood. Ray looked from his captor to his liberator. 'What the hell are you doing here?' he asked furiously. 'You could have got yourself killed!'

'I was worried about you. So, I came to your house to talk to you. And then you came out the door, and I could tell you were going to do something bad, so I followed you.'

'How do you know where I live?'

'You told Luke outside the clinic.'

Ray blinked in shock. 'Yeah, I did, didn't I?'

'I saw you snoopin' around out front. Then he came to the door and all of a sudden you collapsed. He dragged you in, and I thought, that doesn't look right. I have to go help.'

Ray's scowl softened, before he threw his arms around the giant. 'Thank you, Gog,' he said, into his chest. 'You saved my life.'

Gog draped a heavy paw over Ray's shoulders and patted his back.

'What about him?' he asked over the top of Ray's head.

Ray stepped back, and after a few moments to regard Brooks' sorry state – he raised the gun. Brooks lifted a defensive shuddering hand that dripped with blood. 'Please. *No-o-o*,' he whined.

'Oh, I think – yes.'

41

It was late, and Jellicoe Square was deserted by the time he made the journey across town. The small gardens at the square's centre were dark and silent but for the cry of a lone unseen fox. Ray stood in the doorway of Lombard House, an imposing period building, originally intended for use as a family home rather than the apartments it had eventually become, and pressed a button marked Flat 6. After a short wait, a buzzer signalled the door's release.

Ray's footsteps echoed on black-and-white chequered tiles before he began the ascent of the winding stairs. His sick and tired body relied heavily on the support of the wood and cast-iron rail.

The door to Flat 6 was ajar. He entered. There was a small vestibule before a short flight of stone steps. Reaching the top, light from an adjacent well-appointed kitchen, smart, modern and anachronistic, lit a long wooden floored corridor to Ray's left with five doors along its length. The only one that was open was at the far end. Ray walked towards it.

The clink of ice on glass sounded as Ray stepped into a living room that complemented the kitchen's clean lines and minimalist character. 'It's done then,' said John, pouring the brown liquid into two tumblers. He offered a glass. Ray accepted it and nodded. 'You OK?' No answer was forthcoming. 'You don't look too good.'

Ray downed the whisky. 'I've been better.'

'Did he give you any trouble?'

'He won't be troubling anyone ever again.'

'Good,' said John, with a smile and a raised glass. 'Here's to one less monster in the world.'

Ray ignored the toast. Instead, he placed his empty glass on a sideboard. 'Tell me again . . . how did you break in?'

John could not hide his surprise at the question.

'What?'

'Brooks' home. A couple of days back. You broke in. How?'

'I told you, through the back door.'

'So the side gate was open?'

'Yeah.'

'And you broke in and then searched the house?'

'That's right.'

'Did you look in the basement?'

John took a drink.

'No. It was locked.'

'So you were fine getting in the back door . . . but the basement lock was beyond you?'

'I didn't give it my full attention, Ray,' he said, bristling. 'I'd already found the watch. I had all the evidence I needed.'

'*You found the watch*,' Ray said to himself. 'Where was it?'

Perplexed, John tilted his head and looked at Ray for a long time. 'What's going on?'

'I've known you for many years. You're my brother-in-law on paper, but I've always thought of you as just my brother. And my friend. You're a good man and a good cop.'

His tone put an uneasy smile on John's face. 'I feel the same way about you, Ray. You know that.'

'I don't think I ever saw you and Odette have a cross word. I know you loved her as much as me. Which is why I can't work out why you're lying to me.'

'Lying to you?' John repeated, visibly hurt by the accusation. 'What is it you think I'm lying about?'

'You were right. Brooks took Jennifer Moody.'

'I know,' he replied defiantly, raising the whisky glass to his mouth.

'But he didn't kill Odette.'

The glass came to a stop. 'Of course he did.'

'He didn't.'

'He had her watch.'

'He didn't.'

'He'd say anything to stay alive.'

'A murdering psychopath, yes. A liar? I think not.'

'Whatever he told you, he *was* lying.'

'No.' Ray took out the Luger and pointed it at John. 'You are.'

John's eyes grew like saucers. He instinctively raised his hands.

'What the hell are you doing?'

'Come on, John,' implored Ray. 'You didn't break in at all.'

'I think you're confused. Why don't you put the gun down and then we can talk about this rationally.' In an effort to spur Ray to do the same with the firearm, John slowly lowered his glass onto a side table.

Ray cocked the Luger. 'I think we'll talk like this.'

'Have you lost your fucking mind?!' John shouted,

before attempting to force calm back into his voice. 'You're not thinking straight, Ray. You've been through a lot these last couple of years. The trauma. You're not yourself. Look at some of the stuff you've been up to lately. You're not thinking straight,' he repeated. 'Put the gun down.'

'There were hidden security cameras,' continued Ray, unperturbed. 'I checked them. You were never there on the day you said you broke in.' John opened his mouth, but nothing was forthcoming. Ray watched his eyes flick up as he searched for an answer.

'Maybe I got my days mixed up,' he finally said.

'That doesn't sound like you.' John stared back in silence. 'How did you have Odette's watch?' More silence. 'Answer me, *damn you*!'

'Ray, please –'

'Choose your words carefully.' John watched Ray's finger curl against the gun's trigger. 'They could be your last.'

The gesture seemed to take the strength from John's legs. He lowered himself into a well-worn leather arm-chair. And then slowly lowered his hands until they covered his face. He remained like that for a long time, breathing heavily into his palms.

'I fucked it all up,' he finally said, from behind his fingers. 'I fucked it up.'

'What did you do?' Ray asked, with a sinking feeling in the pit of his stomach.

His hands were wet with tears when he removed them. 'I made a mistake. I was angry and tired. I was so tired of it all.'

'Of what?' Ray said, trying hard to keep his voice level.

'Working with my hands tied behind my back. The

system's rigged for criminals. You know that. It's bullshit. No matter how hard we try they're always one step ahead. We get paid a pittance, sacrifice relationships – a marriage! – and they fucking rake it in. I got tired of eating shit!' he said, angrily wiping his eyes. He then attempted to meet Ray's gaze, but couldn't. Instead he looked down at the floor. 'I was broke after the divorce. You know Angie took me to the cleaners in the courts. It started off small. A backhander here and there for something innocuous, nothing that could hurt anyone. But then it escalated. It got out of hand. Before I knew it their hooks were in me.'

'Who?'

'Serious people. People who don't take no for an answer.'

'How was my wife involved in your stupid mistake, John?'

'I got wind of an operation to intercept a drug shipment . . . I told them. She overheard that conversation.'

'*How?!*' Ray growled with barely contained fury.

'I gave her a key when I moved in here after Angie and I broke up. I was so miserable. She must have come here to surprise me, cheer me up. I didn't hear her come in. If I had heard her –'

'What happened?' Ray brought the gun one step closer. John didn't seem to notice. He stared vacantly ahead.

'*Hello.*'

'It's me,' said John. He was taking the call sat in his well-worn leather armchair.

'*What have you got?*' asked the voice on the end of the line.

'Something big.'

'*I'll be the judge of that.*'

'Fair enough. You asked me to keep my ear to the ground for any chatter coming out of the port.'

'*I'm listening.*'

'Border Force found a shit-ton of cocaine smuggled in pallets of bananas on a cargo ship that arrived from Columbia this morning.'

'*Fuck . . .*'

'Yeah, I thought you might say that. Our friends at the NCA have been notified. They're going to follow that shipment to its end point. Sounds like you're going to take a hit on this one. Don't forget I get paid either way.'

'*Becoming quite the greedy fat rat, aren't we?*'

'Fuck you, Tommy. If it wasn't for me you'd be doing a thirty stretch by the end of the day. Don't forget that, *Pretty Boy* –'

'*Don't call me that,*' he hissed down the line.

A muffled crash rang out in the corridor. John quickly ended the call and rushed to the corridor. He opened the door. In the light cast from the living room, his sister stood frozen in her baby blue nursing uniform with her handbag slung over her shoulder. A picture lay on the floor.

'Hey, sis. I didn't hear you come in,' he said, upbeat and warm.

'Yeah,' she said, not returning his smile. 'Sorry about the picture.'

He walked the few short steps to her, picked up the framed photograph she had knocked off the wall, and re hung it so their mother and Uncle Kenroy smiled back at them in perfect alignment.

'No biggie.'

They stood looking at one another. Words unsaid were

weighing heavily in the air. 'Ode . . .' he began, his smile fading, 'I don't know what you think you just heard but –'

'It sounded bad, John. Who's paying you? What are you mixed up in?'

The disappointment on her face crushed him. 'I'm playing a part. It's not what you think,' he said in desperation.

'You were playing it well.'

'You know I got a B in GCSE drama,' he said, with his winning smile, attempting to bring her back with humour.

Odette knew insincerity when she saw it. She checked her watch. 'I have to go.'

'Ode, *wait*,' he said, as she turned to leave. 'Would you wait just a second?' He reached out for her shoulder.

'What?' she said, annoyed, swivelling around.

'Why don't you stay? Let's have a glass of wine. Chill out for a bit.'

'I'm good. I have to get home.' She tried turning. He stopped her again. 'John, please.'

'Don't mention this to Ray.'

She regarded his panicked features in abject disgust. 'I can't believe it.'

'Believe what?'

'My brother, the *bent cop*.' She forcefully turned, shaking off his hand, and headed for the front door, just a few feet away at the bottom of the stone steps.

'Ode.' He grabbed her handbag, pulling her towards him. 'I want to talk about this. You can't tell Ray.'

'*Get off!*' she yelled, tugging at the bag.

'Ode!' They started to scuffle, John trying to hold her in place, Odette trying to push him away. '*For fuck's sake! Stop!*' he yelled, pulling the handbag hard, wrenching it from her hand. She toppled backwards. He reached out to help her, only to feel the material of her nurse's uniform slip through his fingers.

And then she was falling into the void of the stairwell.

Her arms flailed, searching for something to stop her descent, but there was nothing there. She screamed. But as soon as she hit the floor at the bottom of the steps, her legs twisted, her head at an angle against the front door – there was silence.

'Odette!' John shouted, running down to her, dropping to his knees next to her still body. '*Odette!*' He brought her up into a seated position. He felt wetness at the back of her head. Retracting his hand, it was red with blood.

'*Jesus Christ . . .*'

On its side, next to her head, a heavy antique iron that he used as an occasional door stop had blood and hair on its pointed tip.

'*NOOOOOO!*' he screamed.

More tired and weak than he had ever felt before, Ray collapsed into the chair opposite John. '*My girl,*' he sobbed, as he tried forcing air back into his lungs.

'I kept her jewellery and bag, and then I brought her car around the back,' said John, still reliving that awful night two years earlier. 'I wrapped her in a blanket.' Tears rolled down his cheeks. 'But I couldn't leave her in the car. I laid her in the grass. I got rid of the iron and those stupid ski gloves. And then I came back here and waited. I waited and waited. I thought maybe she told someone at work she was coming to see me. Someone would have seen her car out front, or heard us shouting . . . but no one came.'

'You were in my blind spot,' Ray said in a desolate tone, before adding. 'Why Brooks?'

'Everything you've been through. All I've put you through. And then you get cancer,' John said, in disbelief. 'I know you've been consumed by trying to find . . . *the killer*. It's been hell watching you go through that. I thought if I could give you someone it would bring you peace. And then Brooks appeared. If ever there was a man who deserved to die. No arrest. No judge. No jury. It would be our secret. No one else would know. But there would be one less killer in the world and his death would bring you peace. You could finally let her go.'

'How benevolent of you. So you were thinking of me when you sent me into that house of goddamn horrors.'

'You weren't supposed to go in on your own!' John yelled. 'I'd never put you in harm's way like that. We were supposed to go in together. Put him down quick. I could've controlled it if I was there. But no, you had to go in alone – you insisted on it, Ray. That's not on me.' He shook his head in frustration. 'Why did you have to speak to him, Ray? *Why?*'

'I didn't have much of a choice at the time.' Anger was creeping back into his voice. 'I think I know what might bring me some *peace*.' He dragged the sleeve of his jacket across his wet face before he stood and levelled the gun at his brother-in-law. 'Get up.' John raised himself. He closed his eyes and bowed his head. 'Look at me.' Red eyes opened and stared back at him. 'Why did you *really* send me in there?'

'I told you.'

Ray brought the barrel of the gun closer to his head.

After a flinch and a moment's hesitation, John said, 'I was scared.'

'Of what?'

'Being found out. I knew you would never give up. When I saw that table in your kitchen, you were getting closer. Ray Leonard – the best to ever police. It was only a matter of time. But I did want to give you peace. You have to believe that!'

Ray's heart hammered in his chest as his grip tightened around the gun. A minuscule amount of extra pressure on the trigger and it was done.

'You know I'd never hurt her. She was my sister. I loved her,' he said through choking tears. 'I'm sorry. I'm so sorry.'

'Not good enough. She was my wife. Chay's mother. And you took her from us.' He watched John brace himself through the shaking sights of the gun when suddenly – the doorbell rang.

Both he and John looked to the intercom fastened to the wall. A man's face took up the entirety of the intercom's small black-and-white screen.

John looked back to Ray in shock.

Ray released the trigger and lowered the gun, then headed to the intercom. He pushed the speak button: 'Give me a minute.'

'*Yeah, sure. Take your time,*' replied the man in the small screen. '*It's not like I've come miles and it's the middle of the night.*'

Ray released the speak button and the screen went blank.

'Ben,' said John in disbelief.

'Yes. DS Greylag. I asked him to meet me here,' Ray said. 'When I made that call I honestly didn't know whether he'd be arresting you or taking you away in a body bag and arresting me.' Ray sat and nodded to another chair. John sat. 'I've made some mistakes lately. I'm not going to make another. I'm not killing my wife's brother. My daughter's uncle.' John's shoulders sagged in relief. 'You're going to prison. It won't be punishment enough, but after what you've done . . . a disgraced cop who killed his sister – it *will* be hard.'

John shrunk at the thought.

'I appreciate our situation has changed so I need to ask you something. Do you still intend to forget about recent events? Pentecost, Fain, Brooks? Because if not I'll be joining you in prison and Chaynnie will be left with no one. Given the choice, I think she'd prefer to have the man who *didn't* kill her mother around for a little longer, don't you?'

John flashed Ray a look of anger, but it quickly passed when he realized his friend was right. He had taken so much from them. He would take no more.

'You've got nothing to worry about,' he said, sounding hollow and small.

Ray nodded and tucked the gun back beneath his jacket. He got up and walked to the intercom. His finger was poised over the button that granted entry.

'How the hell did we get here, John?' he said, looking back at him.

John shook his head as tears rolled.

Ray pushed the button and returned to his seat.

After a short while a voice called from along the corridor. 'Hello?'

'In here.' Ray called back, without taking his eyes off John.

'I really am sorry, Ray.'

'I know,' he replied with a sad sigh.

42

In the fallout from her uncle John Facey's arrest for causing and concealing the death of her mother, Chay returned to the family home on Gilmour Avenue. Together, she and Ray weathered the ugly truth of what had happened to Odette, their beloved mother and wife, which was splashed across various press outlets for the edification and entertainment of their readers.

But Chay could not find the small comfort that Ray had taken from knowing what had happened. She fell into a deep abyss of grief. Her mother was dead, as was her biological father and now her uncle was gone too. It turned out that he'd never been the man she thought he was – he was corrupt through and through. The betrayal cut deep. How much could one person lose?

Ray spent long hours worrying that he would be the next person to leave her . . . and then his phone rang. Its display said *Caller Number Withheld* – but Ray knew who it was before he answered. As Chay sat watching TV in the living room he gently closed the kitchen door and sat at the dining table, which was now empty and uncluttered.

'Hello,' he said.

'*Bad days. Bad fucking days, Ray.*'

He made no reply.

A loud puff filled the receiver in the long silence. Ray could almost see the smoke leaving Sutter's mouth.

'*Your wife,*' he continued. '*Cancer. Now this. You've upset someone.*'

'Difficult to argue that point, Nick.'

Another puff.

'*What would you do in my place?*'

'Well, that would be easy because I'd know I didn't kill Howard Fain.'

'*You were* sloppy,' the detective said, ignoring the comeback. '*Getting seen was bad enough. I don't know how you got him to write the note; probably put a gun to his head. But the one big mistake you made — the newspaper. You should have got rid of the paper.*'

'I don't know anything about a —'

'*It was open on the table and he was checking the odds for tomorrow's horse race. He was picking his winners, Ray. Does that sound like a man who was about to kill himself?*'

'I'm not going to try to understand the motivations of a suicidal man. But I think we can assume he wasn't thinking straight. An open newspaper on a table . . . I'm not sure that's enough to call it a murder investigation.'

'*I could bring you to Manchester, put together a video parade, see if that face jogs the old bird's memory.*'

'You let me know the time and the place.'

At that, the line was filled with a cynical laugh. '*I know you were there, Ray. I fucking know it.*'

'Well, good luck proving that. I've got a lot on my plate, Nick, so if you'll excuse me. You know where I am.'

No reply. But Ray sensed there was more.

'Yeah . . .' Sutter finally said. '*I don't think we'll be seeing one another again.*'

'What are you saying?'

'*People say I'm a fucking bastard, and they're right.*' Ray heard the glow of a cigarette's tip crackle down the line. '*But I've got my limits, Ray.*'

'So that's it?'

'*That's it.*'

The line went dead.

43

It was three days before Ray returned to the clinic. They had all seen the papers and voiced their distress and sadness at learning how Ray had lost Odette.

'What does it all mean? Your brother in-law. He knows a lot of stuff about . . . you know, what's been going on,' said Luke.

'He knows it all.'

The only other person who does is Gog, thought Ray, *and apparently he can keep a secret.*

Under the umbrella of the truth amnesty and the only rule of Chemo Club, Ray brought Luke and Rose up to speed – the orange puddle in the alley by Pentecost's body, Brooks' basement, Gog's rescue (which blew Luke's mind. Much to Gog's discomfort, labels such as – 'superhero' and 'John Wick' were bandied about. Eventually Ray had to ask him to calm down), and the finer details of John's role in Odette's death.

'Sorry you lost your wife like that, Ray,' said Luke.

Gog and Rose nodded along sadly.

'Thank you.'

Luke asked, 'Will he say anything . . . John, I mean, about that guy in the alley, the psycho in the basement, or Fain?'

'No. He'll keep quiet for Chay and Odette. He owes them that much,' said Ray.

'He owes you too,' added Rose.

Ray gave a nod.

'Good that he's keeping schtum. But what about the woman on Cordwallis Street? The gloves? The car?' Luke asked, full of concern. 'That cop's after you.' Ray stared at Luke for long moments until his face stretched into a smile as wide as his scar would allow. 'So-o-o? It's good news?'

'It is,' Ray finally said. 'Turns out DI Nick Sutter isn't quite the bastard everybody thinks he is.'

'So you're in the clear?' Luke added, beaming.

'Fain is now officially a suicide?' Rose asked, as enthused as Luke.

Ray nodded. 'I'm not going to prison. I'll be here for Chay . . . for a bit yet.'

'How's she coping?'

'As you can imagine, Rose – devastated. She thought very highly of her uncle . . . as did I. But at least there's a small comfort in knowing what happened. For me, at least.'

'Brutal. Absolutely brutal, all of it,' said Luke. 'What a thing to go through. I'm so sorry, Ray.'

'I appreciate that.' Ray looked to Gog who had been sitting quietly. 'Are you OK?'

Gog nodded. But it was far from convincing.

Luke turned to Gog. 'I was wondering why you've been so quiet the last couple of days. I knew it had to be something because you wouldn't be so miserable after the good news.'

'Good news?' Ray echoed.

Gog nodded. 'Chemo's working,' he told him.

'That's brilliant.'

'You must have heard something too by now, Ray?' asked Luke, his eyebrows knitted in worry.

'Nothing yet,' he lied. 'You?'

'I've got a review coming up,' Luke blew out his cheeks and crossed his fingers. 'How about you, Rose? Any news?'

'What's the difference? I'm old. Cancer or no cancer, I'll be dead soon enough, either way.'

'Rose Bisseker, everyone,' said Luke, clapping his hands. 'None of the fun of the fair.' He left what he thought was an appropriate amount of time before he gave in to his inquisitive mind. 'I still can't believe you were in that basement . . . that's insane!' He looked from Ray to Gog in wonder. 'I know he's dead, it was in the press . . . but how did it really go down? How did you end that sick fuck, Ray?'

After shaking his head at Luke's inappropriate enthusiasm, Ray looked to Gog.

Gog gave a small nod of consent.

Ray looked down upon Brooks' sorry state – after a few moments he raised the gun and took aim. Brooks lifted a defensive shuddering hand that dripped with blood.

'Please. *No-o-o.*'

'Oh, I think – yes.'

'Ray . . .' said Gog, placing a hand on his shoulder.

'He doesn't deserve to live.'

'*PLEASE!*' Brooks screamed as blood pumped through fingers that tried vainly to staunch the hole in his thigh.

'Don't do it,' Gog pleaded with Ray. 'You told us a soldier has to have compassion and respect for the enemy. A life had to have value to take . . . you said that. Remember?'

The sights of the gun continued to be filled with Brooks' anguished face. Ray felt its old trigger gradually start to bite into the flesh of his finger. *I think I can make an exception*, he thought . . . but then another thought entered his mind. It was an image from long ago in his past. He saw a gushing wound on a Taliban fighter's leg and the bloodied boot of his friend. What Mac had done that day was abhorrent and criminal. But there was no Geneva Convention here in this dreadful basement. Just his own conscience.

'*Rayyy* . . .' His own conscience and Gog, it would seem.

He released the trigger and lowered the weapon.

'Pick him up and put him in the chair. Careful not to get his blood on you.'

Ray pushed the tray of instruments and the plasma bag to the other side of the room, close to the cabinet, out of reach, as Gog bent down and picked Brooks up with staggering ease. He screamed with renewed vigour.

'One second,' said Ray. With the bottom of his T-shirt he quickly wiped the sharp corners of the metal chair's armrests. 'OK. Put him in.'

'Who is he?' Gog asked worriedly, doing as Ray had asked.

'A murdering psychopath.'

'What are we going to doing with him?'

'Give him a taste of his own medicine. Let's strap him in.'

They both made short work of securing a weak and now barely conscious Brooks. Then Ray looked around the room until he saw what he was looking for. At the back, beneath the record player, he found his discarded surgical gloves along with his jacket and hat. Ray put them all on and then removed a cable tie from one of his pockets. He secured it tightly around Brooks' thigh to stop the flow of blood.

Satisfied with his work, he said, 'Peter,' then slapped him. Slack-jawed, Brooks' eyes fluttered open and his pupils rolled into view from the back of his skull. He looked at Ray in confusion for a couple of seconds.

'Welcome back, sleepy head,' Ray snarled. Brooks attempted retreat. Suddenly realizing why he could not, he wailed in panic-stricken terror.

'I've tied off your leg so you will live, but after about six to eight hours your leg will not. It'll have to come off. That'll be some first-hand experience for you.'

'*Fuck you.*' Brooks winced through tears and gritted teeth.

'Don't sulk, Peter,' said Ray. 'Now, stay awake. I need that face.'

'His face?' said Gog, who looked on, more worried than ever.

Ray went back to the record player and after a short while found what he was looking for.

'He has hidden security cameras. We need to delete the footage of us, and switch them off for when we leave. That's why I need this,' he said, waving Brooks' phone. Even though the strap held his head in place, Ray still roughly grabbed a handful of Brooks' dank hair. He groaned in protest and screwed his eyes shut. '*Open!*' Ray demanded, almost ripping his hair from his scalp. With a shriek Brooks complied and the facial recognition software went to work. Once Ray gained access, he spent long moments staring into the glare of the screen. If it were possible, Gog noticed, his face became even more grave the longer he stared. Finally, he switched off the phone, and threw it back with the wrecked record player. 'You haven't touched anything, Gog?'

'Just the gun and him.'

'That's fine.'

'Oh! And the front doorknob.'

'We'll get that on the way out.' Ray had another thought. 'Forgot to lock it, did he?'

'No. It was locked.'

Confused. 'Then how did you get in?'

'No lock can stop me.'

'How so?'

'I'm a locksmith.' He tapped the pocket of his jacket and the sound of the tools of his trade clinked. 'Never leave home without them.'

'A locksmith?' Ray said, in disbelief. 'I thought you were a bouncer?'

'A *bouncer*? Why?'

'You said you worked in security.'

'I do. I'm a locksmith.'

Ray stared back at the giant in amazement. 'What are the chances?'

'All part of His plan,' said Gog, with a glance upwards.

'I'm beginning to think you might be right. But let's continue this discussion elsewhere. There's a chance the neighbours heard the gunshot.'

'Righto.'

Ray turned his attention to the toppled tripod. 'I just need to delete my footage from the camera's memory card, and we'll be on our way.' He reached down and retrieved it. He opened the small viewing screen on the camera's side and accessed the menu. He entered the page marked 'Files' and deleted what would have been, if not for Gog, Brooks' most recent acquisition to his library of horrors – starring Ray Leonard himself. He was about to shut the screen when he came to a sudden stop.

Gog saw the look on his face illuminated by the light of the screen. 'What is it, Ray?'

'There are other files here,' he said, with a bleak look in his eye.

'What do you mean?'

'Jennifer Moody. The missing schoolteacher. She was the last person to sit in that chair, before me.' He scowled at Brooks, who looked back at them, panting and shaking like an animal caught in a snare.

Ray selected the last file before his own, marked 'Subject Twelve', and pressed play. A sickening gurgling scream of agony filled the room, easily eclipsing the sound of the record player in the background of the recording. Ray had seen some unimaginable things as a soldier and a policeman . . . but nothing came close to what he held in his hand.

'Oh my God,' said Gog, who now peered over Ray's shoulder. He struggled to comprehend what he was looking at. It wasn't a woman any more. Apart from the tangled mess of her long auburn hair, all femininity had been cut away. What remained of Jennifer Moody was a shell of blood, bone and sinew.

'*Exquisite. Simply exquisite,*' Brooks could be heard saying as he zoomed in on her lidless terrified eyes.

Gog turned away in horror and employed the wall as a support.

'I'm going to be sick.'

'Do *not* throw up in here,' said Ray, feeling his own gorge rise.

'*Oh my God . . . Jesus . . . Jesus in Heaven,*' Gog said, gasping for air as the tears started to roll down his cheeks.

Ray closed the screen and Moody's agony was abruptly silenced. As Gog wept, Ray drew a shaking hand over his own pale face, before he turned to Brooks.

'Hey.' The murderer's eyes were screwed shut in tight knots of pain. '*Hey!*' Ray slapped him again, much harder than before, and Brooks came back with a groan from wherever he had been. 'I imagine there are a few of these home videos somewhere in this house.' He placed the camera beside the fallen tripod. 'The next people who come down here will be the police.' Ray removed his hat and leaned into him. 'They're going to lock you up forever. And then *your* life won't be your own.'

Brooks gazed for long moments into the black pits of Ray's eyes. Slowly, through the pain, he managed to bring a small smile to his lips.

'I'll take them all with me.'

Vile bastard.

Ray clenched his jaw until he thought his teeth might crack. He felt the shape of the Luger tucked into the back of his jeans, pressed up against the base of his spine. It called out to him. Acquiescing, his hand circled its grip as Brooks relapsed into another bout of sweat-soaked delirium. Ray watched his features twist and contort. The contrast between the arrogant, self-assured monster he was, and the broken wretch before him, was stark . . . and that thought gave him a sudden realization – *he's terrified for what comes next if he lives. He* wants *to die.* He released the gun. *Let him rot.*

Ray felt Gog's presence behind him. Turning, he could see the Welshman had managed to compose himself, somewhat.

'You OK?' Ray asked. But Gog said nothing. He just stood there looking down at Brooks. 'Gog?'

'I've never seen pure evil before,' he finally said in a scared whisper, as he knuckled away a tear.

'I know. I'm sorry you had to,' Ray said gently, and placed a hand on his arm. 'We have to go.' Ray went around Gog's massive frame and made for the stairs. He was half-way up the concrete steps before he realized Gog wasn't following him. With a grunt of annoyance, he went back down the steps.

'*We have to go, now!*'

Gog, his huge paws hanging at his sides, the bristles of his bowling-ball head scraping the ceiling, was standing unmoved before Brooks.

Arriving at his side, Ray looked up into the Welshman's smooth face. The tears and dismay were gone, replaced by a hardness Ray had not seen before.

'Gog?'

'How could he do that?' he asked, transfixed by the man strapped to the chair. Ray didn't have an answer for him. 'That poor woman.' He started to nod his head as if coming to a decision. 'All right.' Then he reached down and held the back of Brooks' head with one shovel-like hand. With the other he easily covered the man's nose and mouth. Brooks' eyes flew open the moment Gog brought his hands together in an airtight clamp.

Ray reached out to stop him, but his hand had not even covered half the distance towards Gog's grip before he stopped himself. His arm dropped to his side and he watched Brooks' last desperate moments on Earth.

His chest heaved and his fingers shot out from beneath the straps as if he were being electrocuted. His screams could be heard trapped in his throat with nowhere to go. His eyes swivelled and bulged manically, as if trying to escape their fate. Each fraught movement became less and less until he was still. Gog stared into his unblinking, bloody eyes, his hands still fastened tight around his dead head.

'He's gone,' said Ray, placing a hand on Gog's wrist.

Gog released his grip.

Brooks' lifeless face was frozen in terror at whatever greeted him in death.

'That poor woman,' said Gog. 'I had to . . . I . . . had to . . .'

'It's OK, Gog. We should go now.'

44

Ray was first to the stairs. He glanced over his shoulder and was glad to see Gog following this time. They would soon be breathing in clean, night air. As they ascended, Ray thought of Jennifer Moody's last breath of free air before she had been taken. His heart ached at the knowledge of what she had gone through. Poor Jennifer Moo—

Wait.

He stopped mid-stairs.

'Wait a second.'

'What's wrong, Ray?'

'Red hair.'

'Red hair?'

Gog waited and watched as Ray stood frozen, searching a place in his mind.

'I saw her picture on the news. I'm sure Moody had bright red hair? The woman on the camera had hair that was more . . . auburn.' His eyes widened. '"*Is* Moody something to you?", he asked? Not *was*. He said "is". He used present tense! We need to go back down!'

'But you said we needed to go?' said Gog.

'Gog, turn around and go back down.'

Ray's tone convinced him to turn his great bulk around. As Ray stepped off the last stair into the shadowy basement, he noted that the acrid smell of gun-smoke was still present. And (with no small amount of satisfaction) Peter

283

Brooks was still sat dead in the cone of light cast from above.

'Take that shade off the bulb,' said Ray.

Gog did so and the full chilling scene of the room was cast into bright light.

'*Dammit*,' said Ray, gesturing for Gog to hand him the shade. He took it with his gloved hand and wiped the parts that might hold a fingerprint, before throwing it to the ground. He took a breath and then, as gently as the gravity of their situation would allow, he said, 'Just don't touch anything else, OK?'

Gog nodded.

Ray retrieved the camera and accessed its files again.

'Look away,' he said. But a quick glance at the big man showed Ray's order to be redundant as Gog had already averted his eyes. Ray turned the volume down and, holding his breath, searched the remaining files. There were four marked 'subjects' – eleven through eight. After a harrowing time spent looking into the small screen of hellish images, Ray discovered there were no women with bright red hair amongst the poor souls who had been brought to that terrible place.

'She's not on here,' he said, dropping the camera, his voice shaking but with an unmistakable note of hope. '*Jennifer!*'

Once her name had stopped reverberating off the walls there was nothing but silence.

'She's . . . still alive?'

'Maybe.' Ray's eyes came to rest on the large metal cabinet. 'The cabinet.'

In the light afforded by the exposed bulb he could now

see the cabinet's double doors were secured by a small padlock fastened through a metal plate and hoop.

He reached for the bone hammer atop Brooks' trolley and then kicked the trolley and its contents towards the wreckage of the record player. Swinging the hammer, he smashed the padlock off with one violet swing.

Taking hold of the handles, with the sound of Gog's shallow breathing in his ears, he opened the cabinet. When the creak of the hinges stopped, Ray and Gog looked inside with a mixture of anger and relief.

'Looks like more horrible medical stuff, Ray.'

He was right. The shelves were full of all types of medical paraphernalia. Anaesthesia. Pain medication. IV fluids. Anticoagulants. Surgical knives. Retractors. Needles. Surgical staplers and sutures. All items that amounted to a legitimate horror show outside of a hospital.

'*Shit.*'

Ray slammed the doors shut.

He placed his hand on his brow, closed his eyes and bowed his head, thinking.

After some time, Gog said, 'It doesn't look like she's here,' his voice small and frightened.

Ray opened his eyes.

And that was when he noticed them.

'*Wheels,*' he said, looking at the small black castors at the corners of the cabinet's base. He rushed to its side and with his shoulder pushed it along the wall until a metal door was revealed.

'*JENNIFER!?!*' he yelled, smashing at the door with his fists.

But still no answer came.

He yanked at the door but it was secured by a much larger padlock. With the hammer he began to strike it repeatedly. It wouldn't budge. So he doubled his efforts. Strike after strike. Then he felt a hand on his shoulder.

'Step aside, Ray.'

He looked to the soft leather case that Gog held in his hand and, despite the urgency of the situation, gave a snort of laughter.

'Yeah. Of course.'

Gog lowered himself onto a knee before the lock. After a quick inspection he unzipped the 'tools of his trade' and got to work.

With a grace and efficiency that contradicted the meaty hand that guided the pick, the lock's shackle soon snapped the sound of its release.

'I'll take that lock.'

Gog handed it to Ray who put it into his pocket.

They stood side by side before the now unlocked door. The urgency that had driven them until now suddenly evaporated at the thought of what might be on the other side of the sheet of metal.

'Why don't you wait upstairs, Gog?' suggested Ray, not taking his eyes from the door.

'If you don't mind . . . I think I'll stay.'

Nodding his head. 'OK.'

Ray opened the door.

His nose detected the smell of chemicals and human waste. But his eyes saw nothing but black.

'Move out of the light,' he said, realizing Gog's huge form was the barrier.

Gog stepped aside, and through the dim rectangle of

light, a pair of ghostly white feet could be seen at the end of a mattress on the floor.

Ray felt around the inside of the door frame and found a switch. Another, much smaller, concrete space was lit up by an exposed bulb. The room was empty except for a chemical toilet (the source of the smell) and a bed where a red-haired woman lay on her back wearing a thin hospital gown. A sack of clear liquid hung from a hook screwed into the wall above her. A tube snaked its way from the bag into the fold of her inner elbow. Her exposed arms and legs, cold blue in the light, were strapped to the bed. A makeshift cloth gag was tightly wound around her mouth.

She was still as stone.

'She dead?' Gog asked, peering around the door frame.

When Ray turned to him, Gog was surprised to see a faint smile.

'No need to gag the dead.'

On the floor, next to the mattress, was a tray that held a half-eaten sandwich and a box of orange juice. Ray kicked it aside and sunk to his knees.

After gently removing the gag, he put a palm to the woman's forehead. It was ice-cold. He then pressed his index and middle fingers to her throat. After fifteen seconds, he said, 'She's heavily sedated. Her pulse is dangerously low.'

He removed the needle.

'Is she gonna be all right?'

'With Brooks dead she would have been left in here. If the cops hadn't got to her in time –' he nodded at the bag – 'the rest of that would have killed her. She'll come around in a while. She'll be all right.'

With a happy smile Gog stepped into the room and filled it. 'Let's get her up then.'

Ray stood. 'Gog . . .' he said, placing a hand on the solid wall of his friend's chest.

'We gotta take those straps off, Ray.'

'We can't move her.'

'*Why not?!*' he replied, leaning into Ray's hand.

'GOG!' He stopped his lean. 'There's a dead man in the next room!' Softening. 'She can't see us.'

Gog looked down at her, concern crushing his face.

'We can take 'em off and then go?'

'We can't have her coming around and then walking in a daze out into the street. I know it doesn't feel like it but she's safer down here until the police come.'

Gog seemed not to hear.

'Hey! Look at me.' Gog's eyes met his. '*It's OK*. There's nothing down here that can hurt her any more. The police will come. I have to do something first . . . then I'll make an anonymous call. She won't be down here long. She's going to be all right. Jennifer's going to see her family again.'

45

'You killed the bad guy and saved the girl,' said Luke, in renewed awe of the pair of them. 'I can't believe only the people in this room will ever know.'

'That's the way it has to be,' said Ray.

'You're heroes,' Luke added.

'Ray's a hero,' said Gog. 'He saved Jennifer.'

'And wonderful it is that she'll see her family again. But those other poor women . . . their families will be more than relieved that that man is dead,' said Rose. 'Well done, my boy. I'm glad that one of you had the courage to do what needed to be done.'

It would have been easy for Ray to snap at the older woman. Ask her – where was her courage, on that balcony, with her husband all those years ago? But he didn't. Because he knew she was right.

'I'm sorry, Gog. It should have been me. I know how important your beliefs are . . . and now I've burdened you with this.'

'It's not your fault, Ray. I chose to follow you. I chose to go in that house. I . . .' He stopped and looked down at his shaking hands. 'It was my choice.'

'But your beliefs?' Ray repeated. 'You're a Christian. Thou shalt not kill?'

'I know. But how could God create such a creature? Someone who would hurt another person like that. Those poor, *poor* women . . . what he did . . .' He shook his big head. 'He wouldn't be part of that. Not my God. Yes, I took a life. But he wasn't one of God's children – and if he was, then I don't want my place in Heaven.' Surprisingly, a smile, with a missing incisor, spread across his face. 'I'll go wherever you three are going.' The smile faltered for a second. 'As long as I get to see my nan one last time, like my Uncle Ichdyd saw his mam just before he died,' his smile returned. 'I'll go with you.'

With a sudden lump in her throat, Rose said, 'My sweet boy.'

'We'd be honoured to have you,' said Ray, warmly. 'Wherever that might be.' A shadow came over his face. 'Maybe there's somewhere between Heaven and Hell. Somewhere exactly in the middle. A place for people who haven't lived the perfect life . . . but tried their best. Did what they thought was right at the time.' He couldn't help but think of Mac's grisly face. 'I think I'd like that,' he said, his smile returning.

'I have to say,' began a teary Luke. 'I feel very much inadequate sitting in this room.'

'Why?'

'You've all lived amazing lives. You've done amazing things.' After a quick thought, 'Yes, mostly *illegal* things, but amazing all the same. Ray, you fought for your country. You caught criminals, you even dispatched one in the alley across the street.' Ray gave a begrudging nod. Luke continued, 'Rose, you dedicated your life to caring for animals. You had lunch with the Queen. You murdered your arsehole husband –'

'*I did not kill my husband,*' she said with a world-weary roll of her eyes.

'You know what I mean.'

'It was the oven chips,' said Gog, earnestly.

'Yeah. The oven chips,' Luke grinned. 'Gog, you sent a serial killer to Hell. If that isn't the coolest, most badass thing I've ever heard then I don't know what is. I just hope I live long enough to have a story even half as awesome to tell, because right now the only interesting thing about me is that I'm young and have brain cancer.'

'Come on, Luke. Don't sell yourself short,' said Ray. 'You did kill Howard Fain.'

46

Gog laughed.

'I don't get it?' he said, despite himself.

'What's going on?' Rose asked.

Luke was unusually tight-lipped.

'I told you all I went to see Howard Fain in Manchester, Salford,' Ray began. 'I never mentioned the street he lived on. The street Luke mentioned earlier – Cordwallis Street.'

Luke's forehead creased. 'You must have.'

'I didn't.'

'Then I must have seen it in the press.'

'Man commits suicide? Hardly front-page news. It wasn't in the press, Luke.'

'Well, I . . .' He laughed. It sounded nervous and forced to Ray's ears. 'Ray . . . *come on*. What are you saying? You think I busted into Fain's home, injected him with poison and forced him to write a suicide note?' He raised his stick-thin arms. 'Look at me.'

'No, I don't think you did. I think you *and* Rose did.'

'*What?!*' Rose guffawed. 'You've lost your bloody mind. We look like Bonnie and Clyde to you?'

'Pentobarbital,' he said, ignoring her derision. 'It's used in the States to put death row inmates to sleep. In the UK there's demand for it on the black market for people who want to end their own lives. Rightly so, Fain being a doctor, it was assumed he could get hold of some quite easily.

However, there was a detail that I'd forgotten until recently. "*If I was a dog they'd put me down*", that's what you told Donna. I then remembered pentobarbital is used to put animals to sleep. Horses. Cows. Cats. All kinds of animals. But most pertinently – *dogs*.'

Rose looked back at him, unmoved by the analysis.

'You worked at a dog shelter for years. You even said you still pop in from time to time. I think you popped in for pentobarbital.'

Gog, who had been watching it all, jaw on chest, mouth agog, laughed nervously again. 'This has gotta be a wind-up?'

His words hung in the air.

'It's not, Gog. Luke knew I didn't kill Fain from the start. Didn't you, Luke?'

'I knew. Truth or fibs, my lie-detector cannot be beaten.' A cocky smile spread across the younger man's face as he leaned back into his chair. 'It took me all of a millisecond to convince Rose we needed to take a trip to Manchester.'

Ray turned to Rose. Despite his consternation, he asked, 'How? How did you get into Fain's house and make him write a suicide note?'

'Ahhh.' She revealed her sharp teeth beneath a cold smile. 'Well, that's the clever part.'

'Are we there yet?' asked Luke, looking up from his phone.

'Twenty minutes,' said Billy, smoothly negotiating the roundabout.

During work hours Billy had a strict speak-when-spoken-to policy. It hadn't been in the job description when he accepted the roll of Luke's 'Man Friday' but

Luke appreciated it nonetheless because it served to enhance the impression that Billy was a man who could be depended on. And even though he had signed on the dotted line saying as much, Luke, over the years, had learned that he could definitely be trusted with a secret.

'OK. Good. Thanks, Billy.'

Luke sounded uncharacteristically nervous, Billy thought. The origin of his apprehension, who could know? Billy asked no questions. He simply did what was asked of him. On this occasion he had been asked to drive Luke and his 'friend' (the mean old woman from the chemo group, who had been dozing in the back seat for well over an hour now) to Salford, Manchester.

His phone went dark and for a time Luke stared out of the window, lost in his own thoughts.

'How long now?'

'Ten minutes,' answered Billy.

Luke blew out what sounded like a build-up of air in his lungs. He reached across and gently shook Rose.

'What?!' she snapped irritably, as if she had been in the middle of something important.

'Almost there.'

'About time. Feel like I've been stuck back here for hours.'

'You've slept for most of it.'

'I closed my eyes for five minutes,' she lied. 'And do me a favour. You've been looking at your phone the whole way. Your generation and those bloody things.'

'What would you rather I do?' said Luke, in the clipped staccato rhythm of a man from the fifties. 'Listen to *The Archers* on me wireless? Or mebbe I should be out in the sunshine with me 'ula-'oop?'

'Silly boy,' she said. 'Not being on your twit-tocs and your infagrams, or whatever the bloody hell you call 'em, doesn't make me feel old. It makes me feel superior.'

'Well, you enjoy your walks in the park, collecting leaves and birdwatching – in the meantime I'm going to watch a Japanese orgy,' he said, waving his phone.

'And there's the problem with your generation. It's all gawking and no participation. I bet you've never even been in an orgy?'

Luke ran a hand over his exasperated face. 'Let's not start comparing orgy stories, for the love of God, *please*. We need to focus . . . yeah?'

'Yes, yes . . . but I do hope I haven't wasted precious hours coming all this way to see a corpse. I could just look in the mirror for that.'

Ignoring her glibness, 'We talked about this,' he said, frustrated. 'I'm telling you, Fain will be there, alive and well. Ray couldn't do it. He was telling the truth. Trust me.'

'All right,' she said, nodding. 'We best get ready then.'

Rose straightened in her seat, patting down the red and green plaid skirt she wore. She removed her bandana (Luke looked away from the nakedness of her scalp) and replaced it with something a lot more sweet old lady – a scarlet wool-blend bucket hat with a flower made from the same material on the side of its brim. Along with her floral blouse and blue cardigan the ensemble was nothing short of jolly.

'You look like you're ready to deal out some street just-ice,' said Luke, unable to help himself.

'Wolf in sheep's clothing,' she replied, with a jagged grin. 'How about you, my boy? You ready?'

He took stock of his own dressed-down attire – a green hoodie with jeans and trainers – and his face took on a sharp, hard quality. 'I think so.'

'He's a bad man and we're here to do a good thing. Keep that in mind.'

'I don't think the law would see it quite the same way.'

'They had their turn. Now it's ours.'

The car came to a stop under orange streetlights.

Luke looked out of the window. Attached to the corner of the second storey of a small, terraced house was a rusty sign that read *Cordwallis Street*.

'We're here. We're looking for number fifty-seven, Bill. Let's take a slow amble along the street . . . not too slow.'

Billy pulled off.

They soon saw the red-brick house with its weedy little garden that separated it from the pavement. The number fifty-seven was displayed on a front door that held a pane of stained glass in its weathered wood. But most importantly, a dim light shone behind some thin curtains in the room to the left of the door. Howard Fain was at home.

Apart from a woman walking a dog, who turned into a set of steep steps that lead up and away, the street was empty.

'Pull into that spot.'

Billy parked in front of three small, dilapidated garages. Number fifty-seven was now eight houses behind them.

'When we get out, circle the block. When I call, head back to this spot quickly . . . but not too quickly.'

'Understood.'

Luke reached out a hand and placed it on Billy's shoulder.

Billy reciprocated by squeezing the hand with his own. 'Be careful.'

Seeing that Rose was watching the exchange Luke quickly pulled his hand away. 'Yup. Will do.' He reached for the door handle. 'Let's go.'

Once Rose had alighted from the Range Rover – *This thing is like the north face of the bloody Eiger* – they watched it drive away until its red lights faded from view. She was the first to turn and head towards number fifty-seven. Luke put up his hoodie and followed. They were feet from Fain's house when a woman came out of one of the houses on the other side of the street – 'Ta-ra, love,' she shouted, closing the door behind her.

'Keep walking,' said Rose, looping her arm through Luke's.

They passed number fifty-seven. Looking over his shoulder, Luke watched the woman go the way of the dog walker.

'She's gone.'

Rose turned on her heels. They were soon looking at the stained glass in the door. They made another scan of the street.

It was empty.

'Here we go,' said Luke, blowing out another of those big breaths.

Rose ran a hand over the right pocket of her cardigan and through the material felt what she already knew to be there. Satisfied, she was about to initiate the plan until she spotted something.

'*Oi!*' she hissed. 'Take that bloody hoodie off. You look like you're about to murder someone.'

He quickly pulled back the hood. 'Shit. Right.'

Rose let out a tut as she reached up and wrapped her skinny arm around Luke's shoulder and neck. He responded by placing his arm around the middle of her back and tucking his hand under her armpit. Her body went limp and a pained expression crossed her face, with her eyes hidden beneath screwed slits. The low moan emanating from the gaps in her gritted fangs made it seem as if Luke were helping an injured solider off a battlefield.

He knocked on the door.

Long moments went by, filled only with Luke's hammering heart and Rose's ghostly moaning.

Nothing.

He repeated the knock as hard and urgent as he dared in the quiet of the street.

The sound of a door opening within was followed by a dim light that illuminated the stained glass briefly, until a shadow blocked it.

A lock turned.

Rose felt Luke tense. She dialled up her agony a fraction.

The door opened and a dishevelled, tired-looking man in a tracksuit took in the scene before him. It was evident he did not like what he saw. 'What do you –'

'I'm so sorry to bother you but some nutter just almost ran over my grandma. They came flying along the road there –' With a puzzled expression, the dishevelled-looking man followed Luke's hand gesture into the street – 'and they almost hit her but she managed to get out the way. She fell pretty hard on the pavement. She might have broken something. Could I sit her down for a second while

I call an ambulance?' The man blinked at the barrage of words, looking from Luke to Rose.

'*Please.*'

'Ahhh . . .' Fain stuck his head out of the door and looked left to right in a way that asked – *can no one else deal with this?* 'Fine,' he said finally with a huff, stepping aside. 'Come in.'

'*Thank you,*' said Luke.

They began their hobble over the threshold, Rose wailing in pain through the effort.

'On the left,' Fain said over the racket, reversing into the hallway and pressing his back against the wall.

'Come on, Grandma. Let's get you sat down.'

They entered a sitting room that was not a room anyone would choose to sit in (present company excluded). Dust and debris covered every surface and the air was thick with neglect and decay. A TV in the corner, with a layer of grime on its screen, was switched on but muted. A crumpled newspaper was spread out on a small table, opened to the horse racing section. A cheap can of lager from a brand that Luke did not recognize, and an overflowing ashtray with a cigarette burning within, sat nearby.

As Luke lowered Rose into a soiled armchair, he heard the sound of the front door closing. He was on his knees in front of Rose, gently holding her trembling hands when the dishevelled-looking man joined them.

'Thank you for this. You're so kind. I'm Luke.'

'Howard.'

'Thank you, Howard. Have you got a pen and paper?' Luke asked, not taking his eyes off Rose.

'A what?!'

'A pen and paper? I think I might have got the number plate of that lunatic.'

'Oh. Yeah. Gimme a sec.'

Luke heard a drawer open followed by some rustling before Fain reached over his shoulder with a Sharpie and a dog-eared envelope that was partially ripped in a way that suggested someone had given up a couple of inches into the effort of opening it.

'My . . . my hands are shaking,' said Luke, meeting Fain's stare. 'Would you mind?'

Another huff. He made his way to the table, sat, and dropped the envelope onto the opened newspaper. 'Go on,' he said, taking up the can of lager.

Rose made another wail.

'It's OK, Grandma. You're going to be all right. Err . . . OK, OK. It started – I. M. Then I think there was a gap. Five. Zero. R. R. Y. I think that's it.' He watched Fain write the final letter and then replace the pen with the cigarette. 'I'm going to call for an ambulance, Grandma,' he said, turning back to Rose. 'I'm going to leave you for just one second.' He released her hands. 'I'll be right back, Grandma.' He stood and took out his phone. 'Would you mind sitting with her? She's so scared.'

Luke just about made out the words *fucking hell*, muttered under Fain's breath. He stood. His chair made a screeching sound as it was dragged across the threadbare carpet until it came to rest in front of Rose. He sat.

'There, there, Granny,' Fain said with a lacklustre patting of Rose's knee. 'You're all right. You'll be back in the bingo hall before you know it.'

'Hello, I need an ambulance for my grandma, please,' said Luke, stood behind Fain.

Old habits die hard and the doctor Fain once was automatically started looking for signs of trauma. There were no marks on the old woman's legs or hands, no scuffs to her clothes. Her face, yes, it was twisted in agony, but it had no cuts or bruises to speak of. People in pain clutch at the area that's causing it. This old biddy was just rubbing at her forehead and rocking back and forth. *Odd.*

'Where exactly are you hurting?' he asked, sounding interested in her for the first time.

She covered her eyes and weakly announced, '*Everywhere,*' between laboured breaths.

Fain reached for the hand in her lap and placed two fingers on its wrist. She snatched it away with far more force than he was expecting. 'Nothing wrong with that arm –'

'Howard!' He turned to see Luke's panicked face. 'They need your address. What's your address?'

'Umm –' momentarily distracted – 'It's Cordwallis Street. Fifty-seven Cordwa—*Owww! What the fuck!?*' He clutched at the sting in his neck, before quickly checking his palm for blood, but saw none. By the time he gripped his neck again the burning sensation was already subsiding. 'What did you . . . ?' He trailed off when he saw the needle in Rose's steady hand. He looked up into her eyes, which were wide and alert.

'That's a dose of justice,' she said, with a yellow-toothed wolf's grin.

'A *what*?' he said, entirely confused. He went to stand. But Fain could raise his bulk only a couple of inches before he dropped heavily back down. He gave a sharp wince and brought his hands up to his chest, clutching at the flab of his left pec. Suddenly, his face lost all expression, his mouth fell open, and a wheezy rattle came forth. His hands dropped into his lap and his head lolled to the side. His eyes remained fixed on Rose as the world began to decelerate. One by one, he could physically feel each of his organs shutting down, until it felt like his whole body was leaving him, his skin slipping off his bones into a hole in the floor, spiralling away into nothingness.

His head tipped the balance and Fain's body came crashing down off the chair. He was dead before he hit the filthy carpet.

They looked down at him in stunned silence for what felt like an age.

It was Luke who finally spoke.

'Oh my God. Are you for real?'

'What?' She still held the needle before her like a tiny sword. With just her eyes she looked to Luke.

'"That's a dose of justice"?'

'What's wrong with that? It's a good line!'

'A good line?' he repeated, incredulous. 'Who are you, Grambo? There's no way you just came up with that in the moment.'

'I did!'

'Give me a break. It reeks of "here's one I prepared earlier".'

'What about you?'

'What *about* me?'

'Could you have said "Grandma" one more time? Who were you trying to convince? Yourself or him?' Rose said, curling a lip in Fain's direction.

'Don't get me started on performance,' Luke warned. 'All that wailing was *crazy*. It was like the Haunted Mansion in here.'

'Fooled him, didn't it?'

They looked down at Fain's death mask, his eyes unnaturally wide, and his mouth agape in silent horror.

'Oh, yeah. Mission accomplished.'

47

'I wiped down the needle, put it in his hand, and we walked out,' said Rose.

Ray, eyes shut, held the bridge of his nose.

'*Why?* Why the hell did you do that?'

'A thank you would be nice,' Rose countered, aggrieved.

Ray opened his eyes.

'*Thank you?*'

'I should think so. He was an awful man. So we did what you couldn't do.' She wagged a finger between herself and Luke.

Ray turned to Luke.

'*Surprise*,' he said, meekly.

'You almost put me in *prison*.' In the face of Ray's evident anger, Luke looked into his lap. 'You pair of idiots,' he chided, for good measure.

'Now that's unfair,' said Rose. 'At the time, we didn't know you'd been seen in the alley behind his house –' she made a face one might show an adult who didn't know the answer to one plus one – 'wearing *surgical* gloves.'

'Yeah. We didn't know, Ray,' Luke added.

'You went up there to off him,' Rose continued. 'You couldn't. So we finished the job for you. And, if I might say – with considerable panache.'

'You did say you were glad he's dead,' Luke concluded.

Ray looked to Gog. 'Can you believe this pair?'

'I gotta be honest, it does sound a little bit like something they would do.' He shrugged. 'He was a very bad man, Ray.'

Ray blinked, incredulous. 'You've changed your tune.'

Gog said nothing.

As they all waited for Ray's next words he ran a hand over his forehead and through his hair.

'How did you find his address?'

'Ray,' began Luke, unable to hide the fact he found the question cute. 'I work for a billion-dollar shady investment firm – we've got guys. You said Howard Fain, Salford. Probably could have found him with less.'

Ray nodded his understanding, before saying in a tone that sounded noticeably less angry, 'The suicide note. That was clever.'

'Thank you,' Rose replied, feeling she was finally getting the recognition they deserved.

'Standard UK number plate has seven registration characters. Two letters at the beginning, followed by two numbers. And then three randomly assigned to the vehicle. I.M.5.0.R.R.Y. *I'M SORRY*. Very clever,' he said again, sounding genuinely impressed.

'The five was a gamble. But we got lucky,' beamed Luke.

Ray turned to Rose. 'You got the drug from the dog shelter?'

'Correctly deduced.'

'You did make one mistake at the scene.'

'Like what?' she said, defensively.

'He was choosing his winners for a horse race that was happening – the next day.'

'*Shiiiiiit . . .*' said Luke, seeing Fain's pit of a living room in his mind. 'Yeah, there was a newspaper on the table. Yeah. A bloke who was going to kill himself wouldn't do that.'

'Meh,' said Rose, the corners of her mouth turned down. 'It's not enough. Ray's still here, isn't he?'

'She's right. I couldn't prove I didn't do it –'

'But they couldn't prove you did.'

A knowing smile passed between them.

'Get a room,' said Luke, rolling his eyes.

'What do we do now?' asked Gog.

After a moment's thought, Ray said, 'Promise me none of you will do anything like this ever again.'

'All right,' said Rose.

Luke and Gog nodded.

'I want to hear it.'

Luke shrugged. 'I promise.'

'Promise,' said Gog.

'Rose?' Ray said.

'*Yes.*' She sighed. 'I promise.'

'And you can't ever tell anybody about this. I mean *never ever.*'

'First rule of Chemo Club . . .' Luke smiled.

Gog clapped his hands against his knees. 'Righto, then. If that's all sorted? I wanted to tell you all something –'

'Gog,' said Ray, holding up a hand to stop him. 'I don't think I could take another revelation.'

'A what?'

'*Revelation.* A surprising confession.'

'Oh. No. It's nothing bad.'

'All right,' said Ray, cautiously.

'I just wanted to tell you all you've made me hate cancer a little less.'

'How so?' asked Rose.

'Because without it I never would have met you all.'

Rose opened her mouth but the words wouldn't come through the tightness in her throat. Instead she looked away and bit her lip.

Ray looked at the Welshman through a pair of suddenly wet eyes. 'I feel the same way.'

Luke placed a thin hand on Gog's shoulder. 'Me too,' he said, with a wobbling lip.

'Friends for life?' Gog asked.

'Yeah,' Luke smiled.

'Definitely,' said Ray.

'OK,' said Rose, dabbing at her nose with a tissue retrieved from somewhere up her sleeve. 'But only because that's a short-term commitment.'

48

Luke sat next to his driver and gave Ray a wave as they pulled out onto the high street. Rose and Gog had already said their goodbyes for the day so Ray stood alone on the pavement.

He looked down the street towards the alley. It was now just a city alleyway like any other. There was no way anyone could have known it was the scene of a crime. Much like Ray's recent sins, it had been wiped clean.

He looked up and felt the sun on his face. Even though its warmth didn't quite reach the parts of his body that felt cold and depleted of late, he closed his eyes and smiled. It was a beautiful day. The kind of day that new beginnings were made for.

When he opened his eyes, Chay was pulling into the space Luke had recently vacated.

Ray gestured for her to join him.

She stepped out of the old Vauxhall. Had it really been three years since he had bought it for her? Time flies.

'Dream space,' she said, with a sweeping gesture to her perfect parking spot outside the clinic. 'How was it?'

'The usual dull monotony. But it was good seeing everybody.'

'Really?' she said, pleasantly surprised. 'They've grown on you, then?'

'They have.'

'All that time you're in there, what do you talk about?'

'Sorry, Chay. The first rule of Chemo Club is . . . you don't talk about Chemo Club.'

'Ray!' she replied with a laugh. 'Did you just do a film reference?'

'I think I did, you know,' he said coyly.

'Will wonders never cease?'

She was putting on a brave face, but Ray could see the subtle cracks in the facade. 'How're you doing, kiddo?'

'Don't worry about me.' She reached out to him and Ray saw the look of concern on her face as she felt the sharpness of his elbow through his jacket. 'How're you?'

'More of this reverse-parenting thing.' He smiled.

'*Ray!*' she barked, but in good humour.

'OK, OK. It's just . . . I'm at my best when I know you are.'

She thought about that for a time.

'I'm sad, Ray. But I know I'll be able to get through it. Do you know why?'

'Tell me.'

'Eleven years.'

Ray looked confused.

'That's how long you've been preparing me for whatever lies ahead. I'm going to be fine . . . I'm Ray Leonard's daughter.'

Tears came to his eyes.

'*Chaynnie —*'

She threw her arms around him and they held the embrace for a while, dampening one another's shoulder.

Releasing him, 'Shall we head off? Your carriage awaits,' she said, with a smile and a wet sniff.

Ray took a handkerchief from his pocket and gave it to her. He employed his sleeve for his own tears.

'I thought maybe you'd like to join me for a coffee first?'

'Sounds good. Where were you thinking?'

'I know a little place around the corner,' said Ray, offering her his arm.

Chay took it and they set off.

As they walked, Ray suddenly had the strangest sensation that the fingers of his free hand had intertwined with another. He turned and a pair of deep brown eyes, almost black, looked back at him from the face he had loved the most in the world.

'*Sugar.*'

'Odette,' he said, smiling his crooked smile. 'My beautiful girl.'

But then his smile fell away as he remembered the story of Gog's uncle.

'*Oh no,*' he whispered.

'*It's all right,*' said Odette. '*Everything is going to be all right.*'

Epilogue

Six weeks later

A black-clad sea of solemn faces filled every pew, with standing room only at the back as the mourners spilled over into the vestibule. Rose, Gog and Luke (Gog in the middle like a black-suited mountain) sat mid-congregation.

'Today we gather to remember and celebrate the life of a truly good man,' said the old vicar standing in front of the assembled. 'Ray Leonard was a person who touched the lives of so many people. God's plan includes both life and death –'

'Here we bloody go,' Rose muttered.

'– and as we mourn we take comfort in the knowledge that he is with his creator. God has called him home. He is at peace. We must thank God for giving us the life of such a good man. We must trust in God's love and wisdom –'

'Yes, thank you, God. For murdering Ray.'

'Have some respect, Rose,' Gog urged from the side of his mouth.

'I came here to hear about Ray. Not the "God" who saw fit to give him cancer and end his life decades early.'

'My nan used to say "God gets impatient to meet the good ones".'

'My lovely boy,' Rose said, drawing a hand over her black

bandana, 'I think we've all agreed upon the fact we won't be going to Heaven.'

'Will you pair put a sock in it?' said Luke, through lips curled back from his teeth.

Two people from the pew in front turned. One frowned and the other shushed.

'*Shush yourself*,' Rose hissed.

'– Chaynnie Leonard will now come forward to share her thoughts and memories with us. As we listen, let us remember the joy and love that Ray brought into our lives.'

Chay rose, her eyes puffy and red, and made her way to the lectern, her heels loud against the cold stone floor.

'Thank you so much for coming. It's wonderful to see so many friends and colleagues here today. It's a testament to how well-liked Ray was. I know he had a tendency to keep things professional . . . but he was such a loving, caring man . . . he had a big heart . . . although I'm sure he would say his heart pumped blood around his body and nothing more.' A ripple of laughter went through the congregation. The smile on Chay's face sent tears over her cheeks. She dabbed at them and looked down at her speech.

'Raymond Andrew Leonard was a Royal Marine and a police officer who dedicated his life to serving his country and his community with bravery, honour and integrity. He was injured terribly in Afghanistan. He could have come home and taken the rest of his life off . . . but that wouldn't have been Ray. He had to help people. I'm sure you all have a story about how Ray helped you or inspired you to be better in some way . . .' She stared hard at her speech for long moments.

Gog felt Rose and Luke shift uncomfortably at the

words from the pulpit. He was certainly not immune to them, shrinking into his seat (much to the relief of the people behind him) at the memory of what he had done as Ray stood by and watched.

'When my mother first met Ray she was damaged beyond repair,' Chay continued. 'We both were. At least, we thought we were. Over time, with patience and that unwavering level-headedness, Ray picked up the shattered pieces of our lives and put us back together again. For a time, I had the family I had always wanted. Me, Mum and Ray . . . *Ray*,' she said with a quiver in her voice. 'I never called him Dad. I'd had one of those. That word "Dad" doesn't make me smile or feel safe. The word "Ray" does. He was my Ray.' Bringing her lips together in a tight line she looked up into the church rafters and blinked back tears.

'I sat with him in his final days. He was exactly as you'd expect him to be. Always positive. He never complained . . . and that frustrated me. I wanted him to be as angry as I was. I asked him – why aren't you angry? Why aren't you pissed off? He said – Yes, I'm annoyed with cancer. It's going to kill me. But I won't let it take me before it takes me.' She smiled at the memory. 'Have you ever heard anything so fucking stoic in all your life?' she said, church or no church.

Luke had passed the Green Oak but had never felt the need to go in. Taking in the cozy and welcoming decor – plenty of wood panelling, a fireplace (unlit), bit of brass here and there, just the right amount of taxidermy – he thought to himself that he had made a mistake – *this is a nice boozer.*

315

The only shame being that the pretty dappled light that poured in through the big bay windows was quickly absorbed by all the black cloth worn on this sad day.

'What can I get you?' asked the young, shaggy-blond-haired barman, who Luke just about heard over the din.

'Pint of lager, cider and a glass of white, please.'

'Coming up.'

As the barman got to work, Luke took in the fact he too was dressed as if he had just been to a funeral. He hadn't seen him in the church, but he must have been there. Bar staff didn't dress that way for a funeral reception, right?

The place was packed; humid with the crush of bodies. Everyone loudly sharing their stories about the one man who would have hated to have been in this space, thought Luke, with a brief smile.

Looking around – a room full of cops if ever he saw one – he spotted Ray's daughter. She was talking to a tall, ramrod-straight guy. Actually, 'guy' was the wrong noun. 'Chap' seemed more apt. Everybody else in their black attire looked like they were at a funeral. But with slicked-back salt-and-pepper hair and a pencil-thin moustache, this man had the dapper air of someone who had just got off a yacht from Monte Carlo to attend a dinner party.

Luke couldn't hear what was being said but the exchange was clearly one of heartfelt earnest. Chay looked as though she might cry as the chap held her hand in both of his and talked to her with a kindly expression. He released her hand. She touched his shoulder and he made out her words, 'Thank you'. The chap gave her a nod that conveyed deep respect and then turned in Luke's direction.

Noting the abruptness of the turn, that erect posture

and his brisk, smooth, efficient stride, Luke was sure he was looking at a military man.

'Pint of your ale, if you please,' said the chap, with a raised index finger. The barman nodded affirmative as he continued to prepare Luke's drinks.

'Luke Kellner,' he said, offering his hand.

The chap took the proffered handshake with a wide smile full of good teeth and said, 'George Chipton. Friends call me *Fish*.'

Luke noted a few things all at once.

His hand was cool (and as hard as marble) even though the room was continuing to get hotter. And his tie was not black but navy with red and yellow stripes. It was secured with a golden tie-clip with a crest that had the number 40 within.

'Fish and Chipton. That's good. I'm guessing you're a military man?'

'Is it that obvious?' he replied in the kind of RP that made Colin Firth sound like he worked on an oil rig.

'Nah. Not really. I've got a gift.'

'The power of observation, ay? Useful tool.'

'Can be.' Luke nodded at his tie. 'You served with Ray?'

'I did,' he replied, becoming serious. 'He was my Multiple Commander in Afghanistan.' The final syllable was drawn out: *stahhn*.

'What was he like?'

The man thought for a short while. 'The very best of us.'

Luke nodded as if he had expected the remark. 'Were you there . . . in Kabul when he got injured?'

'I was. We lost some good men that day. It was a miracle that Sugar wasn't one of them.'

Despite the grim sentiment Luke couldn't help but smile at the nickname. 'He wouldn't let me call him Sugar.'

'No, I can't imagine he would,' Chipton said, his smile returning. 'And how did your association with Multiple Commander Leonard come about?'

The barman placed Luke's drinks on the bar. 'Thanks,' he said, tapping the machine with a black card. 'We met in chemo.'

'Oh,' Chipton's smile faded again. 'And how's that going?'

'You know what.' A small smile threatened. 'Better than I was hoping.'

'That's good to hear.' Despite the positive sentiment Chipton's face remained stern. 'I'm sorry you've had to go through all that.'

'Don't be. As a friend of mine said – without cancer I never would have met Ray . . . which has been the honour of my life.'

Seeing Luke struggle to hold back the tears, Chipton placed a cool hand on his shoulder.

'It sounds like he had a profound impact on you?'

Luke patted Chipton's hand.

'Oh, you don't know the half of it.'

Luke placed the drinks on the table. Lager for himself, a glass of white for Gog and a pint of cider for Rose, who sounded as if she were midway through another one of her life-affirming TED Talks, thought Luke.

'– it's a cruel thing when a parent dies young.'

'True that,' agreed Gog.

'They don't get the chance to become annoying.'

Gog pondered her words for a moment. 'No. I don't get it. What do you mean?'

'I mean it's nature. One of nature's ways of helping you to let them go. Parents should live long enough to become so excruciatingly annoying their death is nothing short of sweet relief. Think about it – if your perfect parents died, it would kill you. Thankfully my parents lived a long life. I don't miss them one bit.'

'It's a reflex for me to disagree with anything you say,' said Luke. 'But considering your age and how annoying you are – yeah, I think you're right, Rose.'

Gog laughed.

'Gog, my boy, you will laugh at anything,' said Rose, miffed.

'Yeah. I have a great sense of humour.'

'That's not what a great sense of humour is.'

'I'm funny, Rose!' he said, defensively. 'Remember that time Luke asked me have I seen *Ocean's Eleven* and I said no, I haven't seen the first ten yet.' Luke started to laugh as he took off his jacket. '*See!* That's funny.'

'Yes. But you weren't making a joke. You were serious.'

'Doesn't matter. It's still funny.'

'Can we make a toast, please?' Luke asked, shaking his head as he rolled up the sleeves of a white shirt he had once filled, but now looked as if it were borrowed from his father's wardrobe. 'To Ray. The very best of us,' he said, raising his glass.

'*To Ray*,' said Gog and Rose.

They clinked glasses and drank.

For a time they sat in silence, an island of three amongst the surrounding chatter.

It was Rose who broke the lull.

'I hope this many people won't turn up to my funeral. Bloody gorging themselves on me free canapés.'

'Rest in peace,' said Luke. 'No one's going to turn up to your funeral. No friends, no family. Gravity won't even turn up. It'll just be your lonely corpse floating in a vacuum.'

They all laughed at that one.

'Hi.'

They looked up.

'Chay,' said Luke, startled.

'Sorry to disturb.'

'No, no. It's fine. Can I get you a drink?' He started to rise.

'That's kind of you but I'm good,' she said, waving him to sit back down. 'I just wanted to thank you all for coming today.'

'Nowhere we'd rather be.'

Chay smiled back at the giant with tears in his eyes.

'I loved your speech, my dear,' said Rose. 'Especially the last part.'

'Thanks . . .' With an embarrassed smile, she glanced down at the floor. 'Ray spoke of you all fondly. I could tell the way he spoke about you . . . you were important to him.'

'We feel the same way,' Luke said, with a sad smile.

'You know, it's strange, but chemo with you guys, it changed him . . . but in a good way. He seemed lighter . . . even when the cancer got worse. I don't know how, but . . . you opened him up. I wanted to thank you all for that, because our final weeks together were some of the best we ever had. I got to know him better than I thought I ever would.'

She started to cry.

Luke made to rise again, but stopped when the young barman appeared and put an arm around her.

'You OK?' he asked, handing her a tissue.

She nodded, wiping at her eyes. 'Thanks, Miles.' She reached down and the fingers of their hands interlocked. She turned back to the group. 'I hope I get to see you all again.'

'We'd like that,' said Gog, smiling his missing-incisor smile.

'Take care,' she said, before walking away, still hand in hand with the young barman.

'Lovely girl,' Gog said.

'Yeah,' Luke agreed.

'She'll do Ray proud, that one.' Rose took a swig of her cider. 'As have we . . . up until now.'

Luke gave her a questioning look.

'We made a promise. And we have stood by that promise. Ray is now gone. He's up in the electric ether somewhere. So the question is . . .' She smiled her wolf's grin, which slowly was mirrored on Luke and Gog's faces. '. . . who are we going to kill next?'

Acknowledgements

The things we do and the choices we make – it's all about family, isn't it? Janet, Chris, Jonboy, Keith, Shan, John, Gemma – I love you.

Phylicia. You have my heart.

Thank you to my editors. Bill Massey, my first line of defence. Rowland White and Ruth Atkins at Michael Joseph were as sublime as ever with advice that put my forehead in my palm, 'Why didn't I think of that?!' (a special thanks to Ruth – who is just so lovely and so brilliant – you're the best). Having these three brains at my disposal is like handing the test to the teacher who says – This is all wrong, here are the correct answers. Basically it feels like cheating, ha!

For the copy-edit, Nick Lowndes and Debbie Hatfield, with a skillset that baffles me, made this novel reader-friendly. Debbie's attention to detail is mind-blowing. To a dyslexic like me, she's basically a superhero. My thanks also to Jill Cole, for her excellent proofreading.

To my agent Paul Stevens, I needed to put my own voice out there unfettered by the restraints of TV, and you gave that to me. I still can hardly believe it. Thank you for believing in me.

Unlike the research for my first novel, *Call Time*, which essentially involved googling what an eighties mobile phone looked like, *The Last Laugh Club* was a different kettle of fish.

Being a Royal Marine? Nope, not a clue. Frustratingly, as much as I would like to gush, for obvious reasons, all I can say is – thank you, Will. You were incredibly gracious with your time, especially when considering where talking to someone who is writing a book ranks in the importance of your day-to-day duties. Bloody legend.

Being a police officer and police procedure? Damned if I know. Cue Ex-Detective Sergeant Lyndon Smith of the brilliant Consulting Cops. Every cul-de-sac I entered, big and small, Lyndon and his crack team of consultants got me out of there. Special thanks to Ex-Detective Constable Sheena Service (I know. Great name) who showed incredible patience walking me through how the Police National Computer works. For pretty much everything else Ex-Detective Inspector Steve Keogh was my go-to. Been there, seen it, done it, doesn't quite do Steve justice. A fascinating man. If you are writing a novel that involves police procedure I can't recommend his book, *Murder Investigation Team*, enough.

Veterinary practices? I have two French bulls (and if you have French bulls you already know this), which means I'm at the vet all the time. But that still wasn't enough to provide an answer to a pair of somewhat sensitive questions. Enter Dr Nikki at my local vet's. I took Frankie to get her three-month anti-itch jab. At the end of our appointment I asked Nikki, in what I hoped sounded casual, and in no way serial-killery, how easy is it to access pentobarbital at the clinic and how much would I need to kill a human. Needless to say Nikki's colour drained. Eventually, after telling me 'this is highly unusual', she gave me the information I needed. But since that day I suspect she has had her suspicions about me. So I'd like to take this opportunity to say – see, Nikki, I told you I was writing a book, ha!

Finally, and by far most importantly – prostate cancer and chemotherapy. I do know about these subjects, because my stepdad, Ray, had them.

What I learned through Ray is that cancer treatment is all about options. The oncologist never told Ray what to do, as they could not guarantee success. It was always up to Ray to make a choice. The option that presented the biggest chance of survival was always the hardest. The most invasive. Ray always chose that route. And that's why he is still with us.

Not only did Ray give me an invaluable, and unique, first-hand insight into his cancer journey, but he also gave me the idea for this book. He was in the middle of one of the hardest periods of his treatment and was off to the shops to get some 'comfort biscuits'. As he put on his jacket, he said to me, with a wry smile, 'No one better mess with me today, Steve. I'm a man with nothing to lose.' A quip that planted the seed in my mind for *The Last Laugh Club*.

You're an inspiration, Ray. I'm very proud of you and I love you.

As for you, dear reader, thank you for letting me into your life for this short window. I don't take it lightly. It's an honour and a privilege to be in your hands. Can I just say, if I write a third novel, make sure you purchase a copy. That's not a threat, but do keep in mind, I know how much pentobarbital it takes to kill a human :)

On a station platform, with nothing to read,
and a four-hour train journey stretching ahead of him...

That's where the story began for Penguin founder Allen Lane.
With only 'shabby reprints of shoddy novels' on offer,
he resolved to make better books for readers everywhere.

By the time his train pulled into London, the idea was formed.
He would bring the best writing, in stylish and affordable
formats, to everyone. His books would be sold in bookstores,
stationers and tobacconists, for no more than the price
of a ten-pack of cigarettes.

And on every book would be a Penguin, a bird with a certain
'dignified flippancy', and a friendly invitation to anyone who
wished to spend their time reading.

In 1935, the first ten Penguin paperbacks were published.
Just a year later, three million Penguins had made their
way onto our shelves.

Reading was changed forever.

—

A lot has changed since 1935, including Penguin, but in the
most important ways we're still the same. We still believe that
books and reading are for everyone. And we still believe that
whether you're seeking an afternoon's escape, a vigorous debate
or a soothing bedtime story, all possibilities open with a book.

Whoever you are, whatever you're looking for,
you can find it with Penguin.